The Policy

c. i. **downs**

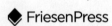 FriesenPress

Suite 300 - 990 Fort St
Victoria, BC, V8V 3K2
Canada

www.friesenpress.com

ISBN
978-1-4602-8092-8 (Hardcover)
978-1-4602-8093-5 (Paperback)
978-1-4602-8094-2 (eBook)

1. Fiction

Distributed to the trade by The Ingram Book Company

For My Parents

Part I: 2009

Chapter 1

Life is fucking hard.

For Rory the anticipation of the drink was more savoury than the act, and yet, neither ever lasted longer than the other. Prying a few minutes from the hours of the week, when one has a young child, was a rarity, but the two ounces of smoky single malt on ice had an essential purpose. An essential satisfaction. The all-in-one erasure and strengthener of the moments that came before and after those in which he sat alone at the bar, drifting between contemplation and complete vacancy.

The memories "The Woodbine Bar" conjured weren't exactly glorious ones for Rory, but there was a faded comfort in knowing a place where his energy did not feel like it had been seized from him—a place where the spectre of life's many liens against true freedom wouldn't follow, where he could remind his body that he was still in control of its peripheral functions with a blaze of scotch down his throat.

Rory once knew the owner and was also considered family among the regulars. But short years took many of them away; on to greener pastures or under new management. Both proficient and explicit killers of being. Linda, the bartender, was the only one left who recalled his face anymore, and it gladdened him to now be counted among the forgotten— indistinguishable to the new breed of barflies. When he really thought about it, his long expired tenure was almost like he'd once owned shares in the place. But they were the kind that returned no dividends and that were worth no profit. Keep giving until you're cut-off, was the silent motto. And as he looked around he couldn't help but think he had been a major contributor to the refurbishments the old bar had been in dire need of— way back, when he gave more than he had to give.

The lighting from dimly lit wall lamps poured out from behind yellow cloth shades on to whole-wheat wallpaper and cedar paneling. It blended with the soft spotlight haze of small, blonde-tinted pot lights in the ceiling and imitation oil lamps on the tables which gave off a copperish glow that coalesced with the cushy brown leather wrap around booths and darkly stained, shiny wooden stools and chairs. The effect made a person feel deep and subterranean, out of reach of nature's elements, unknowing of how bright the light outside could be.

Elvis Presley's "Suspicious Minds" softly came from the digital jukebox, and a few patrons sat joking and reminiscing of a time when only so many 45s could be kept inside. When everything wasn't at your fingertips and immediately accessible.

Linda was behind the bar, putting away wine glasses and beer mugs. She had thick, dark eye shadow that made her look sad—a dismal connotation she could cut through by always being chipper for a chat, no matter how small the talk was.

"Tough couple days, Ror?" she asked.

"Nothing out of the ordinary, but thanks for asking."

"No worries. Can I get you another?"

"I'm good, Lin—one quick one, and I'm off."

She laughed. "Sounds like my ex-husband."

Rory liked to see her smile. It was worth more to him than the drink. He removed his attention from her and fished the twenty-dollar bill he allotted himself for the drink out of his wallet and laid it on the bar. "Keep the change. The tip's for that inspiring smile."

By the time Rory finished speaking, she was already at the other end of the bar and out of earshot, but it didn't matter. She was obliged to tend the needs of many, not just one man who came in looking for something, but didn't know exactly what that something was.

He got off the stool, collected his jacket, and scrounged for his keys. The drink had made him a little dizzy after working a long day that lapped into the night. Rory's tolerance had weakened over the years, and he thought any bystander watching him would think he looked like a fool, fumbling around in his pockets as if he'd just finished a shift of drinking instead of actual, honest work.

He opened the door, and the winter wind slapped him across the face with sharp, icy nails. The cold penetrated the fabric of his pants and thinly insulated jacket. He could feel it wrap around his legs and arms and nestle into his joints and muscles, irritating the light ache from being on the go for twelve hours. *No matter how many years I've spent in this city,* he thought, *I am never ready for this shit.*

He got into his car and fought to turn the engine over. Like it did his legs and arms and organs, the January deep freeze had set in to every piece, every pedal, every hose and every nut and bolt of the car. It took a minute but the car finally came alive, and after giving it a few minutes to warm up, readying it for motion, he puttered out of the parking lot. His old Nissan was a well-wintered trooper and it forged slowly through the punishing headwind and the un-cleared snow and ice that grabbed at the tires like a poorly effective glue trap. *Why do they always have to wait until two days after the forecast says it'll stop snowing to get the ploughs out? City bloody Hall, bunch of bastards,* he thought.

Sleepy eyes were weighing him down, and the idea of pulling over for a nap called to him, but he was jolted alert by the sound of his cell phone.

The screen read "MARISA."

He pulled over to the side of the road to answer. "Hello?"

"Mr. Gunn, it's Marisa. Are you going to be home soon?"

"Yes. I'm about five minutes away. Why?"

"I'm in kind of a rush tonight. I'll see you in a few. Bye."

The phone went dead. Rory thought it a bit abrupt but didn't let it worry him.

The headlights from her idling and warming car were on when Rory pulled up, and Marisa was outside smoking. He got out of the car and made his way up the stairs of his derelict back porch. Marisa seemed tense but not in a nervous way—it was more penitential. She butted out her cigarette and tried wrapping her sweater tighter around her slender frame; she wasn't dressed for the cold.

"I remember when I didn't think I was crazy for going outside for a butt in minus-thirty," Rory said.

She snickered but didn't seem interested in talking about habits. She opened the back door, leading Rory into the house.

"Is everything all right?"

She left the question without an answer and went into the adjoining room to get her book bag and winter clothing. She was speaking to herself, but so quietly that he could not hear actual words. She came back dressed in her heavy jacket, toque, and woollen mitts—ready to make a quick exit.

"Mr. Gunn . . ." She looked Rory in the eye. "There's no easy way to say this, but I can't watch Anna anymore. She had another outburst tonight."

For a second, all the air had been taken out of his world, but he processed it quickly. He leaned against the wall. "Really?" Rory said.

Marisa took a deep breath and exhaled loudly. "She hit me with a toy phone today. Hard." Marisa rolled back her sleeves and showed him a welt the size of a plum on her forearm.

"Oh no," Rory said, shaking his head.

"And the hours are kicking my ass. I thought I could do it at first, but I can't. I'm not getting enough studying done."

What Marisa told him didn't make him angry, not even frustrated. He just accepted it, like many things that weren't worth the effort to fight. Rory knew what she meant. He worked ten-hour shifts, but with transit adjustment, he was gone from quarter past noon until twenty to midnight. How it must affect a student was sometimes lost on him. Not everyone got to work the weird shift cycle Rory did. He used to share swing shifts with another operator but because of the slow economy, they had been consolidated into a team—eliminating their need for assistants while maintaining output.

Most of the other employees had regular work hours from 8:00 a.m. to 4:30 p.m. or 2:00 p.m. to 10:30 p.m. It wasn't until Rory and his counterpart Matt were told of the plans to run their machine on one shift, with no one else to overlap with, that they approached management and requested the odd start/finish times—which, after some hum-and-haw reluctance from management, they were allowed to work.

At first it was contested by other workers. Rory and Matt had three day weekends and no one else did, but ten-hour shifts were daunting, and could feel like being in the plant for twelve hours instead of ten. Eventually the others gave up with their objections. None of them really wanted to be there that long. They just liked bitching and stirring up the shit.

It was by dumb luck Marisa's classes were in the morning and she had afternoons and evenings free. She was the first sitter Rory had ever hired that could accommodate his schedule without him having to use nanny-on-call agencies or other outside services. He dreaded the thought of going back to that. There had been so many problems with them. He suspected one of being verbally abusive but he could never prove it. Another he thought to be negligent, and she gab on the phone—not giving a damn whether Anna was breathing or not. He had finally had enough after he caught one stealing things that were worth nothing.

He walked out of the kitchen absently, swirling potential arrangements around in his head. He pulled a chair from the dining room table and dropped himself in it. Marisa followed him in.

"Are you all right, Mr. Gunn? I'll finish out the rest of the month so you can fill the position."

"I'm fine," he said. "You've been so kind to Anna. And you've tried.

I can't thank you enough for the time you've spent with her. I didn't expect you to stay forever." He looked up at her with a smile.

She smiled back. "She's a great kid. I'll even help you find a replacement."

"Thank you. That means a lot. Now get home, you have class in the morning."

She grabbed her books from the table and backed away towards the front door. "You've got a few days off, right?"

"I do."

"Okay. I guess I'll see you on Monday then. G'night, Mr. Gunn."

"Good night, Marisa."

The door shut behind her, and Rory went to lock it. He felt light-headed again, and he thought he'd gotten up too fast. He went into the kitchen and ran the tap on cold, letting the water run down on his fingers until it was cold enough for his liking. He bent over and took a long, indulgent drink from the faucet, and while he was imagining that it was another shot of whisky his phone started vibrating in his pocket.

The screen read "WORK."

He didn't want to answer, but he did. "Hello?"

"Rory. It's Wyatt." His voice was loud—like he was holding the receiver in front of his face, not beside it. "The loading crew is looking for an order you guys supposedly finished and they can't find it. The ticket has a location, but what we need is not there. Do you remember where you put it?"

"What order are you talking about?"

"Rem-Steel. Says it was completed two weeks ago," Wyatt said.

"That doesn't help much. Could've been moved anywhere."

"Is there any chance you can come back and take a look for it? You'd know what to look for better than anyone."

"I can't," said Rory. "There's no one here to be with my daughter. Can you call Matt?"

"Tried that. No answer."

You don't say, had I been smarter I would've done the same, Rory thought, "I apologize, Wyatt, but I can't help you out."

"I guess I'll have to look for it. A shame to stall the loaders for something you could fix in a few minutes I bet, especially when it's slow."

"I don't know what to say. I can't leave my daughter alone. I hope you can appreciate that."

"I'll have a look then. Maybe we aren't looking hard enough. You have a fine rest of the night."

Rory wasn't even afforded the chance to say goodbye. Wyatt had a way of making people feel like everything was their fault and that things only got done right if he was involved. He was a treacherously cajoling rube who hadn't been in the company's employ for very long as the evening supervisor. He didn't stand more than five feet four inches, but he presented himself like he towered over you, and his foreman's white hat made the authority he had, mixed with his self-importance, made him unbearable.

Wyatt had gone through a weight-loss phase about a year before and had managed to trim a good chunk of his gut off. One day, Rory had made the mistake of complimenting him, and Wyatt had replied, "You asking me out on a date?" Rory didn't think on it too much, but that was the first time he followed an encounter with Wyatt by thinking, *What an asshole.*

Rory considered going back, but he shook the thought from his head and went into the bathroom for a quick rinse in the shower. His attention was on the bigger hole in the boat, not searching for something that had probably been sent somewhere else in error.

His more-than-fair wage and decent benefits at work supported them well, but it just made the mark of comfortable living. There was also a fair amount of a small inheritance left from after his parents passed away, but it was strictly used for Anna's care and wouldn't last forever. And borrowing against his home wasn't an option, unless he wanted to make things harder in the long run—but this was middle-class par for the course, and it gnawed at him, always playing a few strokes behind.

The steam from the shower fogged the mirror. Rory stared into it blankly, watching his reflection run out of space.

Chapter 2

He never had any problem falling asleep—it was how much sleep Rory could actually get that was the problem. Anna had fickle sleeping patterns that fluctuated anywhere between violent tempest and languid protest that could never be predicted. On really good nights she could sleep like a rock for ten hours, but once she woke, no matter the hour, Rory's day began, whether he was ready for it or not.

He would get up as quickly as he could so he could calm her. He thought perhaps it was waking up alone that disturbed her. The idea of sharing a room came up once, to make her feel more secure, but that idea was shot down by the caregiver before Marisa. He was told it wasn't proper or healthy and would make the strain even greater for both of them.

On this morning he slunk out of bed, half-asleep and woozy, barley getting his slippers on before he was out the door to tend to her. This day it was a dull thud that woke him. As he walked down the hall towards her room, the thud stayed as constant as a metronome. When he opened the door, she didn't turn to address her father. Her back was to him. It was her knee against the wall what had roused him.

Her blanket had been cast to the ground along with several stuffed animals—ones she never seemed to care for, but that he placed on her bed anyways, after making it for her. The bottom half of the only stuffed animal she treasured, and wouldn't go without, stuck out from between her torso and upper arm. It was a potbellied bear with googly eyes. An opening in its back allowed for a hand to slip in—thumb and pinky went in the bear's tiny arms, while pointer, middle, and ring fingers went in its head and snout, letting Rory create the illusion the bear could talk. Rory often used the bear to communicate with Anna because the bear got better responses out of her than he did.

"Good morning, sunshine," he said softly. "Ready to get out of bed?"

She remained in the same position but stopped with the thudding and nodded her head.

He sat down on the floor beside her little pink princess bed and stroked her arm. "What do you want for breakfast?"

She said something inaudible into her pillow.

"Did you say *muffins,* honey?" She began to fidget—her face buried in the pillow. "Baby, would you please turn around and face Daddy so he can understand what you're saying to him?"

Anna started to squirm and Rory placed a hand on her shoulder, exuding a soothing reassurance that the tremor would stop. Her straight dark hair was frizzed from sleep but stayed out of her face as she turned to him. Her eyes were small and forever sullen, and her thin upper lip made it hard to look pouty. She always seemed distant, even when her emotions were in full swing. Comprehension was evident, but her response was delayed. He called her his "little deep thinker," always waiting for the right thing to come to her.

Anna was five years old, and from conception she'd had it hard. Her mother, Rory's ex, had been a drinker throughout her teen years and into her early twenties, and she'd drunk while Anna was in utero. It had never occurred to Rory that her drinking was a problem, as he wasn't the most astute of parents-to-be, so by the time he'd had enough sense to ask how many drinks were too many, the damage had been done.

Every time he looked into Anna's tiny brown eyes, he chastised himself for not standing up to her mother while a vodka was poured or a beer was cracked open.

It wasn't long after Anna's birth that her mother abandoned them. The settled lifestyle wasn't what she'd signed up for, and after Child and Family Services started snooping around, asking hard, incisive questions, she decided to pack it in and leave the task to Rory.

The first year was rough. He didn't know where to start, but after first laying eyes on his tiny creation he vowed to do right by her, and nonetheless prepped for the long haul and took his responsibility on the chin. The symptoms of sudden withdraw from the boozing made him shake and sweat periodically, and there were times he didn't think he'd make it, but as his paternal instincts took over, the symptoms receded. The continued CFS investigation was a great deterrent and sponsor for his sobering-up. And after eighteen months of not finding any evidence that indicated Rory was an unfit parent, and that Anna should be remanded into foster care, the agency gave up, but they warned of unannounced visits. An injunction that kept any kind of booze, even rum balls and Christmas fruitcake, out of Rory's mouth for three solid years. It wasn't until he felt in absolute control that he started stopping by "The Woodbine" occasionally.

By the time his ex had bolted Rory had been hardened to being ditched. It didn't help that family was scant. Growing up there was never any sense of togetherness he could draw from. He simply made it up as he went along. His parents had been very private people, even from their own relatives. Sure there were out-of-town aunts and uncles, handfuls of nephews and a couple nieces, cousins removed and displaced, but he didn't have it instilled into him to keep in touch, and therefore he could never consider them to be close—much less people he could call on when he was in a bind. Rory remembered his father always saying that his brothers couldn't be trusted, and that his mother was an only child; no family ever spoken of. His father's mother was still alive, but had horrible Alzheimer's, and even if Rory had a chance to have gotten to know her, there still wouldn't be anything there for her to remember of him. It was in his only sibling, Emily, that he could count on for any sense of family or for help when she was able to give it.

"Did you say *muffins,* you little munchkin?" He poked at Anna's belly, and she nodded, smiled, stuck her finger in her mouth, and picked her teeth with it. "Well, I'm sorry, sweetie you ate the last one. Will pancakes be all right?"

Her smile became bigger, her nod more pronounced. It was going to be a good day.

"Okay, then. Let's go brush our teeth." Rory got up and extended his hand. She sat up, hopped out of bed, and placed her hand in his, letting him lead the way, her bear bringing up the rear.

The bathroom floor was covered in memory foam mats that Anna loved—"marthmallows" was how she described them. A step-up was against the cupboard so she could see in the mirror. Climbing up the stairs and stretching across the vanity, she reached for her toothbrush and toothpaste. It was a pretty messy effort, but she was thorough and cleaned up after herself most of the time.

After they finished, Anna took off for the kitchen. Rory followed, rubbing his eyes and yawning. His body wanted to lie down for another couple of hours, but he forced it into motion. He turned on the stove to heat the skillet and melt a chunk of butter while he prepared the pancake batter. He then opened the fridge. "Apple or orange, baby?"

"Ornge pleeth." Her speech had developed slowly and with a tender lisp, but Rory loved the way she spoke—innocence incarnate. He had seen people struggle to understand her, and when they acted like they understood, he felt closer to her because he could interpret what she had really said, like it was a private language.

He poured her a cup of juice and set about brewing a pot of coffee. She sat on a stool at the island in the middle of kitchen, her legs swinging as she spoke softly to her bear. He knew that he should scold her for hitting Marisa, but it would only put Anna in a grumpy state. And the chances that she'd even remembered doing it were slim at best. Rory couldn't find a reason to punish her for an act forgotten.

"What does Mr. Boo have to say this morning?"

She conferred with the bear. "Mithter Boo wanth to know whath is to-day."

"Well, after we eat breakfast, we have to get ready to go shopping. Maybe we'll go see a movie later or rent one off the TV. What does Mr. Boo think about that?"

She turned to the bear, put a hand over her mouth, and leaned in toward Mr. Boo to explain what was just said in terms the bear would understand.

The coffee had finished, and Rory poured himself a cup. He was about to start pouring the pancake mix into the skillet when he heard a noise coming from his bedroom. The text alert on his cell phone was going off, and by the sounds of it, there was a series of texts being sent at once. He put down his coffee. "I'll be right back. Remember, no going near the stove, honey." She didn't pay attention—she was still conversing with Mr. Boo.

He picked up his phone and pulled the charge cord out of the bottom and touched the screen. *Eleven new messages—what the hell?* They were from three of his co-workers. Two of the messages read, "Are you up?" The other nine formed one long dissertation that ended in the same question as the other two. He typed "yea" to all three, and before he could even start reading the series, his phone rang.

The screen read "DOM."

Dom was rattled and rushed his sentences. The phrases "shit has hit the fan" and "walking around like he's ten feet tall and bulletproof" came through the phone at tremendous speed. And the words "laid off" smacked Rory dizzyingly. He tried to get Dom to take a breath. "What are you talking about, Dom? Would you slow down?"

The phone went quiet, and Rory could hear cars and trucks passing on the street through the receiver.

"This isn't right, Ror. That conniving son of a bitch isn't going to get away with this. Mitchell, Dan, Carl, and Frankie were all canned this morning. They were given a shit severance package. Three weeks pay, can you believe that? And then they were told to clean out their lockers and leave the premises. What the hell is that shit, man?"

Rory worked it over in his head. It didn't really make sense why four guys who had a combined thirty-nine years with the company were let go, but at the same time, it did. "It could be just that they're the most expendable, I guess. I don't know what to say, man. Nothing we can do about it. You remember when they let McAurther and Boise go and put me and Matt together? We all figured they didn't need all of us at the brake and sure enough, one day—*poof*—they were gone."

Rory heard Dom light a cigarette and take a long puff, and Rory could imagine the smoke escaping his mouth as he spoke. "This is utter shit, man. We need a bloody union in this place. I've said it before, but this time it's serious. We need to do something about this now before we end up like those poor buzzards."

"Hold on, now. Please tell me you didn't do anything stupid. Words like that will get *you* an envelope and an escort out of the building too."

"Whatever. When you in next?" Dom said.

"I'm not in until Monday, took a couple holiday days."

"What about Matty?"

"He did too. It was slow. You know that." Rory could tell Dom's skin was crawling and that he needed to cool down soon, "Hey, man, tell you what—come over after work, and we'll talk this out. Don't freak out in front of them."

"All right, I'll see you after work."

"See you later."

The phone clicked over, and Rory's true reaction set in. He slumped down onto his bed and stared into his closet mirror. He didn't want Dom to hear any kind of strain in his voice, but what Dom had said scared him to the bone. Any man who worked pay-check-to-paycheck would be. Having to hunt for a job with so many payments to make and families to support was nerve-wracking, but labourers had to be practical and not let the uncontrollable elements faze them. Work shortages were nothing new. Everyone experiences high season and low season. Steady was all right, but it also meant things might not get better. And that made the worse much more frightening.

Even though it wasn't pleasant, the termination of four workers did create some wiggle room. "Housekeeping," management called it. They did it when a few dollars needed to be dropped off the books. And Rory knew that asking specifically why those four individuals were chosen wasn't productive, he knew why. They were shit disturbers, a bit like Dom. And Rory examined the four workers in question for anything he might have in common with them, in case traits of his own might need toning down. *Work hard, head down*—that's what would keep you employed. It was an adage Dom could only half abide. For him, having one's head down was like having it under a desk.

Rory was so engrossed that he hadn't noticed that Anna was in the doorway watching him.

"Brwekfast, Dwaddie."

He quickly switched emotional gears and broke away from the ordeal; accompanied his daughter to the kitchen. "Of course, of course, of course, how silly of me."

After eating, Rory put *Aladdin* on for Anna to watch while he showered. He would get her organized after—it was easier that way.

He was patting himself dry, running the hot water for a shave when the phone rang. He wrapped his towel around his waist and went to answer without looking to see who it was first. "Hello?"

"Mr. Gunn? Clive Strome here." Clive was the operations manager at the plant.

"Hey, Clive. What's up?" Rory knew exactly what was up. He just didn't want to give that impression, as Dom had been throwing a red-button word around, and if something drastic had been done, Rory wanted no connection with it.

"Well, we've had quite the morning over here, and I'd like to ask you to come in tomorrow for a plant briefing. Ten o'clock. It won't take very long—maybe fifteen to twenty minutes. Will you be able to attend?"

Rory didn't feel like he was being given much of a choice. Clive made things that were most definitely mandatory, sound optional. It was annoying. "What's it all about? I'm booked off until Monday and I don't have anyone to watch my daughter."

"Well, it would be much appreciated if you could make arrangements. We have some restructuring happening and we would like all employees present for an information session . . . to give them a chance to ask any questions and others things of that nature."

Rory tightened his fist instead of audibly grinding his teeth. "I'll be there."

"Perfect. See you tomorrow."

Rory hated how conversations went with that man. He was the master, and the workers were his dogs. He was extremely tall and wide in the shoulders. His big white beard, which extended well beyond where his neck met his clavicle, conjured an image of Zeus— especially when he threw phrases like "tight fiscal quarter" and "don't worry, we're looking in to it" and "my hands are tied" around like lightning bolts meant to ward off nosy questionnaires.

Rory hung up the phone and went to his dresser. He wanted to punch a hole through it, but the scar tissue in his hands and the twinge in his knuckles made him hold back; reminding him it wasn't the best way to dispel frustration.

He changed and went to the living room. Anna was rocking back and forth on the couch, clutching Mr. Boo tightly. He called to her and told her to have a quick shower. She didn't acknowledge him. The movie was less than a half an hour in, and even though she'd seen it dozens of times, she was hooked. Nothing else mattered. If she was peaceful and occupied, he was content—discipline over trivial disobedience was something she never incurred from her father.

He went to her room and got out her jeans and a long-sleeved flowered top and the knitted sweater she'd been given by Rory's sister, Emily. It was supposed to depict Mr. Boo, but the eyes were too far apart, and it looked more like a brown frog with claws.

He came back in, and Anna looked over to him. Mr. Boo was packed underneath her jaw. She motioned for him to come and sit with her. He snuggled up with her, kicked his feet up on the ottoman, and quickly forgot the phone had even rung that morning.

* * *

Rory had just finished bringing in the groceries after running their errands, and Anna had run off to her room and shut the door. She wanted to play alone for a while, and Rory didn't mind. She was pretty good by herself during the day, and if something were to go wrong, he would hear a yelp or a scream. Silence wasn't an indication of trouble in their house.

He was putting the cereal boxes away when the knock at the front door came. It was Dom, hunching his shoulders in uncontrollable shiver. "Jesus! It is cold out here."

Rory moved aside and let him in.

Dom smelled of stale cigarettes. He kicked his boots off onto the floor mat, dropping a good two inches in the process. He still wore his work clothes, and they were filthy.

The issued Dambar apparel always started as comfortable, loose dark-blue coveralls, but eventually turned into a tight, drab garment once it was washed a couple times. The rips and tears were touched up with darker patches that came off easily. Dom had told Rory he washed his at home, that he didn't like leaving the coveralls at work because he was convinced someone was taking what uniforms the cleaning service brought back for him, and he hated getting lectured by management for being in his street clothes when he didn't have a uniform to work in— even though he despised the Dambar Steel logo and name bar.

Dom was a few years older than Rory at thirty-five, but he looked like he was pushing fifty. Dom was a hard worker, but his drinking, philandering, and fighting were all approached with the same vigour. He had the personality of a giant and a fuse on his temper so short, that if it were to be lit, would set off the explosives instantaneously.

It was years earlier, when Rory had first started at Dambar, that the two of them built on their acquaintance as more than co-workers. A few weeks in Dom, having conducted his preliminary assessment, had invited Rory out for some drinks after work. It was that night that Rory met the quickly ferocious and volatile Dom. Towards closing time some drunk had started accusing Rory of sly glances aimed in his girlfriend's direction and he was in Rory's face, pointing and spitting and yelling. Once Dom caught notice, he interjected. There was not a word spoken. Not a hint made at parley. Just fists, feet, elbows, knees and blood. By the end Dom had broken the drunk accuser's nose and kicked free a few teeth. "I don't stand for that kind of shit, my friend," Dom said as they fled the bar. It was that moment, lungs and legs burning from running, that Rory knew his new friend was a good one to have, but to also stay on guard and in fear of the feral side of him.

"Sorry that I don't have any rye to offer," Rory said.

"That's fine. I always bring my own." He laughed gravelly as he pulled a small flask from his jacket. "I'll take a glass, though. And a Pepsi, if you got one?"

"I think I have a can."

"Excellent."

Dom took his coat off, draped it over a dining room chair, and took a seat at the island in the kitchen.

Rory placed the drink in front of Dom and had a water for himself. "I got a call from Strome this morning," Rory said.

Dom took a big swig. "What a prick that guy is. You wanna know what he did to those guys? Brought them in one by one, handed them envelopes, and that was it. Not even eased into it. Point blank. That's just not right, man."

Rory looked down into his water and swirled it. "There's nothing we can do about that. If management sees fit, right?"

"It shouldn't be like that, man. I've been looking into ways around it. I've been looking into stuff. Did you know that the company is buying up all sorts of little business' all over the country? And out of every acquisition, every affiliate, ours is one of two shops non-unionized." Dom said like they were under surveillance—as though even the private residence they were in wasn't a safe place to discuss it.

"They must be doing something right then."

"Or something wrong," Dom shot back.

Rory considered his friends point but ultimately brushed it off before he gave it too much thought. "You've got to be careful with that 'stuff.' If they even got wind about the word being kicked around, they'd be sniffing the air, and you know they wouldn't hesitate to get rid of anyone involved just to set an example. You know full well they have their ways, that the rats in the building wouldn't think twice about giving you up if they thought it got them a tiny brick of stale cheese to nibble on."

Dom finished his drink and brought the glass down with a little irritation. "All I'm saying is that we need to do something, protect ourselves somehow. What if it's me next, man? You know they don't like how loud I am, and I know you've heard Strome say that he silences the loud ones. Or even you, man—what would you do with Anna and all?"

A cough from the hallway stopped Dom's rant cold. His mounting vehemence had attracted Anna to the kitchen and, acknowledging the concern in her morose and frightened eyes that were hiding behind her bear, capped his stream of disaffection. She ran over to her father, and Rory picked her up. She buried her face in his shoulder.

"We'll pick this up later," said Rory. "I have to come in tomorrow morning for the meeting."

"Okay. Think about what I said though." Dom grabbed his coat and went to the door to put his boots on. "I didn't mean to scare her."

"It's okay, man." He nudged Anna. "Honey? Would you like to say hi to Uncle Dom?"

She writhed around a bit, not moving her face from where she'd planted it. When she got frightened, she wouldn't talk for a while. Rory made a gesture to Dom that it wasn't his fault and not to take it personally.

Dom accepted, "Well, I guess I'll be seeing you later my friend."

"Night, buddy," Rory said.

Rory shut the door, and a huff of cold air squeezed in. He set the lock and watched through the window as Dom walked to his truck, undoubtedly swearing about work under his vaporous breath.

Chapter 3

Rory had called Emily, who lived close and on the way to the factory, and worked similar shifts at the hospital, to see if she could watch Anna while he went in for the meeting.

"I absolutely loathe how you have always leave things to the last minute." Emily said over the phone. "But how can I say no to that face?"

"You're not the only one." Rory said—falling just short of bitching, but still with enough acidity that his sister knew she wasn't the only one being put out.

For the most part Anna had problems with women. Rory didn't find it odd considering that her birth mother was a miscreant and a ghost. And different women were in and out of her life so often that focusing on one and being able to tell them apart, rather than thinking of them as the same entity, had to be confusing for her. Though he did find it strange that she trusted Emily so unguardedly. He thought it could have been surroundings—the fresh, vague familiarity with Emily's apartment was never associated with the encounters she had with the myriad caregivers who came and went, from the place she called home.

It snowed heavily through the night and into the early morning. Morning rush hour had passed, and the cars that had gone through the streets earlier had carved out six-inch mountains of snow that ran along miniature ravines of imprinted tread. Navigation was horrible, and changing lanes proved risky—even with the grip of winter tires. Rory pumped the gas evenly so as not to spin out or get stuck. Anna sat in the back, breathing on the window and then melting the frost that had collected with the tips of her fingers.

When they got to Emily's, he left the car running in a loading zone and took Anna up to the apartment vestibule. Emily was waiting for them, her curly hair bushed and sleep tossed, her eyes barely open from just waking.

"I don't think I'll be long," Rory said. "Hour tops."

"No worries," Emily said with a yawn. She bent over to pick up Anna. "Hey there, munchkin."

Anna had a big smile on her face, and she turned to say goodbye to her father.

Looks to be another good day, he thought. *Two in a row.*

During the rest of the ride, the severity started to set in. Rory knew how tough it would be supporting his little girl if he had to start over. The house, the bills, the car—everything would be compromised. The banks didn't deal in pity, and the thought drained the blood from his face. He felt ill as he drove past the big blue sign that read "DAMBAR STEEL."

It was 9:45 a.m. when he parked his car. There wasn't anyone outside smoking, and he thought that given the circumstances, seeing no one outside calming their nerves was a good sign. He went into the locker room to get his hard hat and work boots. Since he wasn't staying long, he chose not to put on his uniform.

Walking through the plant Rory could hear the quiet commotion of his coworkers gathered in the driveway, and the sound grew more distinct the closer he got to it. *The machines aren't running, but at least the heat is,* Rory thought.

Recession was reverberating through not only Canada's financial structure but the rest of the world's as well. The word *austerity* was peppering every article about the economy, and it scared people. Rory and the others had no idea what it meant exactly, but they'd witnessed the cold axe of unemployment lop off a few of their co-workers' heads, so they at least had an inkling of how they figured into the definition.

It looked like the whole crew was there, minus those who'd been given walking papers. Fifty-nine guys left. All present, waiting for the announcement to be made and have their anxieties quelled or confirmed.

The shop was like the hull of a retired shipping vessel, thick dust covered the support beams and ceiling. It was full of out-of-date equipment that was marked with many old scars, rife with dents and chipped paint never tended to because it didn't affect the function of the machine. Time capsules of old cigarette packages, crushed pop cans, crumpled paper, inkless pens, and worn out plaid garden-ing gloves had been swept, tossed and forgotten in all of the incon-spicuous places workers could think of—anywhere that wasn't the garbage can.

Dom was standing at the back with his arms crossed, leaning in as he spoke with a few others. Reg and Cy were in their late twen-ties and worked on a machine that flattened coiled steel into sheets cut to any size ordered. It was the bread and butter of the plant, and everyone wanted to get on that machine, but seldom were there openings.

The other guy standing with them was Richard. He'd been there for a little over thirty years. He'd learned the ins and out of most of the machines in the place, and if you wanted to learn something, he was the guy to teach it to you. He was a patient and level-headed man, the kind of person who earned the esteem of others without trying to.

Richard was not so old as to be considered out-of-date, but the arthritic crook in his fingers and the heavy creases on his face showed the wear that the years had taken. His sense of humour and practical jokes elicited laughs all over the plant, and if one could hear laughter off in the distance, Richard was most likely a part of it. He used to say that telling someone a joke and making them laugh was the easiest way to get to know them.

No subject was sacred enough for Richard to avoid tackling it with humour. He often satirized the fragile barriers between who he called "the immigrant conquerors" and those indigenous to North and South America—drawing attention to the history so it wasn't forgotten. He wasn't a vindictive man by nature, but he had grown up during a horrendous time of segregation in Canadian history, as his family was among the first to leave the reservations and live in the city centre. It was during a time that would've left a toxic impression of society on anyone, yet it was a toxicity that not everyone had to test. It was that endurance what made his calm, in moments that should rumble with anger, so admirable to Rory.

Richard's bloodline was Ojibwe—one bound to the earth under foot. More so than anyone he called co-worker could say without there being less than a granule of truth to it. Richard often referred to that earth teasingly, but always with an undercutting trenchancy, as stolen land. Others would often say "get over it" or "move on" but that only made the credence that much more indisputable, especially to Rory. It was sometime during the mid-eighties, in an exercise of indignation, that Richard hung a magnificent pencil-sketched eagle above his work station as both an emblem and a caution. It was aimed towards the closet racists he supposed were numbered in the many at Dambar, and he quietly dared anyone to tell him to take it down. But no one ever did, and its hung there ever since, above his work station, gathering a faint hue of carbon dust that he would carefully wipe away with a soft cloth when it got too thick. Richard always gave people a chance. He never cursed a person right out of the gate. To him that was too easy, too common. But as soon as they exhibited some form of social ignorance, he would put them in their place. Not many would seek to further an argument about race relations with Richard, and he had become an expert on when to use leverage and when not to. It was an attitude that gave the tightly tied ponytail that ran down his back—so thick and diesel-smoke black no matter how many years had passed—the intimation of a leather whip whose latent lash of equity was only an malignant comment away from being cracked.

Richard was a Dambar historian of sorts and spoke of the way things had always gone in the shop—like it was a nepotistic boys' club for Caucasians. Family ties that enabled those who possessed them to do little in the way of the heaviest, hardening, debilitating work around the shop. He could never escape the name of minority, reminded of it everyday by almost every face he looked into while there, and while he toiled when others that should be helping had their feet propped up on a desk.

In the early-nineties he and another man, Lenny Fallon, had tried to organize a union meeting. It was to be an information session that would be put on by a local union outfit. Richard and Lenny were told by many that they would show up and listen to what had to be said, enough so that they thought success was in the cards for sure. But instead, their intentions were made known to the plant super-intendent by some bootlicking stooge or stooges. Word was that all attendees names were going to be written down and handed over to management for further review—whatever that meant. After that got around only a handful of guys showed up to the meeting, rendering the effort fruitless, and Richard and Lenny had to go back to work defeated. They thought that for sure they would be termi-nated—or at least sentenced to filthy, mindless, backbreaking work until they gave up and quit. Instead it was just silently acknowledged that those kinds of politics were not acceptable at Dambar, and the events kept the word "union" out of their mouths for the ensuing decade. They didn't want to believe it, seeing as the workforce acted so chummy most of the time, but the bottom line was that there was indeed a lack of community in the shop. A false colony of fel-lowship that, without camaraderie, temporary or full-fledged, made the idea of unionizing a futile one. It was only after Lenny suffered a fatal heart attack, sitting in his chair at the flame cutting table, that Richard accepted that the glimmer of any hope of unionizing was being carted off and loaded into the ambulance along with his defiant friend. It was that that kept his consorting with Dom's next-generation of rebellion talk to no more than hushed stories of how it went down when he had tried.

Rory approached the group and assumed that whatever topic Dom was canvassing them related to what was spoken about the night before. They simultaneously made eye contact and Dom gave a wrong-sided salute that Rory acknowledged with a nod of the head.

"Hey, guys," Rory said.

"If these fuckers are going to have us stand around," said Cy, "I'm going out for a smoke." Cy turned for the back door. "Hey there, Ror. So glad you could join us." His tone was always steeped in sarcasm.

Rory saw that the plant superintendent, Gregory 'The Dub' Dubinsky, was standing with Wyatt at the front, facing the pack of workers that either had been told to stop working, or that were in early from other shifts.

Gregory had worked his way up from the bottom over the last fifty years, watching the company expand, be sold twice, and employees and management alike come and go. Years had weathered his frame, and his bowlegged walk made him lean to his left side. He took no bullshit and never wanted to hear excuses, because he'd heard them all before and he was not in the business of sympathy. He was respected and hated all in the same breath, though no one could say he didn't know how to maintain a strict environment. He was the same superintendent who had crushed Richard's pursuit of a union. None of which Rory ever witnessed for himself—because in his last stretch, 'The Dub' had become lax and comical, not giving a young guy like Rory much of a glimpse into what it was that made him merit sneers and acrimony from the veterans.

"None of the office staff are out here with us," Rory said.

"Guess this doesn't affect them," Richard said, shrugging.

Dom was shaking his head. "Horse shit."

Rory looked around and gave a slight tip of the hat to those he made eye contact with. Then he saw Clive emerge from the door that joined the office to the shop floor and the crowd hushed as he approached.

Clive cut to the chase. "Thank you all for coming in. As some of you know, the company has had to make some adjustments to deal with economic strain in the industry." Stone-cold accuracy and succinct delivery, not a choke or a fumble. Clive had come prepared to deliver. "We are trying to keep everyone gainfully employed through this period of uncertainty as we are starting to feel the squeeze. There will be a little reshuffling of personnel but our goal is to disrupt as little as possible."

Dom leaned over to Rory and said, "Billion-dollar company feeling the squeeze of a few guys at forty-four grand a year? That's not saving them from bankruptcy." He rolled his eyes up and pinched his nose like the smell was too strong for him.

"We don't want to alarm anyone," Clive continued, "but we need to be patient. Overtime, weekend or otherwise, and all shifts outside the regular Monday to Friday eight-hour swing have been suspended for all employees, save for Sunday night start time for the midnight shift. The company has also seen fit to rescind the attendance incentive and annual bonus programs until they are deemed stable enough to furnish."

A collective gasp came from the crowd, accompanied by some more expletive reactions. Clive didn't give them a chance to quiet down on their own—he just raised his voice for the last part. "And Gregory Dubinsky has decided on retiring as plant superintendent."

It was a long time coming, Rory thought. There had been a two-year stay of retirement, and this seemed like the right time to call it quits. The old bugger had played it well. His salary getting dropped during a recession made it look like he'd jumped on a grenade to save the jobs of one or two more guys. *Now that's what I call going out with a bang,* Rory thought.

The group began to get louder, but Clive wasn't finished and he raised his voice even more to cut through the yammering. "He will be succeeded by Wyatt Burnaby. Thank you for your time and understanding." Clive turned back towards the office, not giving any time for questions like he'd said there would be.

The gathering slowly dispersed, shambling back to work and to the change room as the information sank in. They looked like residents of a convalescent home who didn't know what to do with themselves after being allowed outside without supervision.

"I figured that Wyatt was up to something when he came here and got that foreman position so quickly," said Richard. "I just couldn't put my finger on it."

Rory thought he saw a bead of sweat evaporate on Dom's face before it could run down to his chin. It was an almost certainty that he was going to lose it this time—circumventing empty threats, straight to war cries. He looked like he was going to push through the crowd and rush Wyatt, whom he would take out low, at the knees, before chasing down Clive and maul him as if a mountain lion had caught a lamb.

It actually made Rory happy knowing that he wouldn't need to work the ten-hour shifts for a while, it might be a chance to finally get some proper rest, but he didn't want to say anything about it around Dom in case it sparked a proximity slaughter.

"This is shit," Dom said. He turned and lumbered to the back door, collecting Cy and Reg on his way.

"That one's got to learn to take it easy," said Richard.

"Actually, I think that walking away was a tremendous display of restraint on his part," said Rory. "I thought we were going to have to pull him off somebody." Rory watched as the three of them exited. "What were you guys talking about before, anyhow, if you don't mind me asking?"

Richard made a gesture towards the locker room. He pulled Rory closer and whispered, "Let's go somewhere a little less populated."

They walked to the back in file and Richard checked over his shoulder and behind them several times to make sure they weren't followed. When they entered the back change room, he took a sweep of the stalls and shower room. He beckoned for Rory to join him at the lockers and pulled out his wallet. He opened it but took nothing out.

"Dom's talking a lot about unions," Richard said in a low tone. "He's really fired up, and if he does something rash, he could end up making a big mistake that costs more jobs than just his."

Rory took a second and inched closer. "C'mon Rich, I've heard it ever since I started here. From you more than a few times. You can't blame him for running with it, the way things are looking now. Maybe he's got a point."

"This is not the time. Too many folks are worried about life outside of here. The company would cut us down before the idea could even be considered by most guys anyhow. These things don't happen overnight."

Rory thought a moment and leaned against his locker, thumbing the keys in his pocket. "You better calm him down, then."

Richard's wallet was still out, the corner of a twenty was between his fingers. In the same instant Rory was going to ask why, the outside door swung open, and in came Wyatt.

Richard pulled the twenty from his wallet. "Here you go. Better believe I'm not making that bet again." He put his wallet back into his coveralls' pocket and went for the door to the plant. As he passed Wyatt, he said, "Those Maple Leafs are crap this year."

Rory didn't falter. He pocketed the twenty and turned his attention to Wyatt. "Congrats on the promotion."

"You seen Cy, Dom, or Reg around?"

"I can't say that I have. Richard just came back here to pay what he owed, and I'm going home."

Wyatt eyed the washroom like a bloodhound that had lost the scent of its quarry. He looked back to Rory, gave him a cursory thank you, and left to pick up the trail again.

Rory rolled his combination lock over and wondered if the thank you was for the congratulations or for the straight answer about his wayward co-workers.

He opened his rust-orange coloured locker. *Don't do anything stupid,* he thought as he looked at Anna's baby picture staring back at him from his locker door. Her smile was both a catalyst and an inhibitor. He was torn between what had been said by management and what was being talked about by his coworkers. If it wasn't too heavy to lift at first, it had started to put on weight.

Rory had called ahead so Emily would have Anna ready. He didn't want to have to leave his car running and unattended in the loading zone or find a parking space. When he arrived they were waiting in the entrance to the building, and Emily was crouched down, saying something to Anna, who was pressed close into the corner of the glass door and the wall that had the buzzer and codes for the tenants.

Emily pointed down the steps at Rory's car and tried to take Anna by the arm, but she stubbornly shook and pulled away.

Rory got out of the car, addled by his daughter's despondence.

Emily opened the door for him. "She started acting like this not long after you left. I could barely get her in the apartment."

Anna didn't turn from her corner, even with the presence of her father.

"Has something happened, Ror?"

Rory looked at Emily and shrugged his shoulders. "I have no idea. We lost Marisa as a sitter but she doesn't react to those kinds of things." He went to the corner and placed a hand on Anna's head. "Sweetie. Darlin'. It's time to go."

Anna turned slowly, avoiding his eyes, acting like she'd done something wrong but was not going to admit it.

Rory tilted her head up so she could no longer avoid him. Her cheeks looked puffy and red with a rash. There was a hollow emptiness he'd never seen in his daughter before. "What's the matter, darling?" Rory could feel his eyelids get heavy and his sight blurred with oncoming tears, but he didn't want to upset Anna further so he picked her up and held her tightly. Then he turned to his sister, "Thanks for watching Anna, I'll call you later."

"Okay, see you two later." Emily said—trying to get a response from Anna with a funny face, but to no avail.

Rory strapped Anna into the back seat and shut the door. He wiped the tears from the corners of his eyes, waved to Emily, got in the car, and carried on home. The car was silent except for sounds of the traffic.

Part II: 2010

Chapter 4

Fourteen months had passed since the announcement, and the crew at Dambar still hadn't fully recovered from the scare the recession brought. They walked to their stations with their eyes on the ground and hands motionless at their sides. The mood was dour. What conversations they did have were sparse.

Dom had, against his will, successfully put a lid on his objections while at work. Cy and Reg might have provided an audience for him while they were at the bar, but the two didn't encourage it and they both noted that Dom had lost course and was acting a bit cuckoo, going on incessantly about programs he would watch on "The History Channel" that depicted and paralleled his beleaguering woe and spite. They could only tell him to shut his yap so many times before they got sick of saying it—letting him run his mouth until he lost his voice. Rory had even himself seen Dom sunk into the seat of his overhead crane, sulking and plotting to himself.

One plus for the workers was that the plant didn't experience a drastic dip in sales during the recession. The year around contract orders were enough to keep everyone busy, and no one else had lost their jobs. Business was slowly picking up again. And that helped to relieve some of the tension that had had their necks stiff and backs arched.

Rory had done the same as everybody else: wait soundlessly in hopes he didn't warrant a re-evaluation of his merit within the company. Management held all the cards and were doing whatever they wanted, addressing issues as they saw fit or not, and it looked like inattention was the preferred course of action—that kinks work themselves out eventually.

A few new pairs of hands were brought in to help where the plant was getting a little swampy. They were hired through an outside agency—ties that could be easily cut. No benefit payments. No holiday or sick time to pay out, either. There was always someone scraping bottom who wasn't seeking long-term employment, who would come in for minimal pay a couple days a week. Most of these types had questionable mental health issues and shadowy pasts. They tried to integrate, but their hygiene made them fit to live with strays and their attitudes were gruff and prone to saying weird and sadistic things. True or not, that was how they portrayed themselves. It was cause for a lot of friction with the employees, keeping their distance, trying not to stir up trouble with the skittish and unpredictable short-termers. The workers' concerns were brought up, but it didn't bother management—muscle was muscle, and the cheaper it was, the better. They didn't have to work with the question marks.

Rory was at his machine; a hydraulic press brake. It was a hulking, mighty automaton that formed steel into angles and complex shapes. Most of what Rory made was used in agricultural equipment. His blue giant might have been obsolete by industry standards but it still did the trick. Newer, more sophisticated machines were being produced that required little human labour—Rory looked at pictures of how easily everything seemed to run with the German engineering, but when he asked management if his blue giant would get a high-end replacement, if it were to crap out, he was told to keep dreaming. He figured it probably had something to do with the size of the thing. It once was used to form massive parts, but now the majority of the work was small enough for one man to complete solo. The brake was powerful enough to smoosh anything made of soft tissue into paste and could grind bone to dust under the 350 tons of force the gigantic hydraulic cylinders commanded. Rory had heard his share of horror stories, even witnessed many skin-tearing pinches, that a lax attitude and slow reflexes can precipitate around such mechanics.

He was in the middle punching some numbers into the brake's computer box, making adjustments to the order he was working on, when Dom came up behind him and just started talking.

"Another new guy got brought in today," he said. "That makes three in as many weeks. Some of them are doing more than just grunt work, too. I saw the guy helping on midnights up in the crane when I came in this morning, and when I asked about it, all I was told was that 'he was qualified.'" He made the quotations gesture in the air. "I don't think these guys are the average rummies off the street that we're used to getting in here."

Rory was trying to concentrate but knew it wasn't going to happen when Dom was around, so he stopped what he was doing. "Yeah, crazy. It finally looks like this place is getting back to normal."

Dom delayed his response as he scoped the driveway for any sign of authority. "I've heard a couple rumours lately, don't know if you have, but I thought I'd run them by you."

Dom turned his head side to side like an owl, and almost right around, watching for people watching them. It didn't matter that the brake was located in a sequestered area of the shop, Dom needed to know there was no one around who could get the drop on them. Rory just waited for him to be content enough to continue.

"I heard from guys on the line that there have been hints the company is asking for funding from corporate to install a new proto-type, state of the art cut-to-length line. Something that will cut half inch coils and that apparently *stretches* the steel out."

Rory looked at Dom like he was playing a trick on him like some of the old guys so often did to a rookie. "Go ask maintenance for the left-handed monkey wrench" was one; "Go get the pipe widener," another. "Go get the plate stretcher" was the most common one, and Rory had fallen for it so many years ago when he had started. "Yeah right, bud," said Rory. "What do you take me for? This place is so tight with cash that you'd have an easier time getting a blue whale through a bull's asshole."

Dom moved in close and stared up at Rory. "I'm not fooling around."

Rory knew when Dom was joking, because he would start laughing as soon as he pulled it off—even if the joke failed, he wouldn't be able to contain himself. But now, there was no hanging on and squeezing every chuckle out of anything. When Dom postured, Rory knew he meant to be taken seriously, but he also knew Dom could take a lot of nonsense at face value and try to use it as legal tender. "Okay," said Rory. "I believe you. Would you please stop staring at me like that? You look like you're going to hit me."

Dom didn't ease his shoulders or his fists. He was all fired up and the probability that the information wasn't going to pass clearly from his brain through his mouth was high. And to keep it as clear as it could be kept, Rory told himself that interrupting him again would not be prudent.

"Marsh told me last night that he overheard Strome and that bulbous fuck Wyatt when he took some orders in. He didn't mean to listen, but what caught his ear made him stay and eavesdrop."

Dom inched closer, and out of habit, Rory stepped back.

"Would you come here? I'm not going to attack you. I don't want anyone to hear us talking. Marsh has only told me, and I said I wouldn't tell anyone." Dom had one of the biggest mouths in the shop. Some guys called him "megaphone" but never to his face. It was hard to believe he was the one getting exclusive information that wasn't meant to be leaked. "I'm only telling you because it is pretty heavy stuff."

"Out with it, then." Rory was tired of all the buildup. He needed to get back to work.

Dom looked around again and cleared his throat with a fake cough. "Marsh said he came in halfway through, but he heard something about shutting down the line and a big excavation process. He also heard them say something about needing another coil pit for influx. That's all he stuck around for. He didn't want to get caught with that kind of intel, so he quietly got out of the office back into the shop before they were aware of him."

Rory processed the circumstances and consequences. If what Dom said was true, shutdown might mean more layoffs, but a new coil pit would mean more room for stock, which meant more work. One thing was sure, he definitely didn't want to get into a full-blown discussion about something that could very well just be talk.

"You need to sit on this," said Rory. He grabbed Dom by the shoulders and stared right back into him. "Dom, you need to keep this quiet. Got it? I'll go and speak with Marshall, and then I'll get back to you. *Do not* spread this around."

Just as Rory let Dom's shoulders go, Wyatt came around the corner by the driveway. He was moving quickly and coming right for them. The two of them were good at hiding their nerves. Years of hearing high-decibel impacts, sometimes for hours on end, had made those nerves as indestructible as the steel.

Dom walked away, and Rory returned his attention to his machine. Wyatt and Dom did not get along. The professional courtesy between them was about as legitimate as a prostitute's child. Rory thought Wyatt would stop and interrogate Dom first, but he walked right past him, not even passing a glance, and went for Rory.

"Not a lot of work out here? I think I could find something for you to do if that's the case," Wyatt said.

Rory hated answering Wyatt when he was demonstrating one of his exercises of impudence. "Just making a few adjustments," said Rory. "Dom had a question about getting a few angles bent up for a trailer." Not the best cover, but it would have to do.

"You going to clear that with me?" Wyatt huffed. The transformation into a fast-and-loose superintendent that Wyatt had been undergoing since his promotion had completed. He had begun to walk even taller in the last year, but he wasn't fooling anyone who knew him before the promotion, and his poisonous adulteration of an otherwise fine smelling aftershave followed behind him—its reek a reminder of who he really was—a bumbling fool, a poor man's Inspector Clouseau with the attitude of a wound-up Pomeranian. He was rarely seen coming, but you knew where he'd been. He would wear the same clothes every day, washed or not, but that was something no one could really be sure of, because his ensemble was all black Dickies work attire. And if he was trying to be intimidating, he was going about it the wrong way.

Rory didn't feel like playing his game. "He just asked me if I was able to make the angles."

Wyatt eyed Rory. "It's okay with me. Just fill out the proper paperwork." The idiot was making it like he'd done Rory a favour. "Anyway, I wanted to see you about your holiday request for next month. I had to deny it."

"Oh . . . May I ask why?"

"The schedule is booked solid for the next six weeks. We can't afford to have you off. Sorry," Wyatt said as he tottered off swiftly without giving Rory a chance to appeal.

Rory took the slip of paper that had a big red line through it and the word *declined* written in a limp-wristed, almost illegible scrawl. He crumpled it up and tossed it in the garbage. Hysterics would do him no good. Wyatt relished watching workers bitch and moan, and that was a satisfaction Rory was not willing to give him.

As Wyatt tottered back to his office, Rory cracked a smile when he saw Dom up in the crane, screaming silently in Wyatt's direction and waving both hands back and forth with his middle fingers extended.

When Dom looked down for a reaction, Rory nodded in approval and flashed a "thumbs up" before turning back to his machine, and continuing with his work.

The denial of his holidays began to eat at Rory. *This is not good,* he thought.

The time off was needed so he could take care of Anna while her new caregiver was away for a holiday of her own.

Rory figured there wasn't a point in telling the new caregiver, a sweet girl named Chelsea, about the denied vacation. He wouldn't feel good about if she canceled her plans to accommodate him—which she would most likely do if she knew he couldn't make arrangements. It was the kind of person she was—always putting other people before herself.

He figured he'd better try Emily first, before getting ahead of himself. To stay out of sight he ducked in behind the cover of his machine and dialed his sister.

"Hello?" said Emily.

"Em, it's Ror, I need to ask you something real quick. Do you know what you'll be working next month? the twelfth to the sixteenth, specifically."

"I have absolutely no idea, why?"

"I need someone to watch Anna. Chelsea is going out of town and I just had my holiday request kiboshed. Do you think you might be able to give me a hand?" Rory crossed his fingers but braced for disappointment.

The phone stayed quiet, "I really don't know. We've been bogged down and working short-handed lately, and if things stay like this, I know I won't be able to do it."

"You know what, that's cool. I just needed to ask." Rory said—hiding his worry.

"If anything changes I'll let you know," said Emily.

"Thanks. Okay, I've got to go. Talk later."

It didn't surprise Rory that Emily sounded a bit hesitant. Not only were a nurses' hours worse than his, they required a lot of energy, and after a day at the hospital, taking care of another person who required a lot of attention, would just be too much.

And Anna had become more difficult to handle. She swung into a crazed and irritable states more often, and without warning, and got easily frustrated with people.

All the doctors he'd been to in the last year had said the same things: that her accelerated degeneration was not normal for children with fetal alcohol syndrome but that everyone with the affliction took to it differently. There was nothing to be done except prescribe various medications that did nothing except knock her out—something that Rory, and Emily, did not agree with.

Anna had turned six and would be turning seven in a few months. The discussion whether she could attend school had come up but it didn't last long. The one school in the city designed for kids with learning disabilities, together with paying a regular caregiver to be around while he worked, was way out of his affordability—it was one or the other, not both. There was no way around it, and making do was becoming more and more insurmountable every day.

It wasn't just the growing intensity of Anna's tantrums that he was contending with either. He had also been repressing the intensity of his proliferating physical pain and his broken-down, in-need-of-repair emotions, and they were slowly and silently taking their toll—but through it, not once did he yell, not once did he blame her for anything—soldiering forth was his specialty. He would adapt again—even if it crippled him. *I'm thirty-two years old, how can I be this fucked up already?* he thought.

He searched for ways to alleviate his discomfort. He read about holistic healing practices and meditation classes that might relieve the stress, but the mantras and breathing exercises exhausted Rory. He tried massages, but they didn't get deep enough. He inquired about his insurance coverage for physical therapy, but it was so little that he could only use it for two sessions—unless he were to hurt himself at work—but the pain was all over, not just in one specific area, and he decided that doing anything to himself deliberately would be idiotic. Time was too scarce a commodity for him. And taking up any kind of class or long term treatment, and leave Anna without, was something he couldn't justify.

In an effort to try something that didn't have a cost, he went to a meeting at a local church, but he came out feeling even more emotionally depleted and vulnerable, instead of comforted and calm. The others at the meeting who had children with similar problems told him things would get better, explaining how the ailment had developed over time with their children, but he didn't buy their stories. They never fit his own. Some of the other attendees' children had mild cases, and most of the parents had unknowingly adopted children with FAS already in place. They hadn't been party to the problem, so they had nothing to admit to themselves. And Rory figured that if they had known about the child's problems, they would've just chosen a better model. None of the people around him could identify with what kind of knotted ball of yarn he was trying to untangle on a daily basis.

After that he had stopped looking for cures. There were none as far as he was concerned. He just needed to cope. To find and focus on the redeeming qualities of the pain, for both his sake and for Anna's. He owed her at least that.

He had grown a beard to cover his grimace, and the stress had begun to salt it around the corners of his mouth and on his chin. Anna hadn't taken to it well at first, but she'd gotten used to it.

All that he was twisting around in his mind was being made worse by the pang of hunger in his stomach. He looked at the clock—it was another 45 minutes before he could sit down for a lunch he needed, so he could get out of the funk Wyatt had put him in.

Chapter 5

In the Northeast corner of the building, towards the back, well removed from sight of the front office, was the workers' parking lot and lunch and change rooms. The lunchroom wasn't a very well maintained one. The floors were streaked with boot scuffs, and the tiles' finish had been scratched away by the legs of cheap chairs that were rarely replaced or updated. The tables weren't any better. They were levelled by folded paper that wouldn't provide sturdiness for long. Some workers ritually sat at the uneven surfaces to eat, but never would you see a bowl of soup in front of them. All it would take was one wrong move, and it would be all over the place.

Another nuisance commonly dodged was the spot under the ceiling fan that hung in the centre of the room; it wobbled perpetually from improper installation. Workers avoided having to eat underneath it and teased the one who came late for lunch who had to, as they believed one day it was bound to detach, and plummet into a plate of food.

The cabinets were made of particle board, and the handles that hadn't already fallen off were barely hanging on by screws that just needed a little tightening, but weren't problematic enough for anyone to take the five minutes to fix them. The walls hadn't been painted in ages, and they were coated with a sallow stain from when smoking had still been permitted indoors. And in all the rooms there were signs posted that warned of asbestos danger if the floor tiles were disturbed. One was posted right beside the giant clock that kept slow time, and Rory and Richard found it funny that no one saw the humour in its coincidentally foreboding placement.

Of the fridges supplied by the company, one was brand-new, and its white stood out against the disrepair of the lunchroom. The second fridge was a muddy olive green and it looked like it could shield someone from a nuclear blast. The icebox was forever overly frozen, shedding frost every time someone tried to stuff a microwavable dinner inside. The grated shelves still provided support, but they looked worn away, as if eaten by slow-acting acid, ready to give out under too much weight. This fridge was used exclusively by the older employees. Perhaps they quietly identified with it—not too old to be given up on and with just enough juice left to serve a purpose. It was a monument to their resilience, but the day that it failed would serve as a hint that their own requiem would not be far off.

The coffee vending machine was also ancient. It had a picture reminiscent of a 1950s cafeteria display on the front, an inviting scene where the coffee was hot and the biscuits and pie were fresh. But the once-vibrant colours had faded into a hazy light blue and yellow, making it look like it had sat in the sun for years, and that the coffee and biscuits and pie were now cold and stale and inedible.

They called it The Sludge Machine. Every time workers heard someone slide change into the machine's belly, debates raged over whether whatever it was that the workers were drinking could be safely ingested. Some jested that it was the strongest stimulant on earth and that a man could lift a full ton of steel after a few cups. They also claimed it was the most powerful bowel displacer in Canada and, only after years of training, one could harness the immediate explosive call of nature the thick brew summoned. Others told new hires that a cup of joe from The Sludge Machine was a sure-fire way to get sent home sick without having to feign the symptoms. But whatever side was taken, most people ended up drinking it as a last line of defence against weariness, and after one developed resistance to the taste and smell, and were in full control of their bowels, telling the difference between good coffee and what came from The Sludge Machine was nearly impossible.

Since he was on the day shift, and without an assistant, Rory took his lunch half an hour later than the rest of the plant. It got too crowded to enjoy the thirty-minute break when they were all in there. And instead of having to listen to the profane talk and boorish eating habits of his more distasteful coworkers, Rory could turn the radio to his favourite station, 92.1 FM—classic hits from the sixties, seventies, and eighties.

Lunch gave Rory a chance to have a midday disconnect. It wasn't much but it made the second half of the day feel like he was starting fresh.

Just as he was about to dig into his meal of leftover meatloaf, he heard the door to the plant open in the other room. *Great,* he thought. He hated that the washroom and lunchroom were so close to each other, especially when the person using the john didn't think of checking the lunchroom and shutting the door between them before setting about their business.

Rory got up, annoyed by the usual lack of courtesy, and went to shut the door. But in his hurry, he almost ran into Marshall, who was coming into the lunchroom.

"Whoa there, friend. Really gotta go or what?" said Marshall.

"Sorry, man. I was just coming to close the door. I thought, well, you know."

"Nope, just getting a drink."

Rory sat back down, and Marshall went to the old fridge—he was one its steadfast patrons—and got out a Coke. He cracked it open and gulped down about half the can.

Rory was just about to drift back into his lunch break calm when he thought to ask Marshall about what Dom had said earlier. Rory didn't want to surprise Marshall and make him feel cornered, so he got up and did a quick scan of the stalls in the bathroom, the urinals, the shower room, and the locker room. When he came back in, Marshall was still standing by the fridge.

"Hey, Marsh," he said. "I was talking to Dom earlier, and he was saying you overheard something in the office between Wyatt and Strome. And I know how Dom can embellish things. I was just wondering about hearing it from the source."

Marshall didn't move—not like he frozen with fear, more like he was silently lashing himself for telling Dom anything at all.

"There's no one else back here," said Rory. "I promise that I don't intend to use this information to start anything."

"I do believe you, Ror. It's just that maybe what I heard was just office talk. You know, like, 'Wouldn't it be great if we could blah' or some other form of that."

"Yeah, I guess." He didn't want to turn it into an interrogation. If Marshall thought something was pertinent information, he'd say so.

"What was it that Dominic told you?" Marshall said, pulling out the chair beside Rory for a seat.

"He said that there have been a couple whispers about a new cut-to-length line. Something new that can handle a hell of a lot more than the old Triton can. Sounds a little much to me," said Rory.

"Well, I personally didn't believe it, but after what I heard, I can't say I'm too sure what I do believe. One thing I know for sure is that I don't want to go around stirring shit up if they are planning something big. The way I see it is, we can either benefit from the investment and the business that comes with it, or we can get canned for plastering their plans all over the place. This company is a heavy hitter in the industry now, and I ain't so delusional that I think I'm irreplaceable."

"You sure did choose the right person to confide in," Rory said bitingly.

"Yeah, I know. We were at the bar after work, and I'd had a few. Stupid of me."

"Well, I guess we leave it as nothing," said Rory. "I'll have a talk with Dom and pass it off as drunken gibberish and that you don't remember what it was you told him."

Marshall got up and chucked his empty can in the garbage. "Thanks, bud. See you out there."

Rory knew the rumour wasn't going to stay contained. Word spread like wildfire on the shop floor, and it was only a matter of time before everyone knew. All Rory wanted was to prevent Dom from being the one management singled out if they needed a scapegoat.

* * *

On his way home cars zipped in and out and around Rory. Some honked, and some didn't. His body was in the driver's seat, but his brain was somewhere else.

A frosty haze shrouded the streetlights, and even though the snow was almost melted, the night still came early, and with it, the air would get chilly and mist the city.

In faraway thought, he hadn't realized how much slush other cars had kicked up onto his windshield. He could barely see, and he snapped out of it in time to regain control of the car from the now natural pull to the left. The passing car he'd almost sideswiped sped up, and the driver was flashing what Rory figured was the finger, but he couldn't be sure because of how dirty and foggy his windows were.

He looked at his gas tank meter. The needle was bouncing off the empty mark, like it didn't want to accept it was out. The bright lights of a gas station shone through the windshield, and Rory decided to stop and collect himself, get some air, and formulate a plan on how to keep the news he had gotten at work to himself, and not involve Chelsea.

The gas station attendant came up quickly, not even giving Rory enough time to shut off the car and get his window rolled down all the way.

"What'll it be?" the attendant asked.

"Fill it up, please."

"Actually, you're going to have to go on the other side. Our hoses don't reach that far."

Rory had pulled up on the wrong side. *Honest mistake,* he thought, but it made him feel incompetent. He backed out, pulled in on the correct side, and got out of the car. The attendant was waiting for him.

"Sorry about that," Rory said.

It didn't matter to the gas jockey one bit. He just set the pump and went back into his little heated shack.

Rory went around the other side of the car and leaned up on it, paying no attention to the wet dirt covering the doors, and thought back to when Chelsea had come into their lives.

She had been working towards a BA in child development and was on the verge of graduating when she answered the ad Marisa had posted at the university. Upon meeting Anna, Chelsea was promptly smitten. She thought it was a perfect start for her career— even though she would make far less than what her fellow class-mates would be making.

"I work horrible hours. Back and forth, days to evenings, week after week. Is that going to be a problem?" Rory asked when she'd come to his home for the interview.

"I don't think it'll be an issue. I still live with my parents, and I'm pretty much socially inactive," said Chelsea— a slight hint of embar-rassment colouring her face at the admission.

"Are you sure you're not an angel?"

"Not that I'm aware of, but if I start growing wings, I'll definitely let you know."

"I think we're going to get along just fine," said Rory.

It didn't take long for Anna to acclimate to Chelsea, but it was far from easy. Through Anna's violent episodes and demeaning remarks, where a weaker person would have just walked away, Chelsea rode it out.

Chelsea had done so much in the last year that having to tell her he was unable to reciprocate hurt him to the bone. He looked up to the sky, pleading to the heavens, but all he got for a response was the blue and red flicker in the corner of his eye—a flashing sign of a liquor store.

Where all this shit began, he thought.

He could almost taste the whisky on his tongue, and he imagined dumping a bottle of it down his throat and drowning in it, but he shook the thought away. It was not long after Chelsea started that Rory decided to stop going to see Linda at "The Woodbine" for his occasional drink. It had lost its purpose, but every so often he felt that lust for the drink come back to inquire how he was getting on.

Then an image of Wyatt came into his head, ripping up the vacation request and laughing, and it enraged him. He then thought of taking a full wine bottle and cracking it across Wyatt's smug face, leaving nothing but a slight forming bruise on the complexion of the man who continued to stare at him, unfazed. Rory shook that thought from his head too. No need to take any more aggression home. It wasn't healthy for anyone.

He turned back, away from the glow of the liquor store. The attendant was hanging up the hose on the pump. "Cash or charge?" the kid asked.

"Charge." Rory followed him to the shack, paid, and then got back in the car. He took one more look at the liquor store before turning the engine over, putting the car in gear, and driving off, his temptation firmly put into check.

When he got home, Chelsea was waiting in the living room, flipping through a fashion magazine with Anna snuggly by her side looking on at the bright coloured dresses and outrageous ensembles.

"Hi girls," Rory said.

Chelsea got up and gave the magazine to Anna so she would stay occupied. "Hello, Mr. Gunn. How was work?"

"It was work, thanks for asking." Rory looked to his daughter, half expecting some sort of welcome. "Honey? Hello? Anna?"

She still didn't turn to acknowledge him.

"She's just now settling. It was a particularly tough day," Chelsea said.

"You can say that again," said Rory—barely able to hide his own instability.

"Is everything all right, Mr. Gunn?"

Rory felt weak. There was no good way to say it, but it had to be said. It would get harder the longer he waited, but he just couldn't listen to Chelsea tell him that her plans weren't as important as Anna was. "Everything's fine . . ."

Rory watched as Chelsea nodded in acceptance but he couldn't lie to her— she didn't deserve that. "You know what, Chelsea. Everything isn't all right. My holiday request was denied for when you are going away, but don't worry, I'll work something out."

"Oh, well, I . . . you know if you need me . . ."

"Don't let that be in your mind. Forget it. Let's talk about something else, okay? What's for dinner?"

Chelsea was irked and she scrunched her face but chose to move on, "There's a Shepard's pie in the oven. Store bought but I've had them before. Really tasty."

"Will you be dining with us tonight?" Rory asked.

"I can't. I must get home and get ready. I have tickets to the theatre." Chelsea said—in mock curtsey, like it was going to be an elegant affair.

"Do you mind just watching her for fifteen more minutes while I have a shower and get changed?"

"Not a problem," Chelsea said.

"Thanks. You really are a lifesaver."

"Okay, Mr. Gunn. You're on the clock." Chelsea said—tapping the back of her wrist jokingly.

That night Rory had a restless half-sleep and it made for a groggy morning. For a few moments a remnant of his dream popped into his head. He was in a clearing that was surrounded by a forest. Anna was with him and they were looking for something. He remembered her getting a little way in front of him, and when he finally caught up to her he noticed her stuffed bear, Mr. Boo, looking back at him, but its eyes were possessed and it flashed sharp teeth. The image had jolted him awake, but once he felt around and realized he was in his bed, he fell back asleep.

What a crazy dream, he thought as he started his coffee pot. While it started to hiss and bubble, he heard the sound of Chelsea's key turning over the lock. It made him think of when he was young and sneaking in after an all-nighter.

"Morning. How was the show last night?" Rory said quietly.

"It was nice."

"Glad to hear it. I'll be gone in a few. Help yourself to the coffee."

Chelsea stayed over most nights when Rory worked the day shift. At first it was on the couch but Rory ended up buying a pull out bed and cleaning out the den to give her some privacy. It was more convenient for all of them, and the serendipity of the arrangement—one Rory didn't need to suggest, was one of the guilty pleasures Chelsea afforded him.

Anna would sleep until well after Rory was gone, and sometimes he wondered if it was cruel to leave without saying anything to her, but disrupting her peace wasn't worth waking her for a selfish kiss goodbye.

He didn't want to go in to work that day but he looked forward to the times he was on the same rotation as Richard, and the prospect of shooting the shit with the one person who could help him forget his worries got him in the car, out on the road and into the building.

Through the years, the calming nature of their discussions made Rory's respect for him impermeable. It had not been long after Rory started at Dambar that he began working closely with Richard, learning how to operate various machines. It was in that time that they developed a good trust and became close friends.

Rory's lack of family custom made the culture of Richard's ancestors all the more endearing to him.

In the time before Anna was born, Rory was lost. A quarter life crisis was staring him down and his vices were rapping on the door, begging for permanent lodging. He had never before considered the importance of respecting, and being a part of, nature and life. Nothing ever seemed that important.

It was after one of their talks that Rory started questioning his ex about the damage she might be doing to their unborn.

"The things of the past make us who we are," Richard said in an attempt to settle Rory down—after learning of Anna's diagnosis. "We become life with no choice but to accept some of these things. It's how far ahead we can see without being distracted by the things that cannot be changed—that is how we make ourselves in the present and what the new life will have to work with in the future." Richard, having learned the hard way, cautioned that fighting against the past and getting angry wasn't the solution anymore.

It was all testament to the idea that Richard's knack for activism was not gone. There was a latent bitterness in his perspective that wanted to try a coup again, but Rory only ever picked up on when they spoke alone, and whenever Rory tried to call him on it, he would insist that his days of logrolling were over.

It had taken a while for Rory's rebellious desires to abate, but after Anna's birth and the desertion of her mother, Rory traded the torch of social justice for the one of the taxed single parent trying to keep it together against odds not in his favour. Had it not been for the guidance that Richard provided, the challenge of raising her would have beaten Rory long before.

By the time Rory got to work Richard was waiting in the lunchroom with coffee for both of them. He was reading a tiny little pamphlet. It was yellow and had blue writing on it, but Rory couldn't make out the words. "Whatcha reading?" Rory said.

"Oh, nothing too important." Richard shut the book and stuffed it into his breast pocket. He took off his glasses and let them dangle on the chain around his neck. "Something for later perhaps."

Rory didn't pay it any mind and went and got changed. "I had a weird dream last night. I think it might've been a nightmare actually. I was in the woods with Anna looking around for something, she got ahead of me, and as I got closer, her stuffed animal, this bear, looked like it was going to leap from her arms and tear me to shreds. Scared the shit out of me."

When he came back in to the lunchroom, Richard seemed to be staring into nothing. "That dream of yours might not be a nightmare. Bears mean a few different things to me . . . healing being one of them."

"Even if it was planning on eating me?" Rory asked.

"Especially if it was planning on eating you." Richard said with a smirk.

"Well, that's comforting."

"Wyatt was back here this morning. Didn't know I was. He was putting something up on the cork board when I came back in. Didn't say a word. You should go have a look at what he put up." Richard gestured behind Rory to the board that was usually used for shift and position postings.

A new piece of paper tacked to it had the company letterhead at the top. Rory looked at the signature on the bottom first: Grant Campbell, the branch manager. "Aren't we blessed?" Rory said.

"Read it," said Richard.

It was an announcement. "'The company's board of directors has approved the installation of a new state-of-the-art cut to length line,'" he read aloud. "'It is a project that will begin sometime within the two to three weeks with estimated completion in September or October of 2010. Construction will run through day shifts and evening shifts to diminish any possible interference of production abilities. We are excited for the bright future and possibilities.'" Rory just skimmed the rest. "The official declaration of things really starting to cook," he said. He turned back to Richard. "This could be great for us, don't you think?"

"We'll see, I guess."

Rory turned back to read it again, in more detail, in case he'd missed something, but all he was really thinking about was how Dom was going to flip out when he read it. Those were fireworks Rory did not want to miss.

Everyone had read the memo or had been informed of it by 9:00, and they were talking about the new machine fervently. It relieved Rory that Dom was out of the line of fire.

Clive and Wyatt were even fielding any questions people had. It was in that instant that the stale mood everyone had been in for the last while had worn off completely. People were laughing and looked happy again, and Rory welcomed the change, but there was still no sign of Dom—the one guy who should be gathering all the info he could. Rory found it odd for someone who took every advantage he could to avoid his crane.

There was a buzz around Clive and Wyatt as they played the part of company liaisons. The two of them never came off as the most personable people, but when worker relations were the task of the day, they wore million-dollar smiles like they hadn't paid a penny for them.

Rory snuck in behind the throng, pretending to go to the water cistern that was outside the shipping office. He took a few swallows from the upside-down dunce cap cups and peered in through the window.

Still no sign of Dom.

Rory had another swig of water. After a few of the guys had walked away, having heard enough, he seized the moment to get Wyatt's attention. Rory tapped him on the shoulder, taking him by surprise.

"Rory. Didn't see you there," he said.

"Just came for a little water. Hey, you seen Dom around?" As soon as he asked, he knew his choice of words was wrong, as he may have given Wyatt a reason to tear a strip out of Dom.

"He called in and said he was going to be late. Car trouble," Wyatt said.

"Oh. Okay." Rory took one more cupful of water and returned to his machine.

When Rory got back to the brake, Dom was waiting by the desk, sitting back with his feet propped up on overturned pail.

"Funny, I just went to look for you," Rory said.

Dom wore an ear-to-ear grin. "Always in the last place you look—right under your nose."

"Hear the news?"

"I did. And I'll tell you, those idiots swarming Clive and Wyatt are like strays at the pound, barking at everyone that passes by their kennel, wondering if they're going to go to a new home instead of remaining in a dank cage. But what those poor bastards don't know is that in reality, the guy with a big smile that is bending down petting them—the guy they think is going to take them home and provide for them—has a huge fucking needle behind his back."

"You can be very colourful when you want to be, you know that?"

The grin didn't leave Dom's face. "I ain't buying any of this love-in crap, my friend."

"We don't really have a choice, do we?"

"Perhaps you're right." Dom let the smile thin out and fade away. "You know that stuff I was talking about? The union stuff?"

Rory nodded and did a quick peripheral check.

"Well, I found the one that looks good."

Rory stopped him short. "This isn't the place to talk about it."

"Anybody who would have a problem with our conversation is occupied right now. Cy and Reg are totally on board. Richard won't take much, you know that. We need to get these others guys, though. Thirty percent of employee signatures gets a secret ballot for everyone. Fifty percent plus one gets a day in front of the labour board, and over sixty-five percent is automatic certification." Dom's eyes were wide and persuasive.

Rory didn't want to outright tell Dom to get lost and drop it, but he was cornered. "You know that there hasn't been any kind of indication that those surprise layoffs are coming again, and you know as well as I do that everyone has been looking for any indication that they are."

"Come on, man. You aren't a stupid person. You've heard the grumblings about the way Wyatt runs this place now. He's a fraction of what 'The Dub' was, even if the guy was hated. That and all the new faces that aren't just a pair of hands and a back? These guys have fucking training, for fuck sake. And they work for less. C'mon, it looks weird to people, and no one knows what's really going down. They just think they do." Dom got up from the desk and walked towards Rory in an uncharacteristically easy manner. "Look. This kind of thing will only work if you're on board. People in here think very highly of you. And Richard. They would get behind that. Cy, Reg, and I are ... how do I say this? *Overwhelming.*"

"I don't know, Dom. I don't want you to take this the wrong way, but management have never really given me any reason to resent them. I don't see them as treating us unfairly, either. I mean, sure, Wyatt is a fool, but business is business, right? Would you want his job?"

Dom started to get agitated but kept his temper at bay. "They tell us that they're going to install a brand-new prototype machine in this old and filthy facility, and they don't think we're going to wonder about the cost of such a thing? Where the money is coming from? What kind of production and weekly output they're going to expect? Hell, who are they going to get to run the damn thing? You know as well as I do that hardly anyone here is school-certified to run these machines. Shop-taught only gets you so far.

"This project has got to be in the millions," Dom said, his voice rising. "Money that this company all of a sudden doesn't want locked in a vault? Saving their money elsewhere? Like our bloody incentives that they still haven't reinstated, let alone mentioned.

"And what about cost of living increases? You can't tell me that this powerful, conglomerate connected company saved an extravagant amount of cash by withholding those bonuses and economic increases. How do you not see this? You're a smart guy."

"Quiet," Rory said. "Someone's going to hear you."

"I don't care who hears me!" Dom bellowed. "Ror, the math doesn't add up, man. And I for one will not let complacency wash over me. I think you should think about this a little more. Here, this is a web address for more info. Don't write this off yet."

Dom handed Rory a small piece of paper. The address read "unitysteel.com." Dom didn't wait to see what Rory chose to do with it. He just walked away without looking back. Whether to throw it in the garbage or put it in his pocket, that was up to Rory alone.

The idea couldn't go beyond the little circle of conspirators without Rory. Dom needed Rory's influence to sway the train of thought and convince people the movement wasn't just a swift, angry kick to management's nuts. Someone needed to give a level-headed explanation of why it was a good idea to take on a menacing foe that extended beyond Wyatt and Clive.

Rory put the piece of paper deep in a desk drawer, underneath a couple of old wrenches and empty protractor cases—barely useful garbage that could not be disposed of. He knew where the address was if he ever needed it, which he didn't think would be ever. Evidence of insurrection wasn't safe to keep around, but something fleeting in him wanted to know where it was.

Chapter 6

In a last-ditch effort to accommodate Chelsea's holiday plans, Rory asked to work an overnight shift at the plant. There was more room to maneuver and less people to contend with that could slow him down by tying up a crane, or standing in the way of retrieving materials for orders, or prattling on, extending the hours needed to complete the jobs.

It wasn't hard to convince Wyatt to let him work an overnight shift, but it was met with some dubious uncertainty as to why. And after the usual hum-and-haw calculations, he granted Rory the request because he could find no fault or conflict in it.

It relieved Rory when he was so easily given permission, because more than ever, one had to mind their step around Wyatt, and it was as difficult as walking on egg shells in concrete shoes. He'd just lost his wife to another man, and was taking it out on anything with testicles—behaving with off-hand and undue callousness and resentment. It had all been falling apart for Wyatt around the time Rory was denied his holidays, and it didn't take long before the whole plant knew exactly what it was was making their superintendent so nasty. Anyone could see through his window while he engaged in yelling matches over the phone with, who it was safe to assume, was his soon-to-be-ex-wife.

Since the initial revelation, and indiscreet reaction to it, Wyatt had settled. His personal crisis was no longer the cause of trivial infractions and unwarranted, licentious put-downs that were directed towards the employees. But he still had a look in his eye that if anyone had a leg up, or was trying to get one, he would pull them down into shit—just because he could.

The last few hours of his final shift of the week drifted by, and Rory felt the pull of drowsiness. He thought about wrapping himself in his big, cool pillows and toasty down comforter at home. To stay awake he tidied up around his machine, sweeping up all the dirt and carbon dust that had settled over the course of the day. It got filthy so quickly in the shop that one might think miniature dust devils blew through on an hourly schedule to meet quotas of uncleanliness.

Rory would walk out to the driveway to empty his industrial dustpan—a shovel—in the giant waste bin so he could peer over to Wyatt's office window, the same one that the employees would watch his enactments of animated fury at being severed, which looked out onto the shop floor. Several trips and a spotless work area later, Rory saw that Wyatt had come in and was sitting at his desk. He was eased back in his chair with his hands behind his head and was talking to someone out of view—seeming to be in good spirits.

After giving Wyatt fifteen minutes to get comfortable and drink back half his coffee, Rory went into the office to take his chances. Wyatt was shuffling papers, looking for something on his desk. "Nothing is ever where you need it," Wyatt said.

The unfamiliar pleasantness threw Rory for a loop, and for a second he forgot what he'd come in to ask about.

"Yes, Rory, may I help you with something?" Wyatt said, continuing to search his desk.

"Well, actually yes. I mean, I'm not sure."

"Okay . . ." Wyatt said.

The Policy

"I'm in a bit of a pickle, and I need to ask you about next week. As you may recall, I requested some holidays and was denied due to the workload, but I really need them. I can't find anyone to watch my daughter, and my normal caregiver is out of town. I really need to have it off. I even got most of the orders for next week done." Rory felt like he was begging, and it turned his stomach to come off so desperate, giving Wyatt the upper hand. But all other options were exhausted, and the midnight sluggishness was setting in more and more with each second that passed.

Wyatt knew about Anna, but he and Rory never ventured so deep into personal conversation that he knew more than her name. Wyatt stopped reorganizing and sat back in his chair, tilting his head towards the ceiling. After a moment, he leaned back to his desk and searched for his computer mouse, which was underneath a mound of stray paper. He brought up the schedule on his computer screen and clicked through the machine's workload. When he got to Rory's machine, the schedule showed that all the orders that had been allotted time were highlighted with a neutral blue colour that signified they were complete. Then came the week after, which had just as many orders, but only required that a few be completed.

"There is a lot of open time here, Rory. What happens if I give it to you off and sales wants orders moved up, and I don't have enough operators? I'd have some shit to answer for there. Matt would have no one to help him out."

Rory didn't answer. The silence tethered them together. He didn't know if it was a cue to grovel more, and being tired made the game more perplexing. "I'm in a tight spot here, Wyatt. I really need next week off. I'm sure Matt can handle last-minute rushes, Richard's also more than capable of helping him." Rory said, heaping the responsibility onto his comrades, hating himself for it.

"Well, if it's a need and not a want, I can't really argue that, can I?" Wyatt said.

The meaning twisted itself up like a car wrapped around telephone pole. Rory couldn't keep up any more. He couldn't tell if he detected sarcasm or not, and he figured his chances were dwindling.

"I guess so," Rory said.

"Okay. Fill out the paperwork again, and I'll sign you off."

"Really?" Rory snapped awake. "Thanks, Wyatt. I owe you one."

"I'll remember that," Wyatt said.

It went too easily, and something about the whole exchange didn't sit right, but Rory didn't dwell on it. He was happy that at least he got the time off, and he couldn't wait to tell Chelsea the good news.

When he left the office the day shift workers were coming in and getting ready to start. He went back to his machine to touch base with Matt, just so Wyatt couldn't come by later and make something up that would create a rift, like suggesting to Matt that he'd been left to bust his ass while Rory took a leisurely week off.

Matt was a quiet guy, and no matter what kind of news he got, about anything, he always reacted in an impartial and deferential manner. He didn't like confrontation and would shrink away behind some sort of obstruction when one presented itself. It had taken Rory a couple of years to develop the right way to talk to him so Matt didn't feel pressured or attacked.

"Hey, buddy, how's it going?" Rory said.

Matt was punching some measurements into the brake's computer. "I'm all right. Have you seen this layout? This part is going to be hard."

Rory had a look at the schematic and then looked over their machine. "Yeah, I was looking over that. Sometimes those programmers don't think about how awkward these parts can be. Just because their computers tell them they can do something, they think actually doing it is just as easy. But what can you do, right?"

"You're correct on that one," Matt said.

Rory let a minute pass. "Hey, man, I just came from seeing Wyatt, and I got next week off like I needed."

"That's good," Matt said, not turning away from the computer.

"I got us ahead. Hope it's not going to get hectic on ya."

"Should be fine. I'll manage. They pay us by the hour, not the part."

"Great. See you in a week. Take care."

"You too, buddy."

When Rory got home no one was awake. And because of the time of year it was still mostly dark outside, but that proved no aid with falling asleep, even when overtired. All he needed was to be out before Anna and Chelsea got up and started moving around in the house.

Against better judgement, Rory had started Anna on a mild sedative to combat her increasingly choleric temperament in the evenings. The meds also left her easier to handle in the morning, as she would stay dazed for about an hour as the drowsiness of the drugs and sleep wore off. The bouts of thudding and wailing and sobbing had been replaced with a woozy divergence in her that troubled and pained Rory to concede to, but he knew it to be needed.

That day Rory did not dream, at least nothing that he would be able to recall with any kind of vividness. His wake-up was hard and abnormal. From around the blinds on his bedroom window it appeared to be just as light out as it was when he had first laid down, "Man, just sleep for fuck sake," he said aloud. But when he rolled over to check his bedside clock, it read 6:15 p.m. He had slept for ten, nearly eleven hours—right through the season's limited daylight and back into a seasonal overcast grey that descending night sometimes shared with the rising prairie morning.

His muddled senses were roused by a smell that was wafting into his bedroom from the crack between the door and the floor. It was a smell unlike anything he was used to. And in his alarm of sudden consciousness he scrambled, putting on whatever clothes he had left at the side of his bed—gaining his bearings as he went. Still half-asleep and weak in the knees, he came unsteadily into the kitchen from the darkened hallway.

The girls were in the living room, kneeling down at the oversized coffee table and colouring in a book. Anna didn't respond.

"Evening," Chelsea said as she got up from the table. "Or should I say 'good morning'?"

"Yeah, I don't even know . . . I'm so out of it. Sorry to have slept in like that." The sleepy haze started to dissipate, his grasp on time more firm, and he went over to the coffee machine and got a pot started.

"No worries. I had nothing going on tonight."

"How's Anna been today?"

"She's really into that book I got her. That's her tenth picture today. Have you ever tried colouring before? It seems to capture her attention like nothing I've ever seen."

"No." Rory said—turning to face Chelsea and look in on his fully entranced child. "I definitely don't remember any kind of concentration like that."

A blushed look came over Chelsea and she directed her eyes to the ground, hurriedly covering a doting and coy smile that had set itself on her face.

Rory went puzzled. The mood went a mite awkward and he didn't know why. Upon turning back to the cupboard for a coffee cup he caught a quick glance of his reflection from the kitchen window. In his haste he'd forgotten to put a shirt on. He was sure that the exposure was what caught Chelsea off-guard and put some minor lewdness in the air.

"Excuse me a minute," said Rory.

He slipped back into his bedroom and threw on a shirt. Something had happened. There, in the kitchen between he and her. In that small instance of awkwardness something tingled. His amorous traits may have been dormant for quite some time, but they weren't defunct. The bashful look he'd seen in Chelsea's eyes had gotten the gears turning in rusted fascination. And quickly calculating his chances, he wondered if his instincts were right. But just as quickly as those calculations came, he immediately quashed the idea. But again his being pulsed—wanting it to be a truth—it for him, and him for it alike. After all, she'd gotten to know them both, as they had her, and she practically lived with them full time. It wasn't stupid to bet that some sort of feeling could have developed, but it also wasn't a relationship he was prepared to ruin over a misinterpreted exchange.

Upon returning he went straight for the pot of coffee. He thought it best to not address the awkwardness—leaving it behind them, like it had never taken place.

"Coffee?" he asked.

"No thanks. I never drink it after 5:00."

"I probably shouldn't be, either. I'll be up all night now. This weekend is going to be a gong show. What's cooking, by the way? Smells delicious."

"It's a mushroom and ground beef stroganoff my mother makes. It's easy and quick, and I didn't want to disturb you—thought you could use the sleep."

"Thanks for that. Although, I'll tell ya, it sure feels like I didn't sleep at all."

"Ya. Oversleeping can do that," said Chelsea. "Ummm... Mr. Gunn. There's something I wanted to speak with you about. Something we need to speak about soon ... Not now, if it's inconvenient, but soon."

"That reminds me, I have something to tell you. Mind if I go first?" he said— completely forgetting what a solemnly requested disquisition usually meant for him.

"Sure."

"I hope it's not too late, but I got next week off, and you can go on your holiday."

"That's great news, Mr. Gunn," said Chelsea. "Thing is, I don't exactly need the time any more. Actually, it has something to do with I have to say."

Rory bit his tongue while he stirred his coffee and took a seat at the kitchen island, preparing himself for devastation that he was now aware might be getting ready to blow through his home once again.

"I was actually going for a job interview, well it's actually like a job offer," Chelsea said, "but I don't need to go out of town for it anymore." She seemed to see the distress in Rory's face and rushed to make her point. "The thing is that there is this institution in Alberta. Just outside of Calgary, in Canmore. It's called The Webb Institute. Some of my colleagues are there, and the person taking over as director used to be a prof of mine. And I'm being courted by them to take a position."

Rory tried to look happy for her, but he didn't think he succeeded.

"Long story short, because I don't know how to address this

idea—I was telling my old prof about Anna, and what I'm doing here and he was grief-stricken to hear about her and the situation. He wants to meet her. Maybe to help in some way, I don't know. And I want to know if you were interested in meeting with him first." She beamed.

"An institution? Oh, Chelsea."

"I know it sounds crazy, but, Mr. Gunn, it's the frontrunner for care when it comes to those with developmental difficulties like Anna's. I know there to be some bursaries, too. Please, just meet with him and hear him out. For Anna's sake. Who knows, right?"

Rory rolled it around in his head, but he couldn't even think of the proper words to form a sentence. He looked over into the living room at his peaceful daughter—so innocent and unaware of the turmoil, yet so occupied by it. "Give me some time to think about this, okay?" Rory said.

"Not a problem. Here." Chelsea handed Rory a business card. "No rush. No pressure."

He stared at it blankly. The words on it made no sense to him, and he strained to bring them into focus. *Easy for you to say no pressure*, he thought.

"I'm going to wash up, get out of this ratty lounge-wear, and put on some proper clothes for supper," he said as he walked away from the island. No answer came down the hallway after him, but that didn't surprise him. His voice hadn't carried far past the lump in his throat.

Chapter 7

"Thank God that week is over. What do you say we hit The Zoo after work for a quick splash of whisky?" Dom said with a death-wish grin.

"How much coffee did you drink today?" Rory asked.

Dom liked a lot of sugar in his coffee, almost enough to make it syrup, and if the answer he gave was three cups or more, then the dynamite rush of vivacity was just about to peak, right before its accelerated drop off put him into a numb state of shock. Whisky would only serve as the relaxant for his mouth to continue running.

"Enough," Dom replied.

To Rory, that meant the answer to the equation was *too much*. Sober Dom was already as impulsive as a colt put out to stud in a field of mares—a disposition that made those of a more reserved nature uncomfortable with the heightened attention that Dom drew when out in public.

"I can't, Dom. I don't need a quick splash turning into a full scale swim meet. You know that's exactly what'll happen. Plus, I'm meeting with a specialist for Anna in the morning, and I'm a little nervous about it, so I need to be on my toes."

"Specialist for what?" Dom asked.

"It's complicated. This guy I'm meeting might be able to offer some alternative kind of care."

"What kind of care?"

"Dom! Drop it!" The questions ate at Rory's patience, but he knew Dom hadn't deserved the outburst. "I don't know what kind of care. I just..."

Dom didn't posture like he normally would if spoken to aggressively while also in the throes of a caffeine high. He seemed to notice his friend had become irritated and was able to bring it down several notches. "Didn't mean anything by it, Ror. You know I love that little angel."

"I know. Just tired of all these roadblocks. It's like she doesn't know who I am anymore or is choosing to ignore me." Rory said. "And it's my fucking fault."

Dom just stood there. He was too rough to offer consolation. His emotional vulnerability came only after a six-pack, a few shots, and some mediocre afternoon strippers, perhaps a joint. "I'm sure it will all work out," Dom said.

"I will tell you one thing, man," said Rory. "I've been craving a real piss-up lately. Just to let go and lose myself. It's been so long since I've done anything like it, for myself, you know? But every time I think about it, this little pain develops right where my skull and spine meet."

"No problem, man. Read you loud and clear. I'll catch up with you later."

"Hey, Dom?" Rory grabbed Dom by the elbow. "You mind keeping this between us?"

"Sure. Not a problem."

* * *

The early morning sun was bright. Rory wore wraparound sunglasses that allowed no light whatsoever to creep in through the sides. It had taken him two weeks to finally call and set a meeting with the doctor.

The Policy

The night before he chewed on his nails uncontrollably, something he hadn't done since he was a teenager. He tried thinking of where he'd begin and what he needed to say to the doctor, but everything slipped away just as quickly as he thought of it. He felt like he was going to his first job interview—not quite confident but determined to sell himself, even though he wasn't quite sure what about him was worth to buy. And he didn't want to foul it up by saying the wrong thing or by giving the wrong impression.

Chelsea's professor's name was Dr. Henry Abbott. He suggested that they meet at a delicatessen located in a small strip mall in an upper middle-class neighbourhood. Rory knew the place. It was an out of the way, on the other side of the city, but he didn't think there was a point in bickering over a compromise.

Rory felt out of place meeting with the doctor. He didn't know how to correspond with intellectuals well, and it frightened him a little. He thought that scholarly professionals could figure out regular people easily and that trying to hide anything that would give away his lesser standing would be useless against their powers of perception.

The possibility of some kind of hope did lessen the angst Rory was feeling, but he didn't put all his proverbial eggs in his proverbial basket. Relying too much on hope could lead to a catastrophic letdown later on, and it wasn't worth compounding the heartache.

He obeyed the stoplights and traffic signals automatically while he drove to the deli. His thoughts were roaming all over the place except the road, and he didn't know how he would handle good news if Anna were to be accepted—or even if he would send her.

He was told to come alone, and the secrecy made the meeting seem a little dangerous, like he was selling Anna to an experimental medical facility. He hadn't been told what to look for to identify the doctor, not even a certain coloured sweater or hat, and that made the doctor all the more mysterious.

After pulling into the sparse lot and parking, Rory snapped out of his trance and got out of his car. It wasn't an unseasonably cold morning, but he could see each breath he made, and his body tensed like it was colder than it actually was.

The big red door to the deli, tough to open, was due for a little oil on the hinges. He stood at the entrance, relaxing his posture and scanning the tables for some kind of hint as to which patron was the doctor.

It was pretty well empty, save for a few tables of seniors eating breakfast. The doctor had told Rory that it didn't get busy until 11:00 in the morning and that the lack of a crowd wouldn't make it difficult to identify one another.

After Rory's initial scan, he saw a large man get up from a table. The man wore a generous, warm grin and had thick brown glasses that looked like they were a decades old model of a tried and true brand. He started towards Rory with a welcoming hand extended. "Mr. Gunn?" said the man.

"Yes?"

"I'm Dr. Abbott. It is so good to meet you." Dr. Abbott had a voice like a giant: deep and hollow. Yet the way he spoke made his words like soft, playful blows from a feather pillow. It was evident he worked with children and people who required a different kind of attention. He smiled a lot, and Rory didn't know if being put off by that was the right response. The years of being around sullen and cavalier people made him suspicious of excessive cheer.

The doctor shook his hand heartily, his hold so strong it was like Rory was dangling over a cliff and there was no way Dr. Abbott was going to let him fall.

"Likewise," Rory said.

"Please join me." Dr. Abbott gestured towards the table. "Here, let me help you with your coat," he said. "I hope you like caffeinated coffee. Gets me positive. I took the liberty of having the waitress bring a carafe of it to the table."

"Yeah, thanks."

Dr. Abbott poured Rory a cup and pushed the cream and sugar dish his way. The words froze in Rory's throat—he didn't know how to proceed. He wanted the doctor to take control of the conversation, but it wasn't something he thought appropriate to make clear.

"Mr. Gunn, I've heard many great things from Chelsea about your daughter, Anna. Has Chelsea told you about me and what I do?"

Rory waited a second, not knowing if it was a trick question. "Not a whole lot. She told me about the facility, and to be honest, Doc . . . May I call you Doc?"

Dr. Abbott nodded, his giant grin unflinching.

"To be honest, I don't know what I'm doing here. Webb is not something a person like me can afford, but Chelsea really wanted me to meet with you. For what, I really don't know. I'm here to listen I suppose."

"She informed me of your situation," said Dr. Abbot. "Of the troubles with schooling, especially as Anna is at the age where she should be attending." He reached beneath the table and brought up a brown leather satchel that looked like it had, at one point, been strapped across a horses back and been ridden across the country in all manners of weather. "Let me tell you a little about the facility first, Mr. Gunn."

He handed Rory a brochure. It had a picture of someone baking bread and wearing a smile like the one sported by Dr. Abbott.

"At the Webb Institute, the emphasis is on participation in society for people of all ages with a wide range of issues: developmental delay, learning difficulties, poor judgment, and impoverished inter-personal skills. Terms I use to illustrate the issues without using too much technical nomenclature."

Rory flipped through the short brochure, but only the images were sticking in his head, not the words.

"There are, of course, different wings to the facility. One for children and one for our older residents. In our children's wing, there's a staff ranging from volunteers to grad students to other full-time doctors. Together, they provide what we refer to as 'early intervention and alternative education.' It's a special kind of attention placed on the needs of the young ones hampered by some difficulty who may not be able to grow and realize their full potential. We try to make it easier to adapt to those handicaps, as we know some just cannot learn at the rate most do. That includes other, less demanding, challenged people as well."

Rory's emotions began to itch, and he couldn't pinpoint if it was because he was hearing these things out loud or because of the generalization Dr. Abbott was making about Anna, as if he knew her without an introduction. He *didn't* know her.

Rory still clung to her individuality, and part of him refused to let someone to tell him—or at least make it seem like he was being told—that she was headed down an even more horrible, frightening, and darkened one-way street. For a fleeting moment, he thought Dr. Abbott was scolding him and insinuating that his care and love was inadequate and that they had a solution for his inadequacies. He couldn't look the doctor in the eye, lest an imprudent remark escape him.

"Mr. Gunn? I don't mean to alarm or anger you."

Rory snapped from his trance and looked up at the doctor. "You'll forgive my frustration. I just don't like the way you're talking about my baby girl."

Dr. Abbott took a moment to let the dust settle. He took his glasses off and gave the lenses a rub. He topped off his cup of coffee and stirred the sugar in methodically.

"Mr. Gunn, there is something I'd like to make clear here. In no way am I taking anything away from your daughter or from you and the way you have raised her. Chelsea has told me how you are with her. Webb is very interested in employing Chelsea but she's been adamant about helping your daughter. I wouldn't be here today if it wasn't for her convincing me as she did you. I see many cases that I wish I could intervene in, but the situation is handled by another agency, unfortunately. Some people aren't fit parents, and it's impossible to help everyone." He placed his glasses back on his face. "Do you see what I'm getting at here?

"I am quite intrigued with Anna's case because with FAS suffers, I have never heard it making them so—how do I put this lightly?—socially and cognitively detached. Especially with her circumstances, and by that I mean she isn't neglected or impoverished or abandoned."

The drunken half-smile of Rory's ex flashed through his mind when he heard the last word Dr. Abbott had said, and Rory's eyes filled with tears. He tried to push them back in, but the red swelling remained. What the doctor had said came hard and hurt, like he'd never before realized it himself.

"I don't want the stress of fiscal constraints to pester you at the moment," said the doctor. "First I'd like to meet Anna, if that's all right with you?"

Rory collected himself and let the doctor's smile subdue him. "Of course. I didn't mean to come off combative. I just get defensive when it comes to her."

"As do all loving parents. Trust me, I see agony and powerlessness all the time, Mr. Gunn. It truly is as onerous on the parents as it is the child. Which brings me to another question, Anna's mother. I know what Chelsea told me, but I'd like to hear it from you."

"She left when Anna was young. She drank, and I did nothing to stop it." Rory felt her ghost slap him across the face. The sting was real to him, and he wore it as reminder that he'd failed and had to work tirelessly to make amends. "I'd prefer if that's the beginning and the end of that question."

"Of course. I apologize," Dr. Abbott said.

The waitress came and asked if they were ready to order, and Dr. Abbott recited his by heart. Rory was somewhere far away, listening to the muffled transaction.

The waitress and Dr. Abbott were looking right at Rory, their mouths moving but without sound. The doctor put his hand on the waitress's arm, and Rory thought Dr. Abbott must have told her that he wasn't hungry, because she slid her order pad back into her apron and went back to the kitchen.

Rory's heart thumped. He felt clammy and bolted to the chair. "If you'll excuse me."

Rory crashed through the entrance and took a deep breath of the cool morning air. He became lightheaded. He wasn't used to the kind of conversation they were having, and talking about the past made the present more potent.

He took a few more deep breaths. He didn't want to put the doctor off with his erratic behaviour, so he gathered himself and went back in the deli and sat back down for a proper breakfast with Dr. Abbott.

"How would you like to come and meet Anna today?" Rory asked.

"That would be splendid."

Chapter 8

The following Monday morning was dreary.

The construction crew were almost finished their initial excavation, and certain areas were cordoned off by yellow tape. Most of the workers weren't easily distinguishable from the regular shop employees—they were all gruff, bearded or stubbled men with long faces and dark rims under their eyes.

Business was to run normally while the work was being done. That meant it was going to be harder to perform in some areas, as things were moved around and crammed together to accommodate the construction equipment and extra bodies.

All the workers received a memo that said the noise would increase tenfold and that hearing protection was mandatory at all times—a policy that, even before the digging started, was indifferently adhered to. There were many policies that weren't. Words that provided some sort of precedent. Corporate covering their asses, abiding by the laws, setting standards of codes and practices that look good on paper, but never transfer over well to the real world.

The night before had been an especially cold one with a

slight but steady spring rain, and the driveway doors had remained shut all through the midnight shift, and still were. The nauseating smell of diesel generated by the fully loaded trucks inside, revving their engines to build up air in their trailer's brakes, pumping toxic fog from the heavily sooted mouths of the tops stacks into the rafters where it would disperse, unseen to the human eye unless it went by under one of the high wattage lights in the ceiling. It didn't help that the sickening irritation of the diesel burn off increased with the presence of other diesel fuelled construction equipment, and it was so strong and pronounced that Rory got an instant headache when he entered the plant.

Some workers were gathered by the foreman's shack, talking to the foreman hired as Wyatt's successor, Anders Krue, who seemed to be fielding questions like a defendant with TV cameras in his face as he left the courthouse.

Anders was a speciously assertive type, impossible to take seriously. He could be your best friend and your worst enemy at the same time, and it seemingly didn't occur to him that he was like that. It made him absolutely untrustworthy, which Rory figured was a fine enough trait for one to have when trying to move through managerial ranks.

Rory came up behind and saw Richard and Dom at the front of the pack.

"Don't pretend you can't smell that, Anders. Its been like this all bloody winter, always is, and I can't stand it anymore. We inhale so much shit in here and it's worse now with all this other equipment going." Dom said loudly. "And you can't show us that those negative air flows are working?"

"These concerns are nothing to worry about," Anders told the crowd. "These kind of construction projects go on everywhere, and these companies are professional. They have safety protocol to follow just as we do. I assure you there is no risk."

"What is so hard about showing us if those exhaust fans work?" said Dom. "The propeller fan on that one isn't even moving, and I don't think I've ever seen it move! Why can't you just bring in someone to do an air quality test, and shut me up at the same time? We don't have an office we can escape to, in case you didn't know." He was really digging into Anders, and the overwhelmed supervisor seemed to be running out of rhetoric.

"Dom, would you please come into my office and discuss this with me? Everyone else, please get to your work stations."

Anders couldn't help his weakness. He said *I'm sorry* and *please* too much for anyone to think him formidable, but it was the way Wyatt liked it—his job couldn't be threatened by a pipsqueak with a soft touch.

The door shut to the foreman's shack, and Rory watched for a few moments while the two inside interacted. It didn't look nasty, but Dom was irate, and it would be surprising if Anders could pacify him.

The excitement had died down, but the blue fog of diesel fumes still churned overhead. It was an irritating, awful smell to be around for long periods of time. The fumes dissipated easily enough in the summer when the driveway doors were open, but during winter and the chillier spring and fall months when the doors were closed, the exhaust mixed with the air discreetly, contaminating the atmosphere quickly.

Dom was the only one who was consistently zealous about the safety issues, which was almost certainly why his hair was receding and turning white. He fought tooth and nail to try to get answers, but management had learned that it was best to let him wear himself down and let it go.

Rory prepared for the day's work, laying out his protractor and tape measure, slide square, and various digital measuring tools. The brake was cold from sitting idle all weekend, so he fired it up to let it warm for the eighty hours of work it was about to endure.

A slam came from the foreman's shack, and then Dom was marching directly for the brake. Rory didn't feel like dealing with the aggression and placed a hand on his machine affectionately. "You and me both," he said to his blue giant. Rory was almost positive he was going to get the brunt of what Dom hadn't been allowed to air out.

"I can never get a decent answer around here," said Dom. "How fucking professional is that?"

"And you act like that's something new?" Rory walked around his machine, giving Dom half his attention.

"The common sense is right out the window with them. They say they care about us, but it sure doesn't seem like it. I'd like to see them come out here and spend eight hours a day in this shit. I bet you something would change then."

"C'mon, Dom. You know this isn't going to get you anywhere. Just give up like the rest of us." Rory didn't like the way that had come out. It was too defeatist.

"The rest of us? I hear most of these guys on the floor whine about this stuff when it's convenient for them. But when I start to say something out loud, I get no support. They scurry away and eat up whatever excuse they're fed."

Rory didn't respond.

"Sorry, fuck it, forget I said anything," said Dom. "How was the meeting thing with Anna's doctor?"

"It went well, I guess. He came over and met her, told me about this place that he's going to be the overseeing director of, blah, blah, blah. I don't know."

"Sounds promising."

"Yeah, well, it's not an immediate thing. He doesn't go out there and take over for another couple months. Then there's getting established and getting to know the staff. Maybe in the fall, the promise might be a little more solid, but for now it's just a faint glimmer of something. I'm still all over the place about it, anyhow."

"Well, I hope it works out for you, man."

A yell from the driveway caught their attention. It was Wyatt, and he was pointing to the crane in the east end. "It's not going to run itself, Dom!" he bellowed.

"All right. I guess I'll be seeing you later," Dom said as he walked away.

"Hey, Dom?" Rory called after him.

"Yeah?"

The Policy

"Don't put the world on your shoulders, okay?"
"Yeah, I'll give it a shot."

Chapter 9

Cool spring raced by and into an incendiary summer and with it came the threat of heat exhaustion in the plant. The boilersuits issued by the company lived up to their name—they clung to skin in the extreme heat, making movement uncomfortable and annoying. In an effort to escape the heavy coveralls, some people came in wearing lighter street clothes, but were quickly sent to change. By condition of employment, the workers were required to wear the company name and colours at all times—one of the few policies enforced without exception, but not as often by the foremen, as it was by Trent Cluse, the coordinator of the quality assurance department. He was always on the prowl, keen to catch anyone he could get in trouble.

Trent was also the "employee delegate" for the health and safety committee. But instead of representing the real interests of the workers, he made his own rules, and without restriction or worry of repercussion, could say just about anything, about any issue, and making things up to circumvent concerns that would be a cost for the company to update or fix. He was a hide-the-problem-save-the-money apprentice in training, and he was naturally born for it.

He was also the stepson of Clive Strome, so it hadn't taken long for him to be incorporated into the office mix of untouchables that you couldn't challenge without incurring some sort of punishment or ire. He bothered the workers greatly, the way he talked to them and demanded to be given just as much authority as a foreman or manager. But they were accustomed to the way things worked at Dambar. And nowhere was it written that Trent couldn't speak, or do, what he wished.

Suppressing injury claims was Trent's specialty, and through feigned empathy, he tried dissuading injured employees who came to his office to fill out workers' compensation forms. His solution was an ice pack and an hour's rest. He was by no means a certified physician, but he sure did act like one, even though he was known to walk in the other direction if there was a drop of blood at the scene of an incident.

When it came to relational skills, Trent's full stride had really started to show when the crew digging the pit for the new machine hit what they thought was a gas line. Their union steward wasted no time telling them to drop what they were doing, evacuate the building and instructing them not to return until he gave the all clear.

Dom watched it happen from his crane and came down for a closer look and to have a chat regarding what the commotion was about. He approached the digging crew's foreman, who was standing by a door jotting something down in a little notebook, not uttering a word of objection or protest as his workers walked passed him and out the door.

That no one was running around with their arms in the air, calling the crew "pussies" or "babies" or "to get back to work", baffled Dom, and after gathering a few Dambar workers and telling them what was going on, he marched towards Trent's office for some answers regarding why, if unionized workers were allowed to cease operations because of a potential gas leak, the Dambar employees weren't also allowed to leave. Dom and Trent were yelling so loudly that every word said between them cut through the noise of the plant and was heard by Rory while he was at the brake. He stopped what he was doing to watch how the situation unfolded.

Dom was, in front of his peers and in complete contrast to that of the digging crew, insultingly told by Trent to go back to work and not to bother with what was going on with the construction, that it was out of his league. It was the wrong thing to say to a person like Dom, but Trent got a kick of riling him up, and Dom fell for it every time.

Dom launched into a tirade against management's constant dismissal of safety concerns. His volume continued to grow, and it was loud enough that most of the office had heard Dom's piece, and it drew Wyatt and Clive out onto the shop floor.

Without knowing who was behind him, Dom continued. Clive tapped him on the shoulder, and upon turning around and seeing who stood behind him, Dom mouthed something that Rory made out to be, *fuck me.*

Clive and Wyatt escorted Dom off the shop floor and into the front office. When he came out, he looked as red as a tomato and went straight to his crane, not saying a word to anybody for the rest of the day.

Dom was like a neutered dog after that. His voice was barely audible when he spoke to anyone. He came into work right as the buzzer sounded and left promptly at 4:30. Rory tried speaking with him after the gas line episode, but all Dom said was that Clive had handed him the classifieds section of the newspaper and told him to make a choice. Dom didn't elaborate on it, nor did Rory push any further.

A few days later a heat wave enveloped the city, and no one could remember it being so hot in the plant before. There were a couple water outlets that were connected to the building's water supply, located throughout the plant, but when it got so hot that the risk grew of workers dropping from constant exertion, water bottles were provided so they could stay properly hydrated at their work stations.

It was Trent who was in charge of filling the large cooler with ice and bottled water in the morning and he full well knew the provincial health and safety regulations—they stated that water and extra breaks were obligatory once the humidex chart, which measured the impact humidity had on the temperature in the plant, reached a certain degree. What he also knew was that he wasn't violating any human rights by waiting until the exact moment that law required the company to hand out water to the employees, and he would fuss if anyone suggested it be given one second sooner.

The cases of water were bought at a Costco a few blocks away and were cheap enough that the bill was peanuts compared to the kind of money the plant took down in a week, let alone three months of summer. Yet Trent couldn't see past his own sense of bloated and disproportioned importance at Dambar.

By noon of the second day of the sweltering tide, the heat was rapidly rising to suffocating levels, but staying just under the mark for water distribution. Rory noticed the engineers, in from Chicago, who had designed the new cut-to-length line, and were running preliminary diagnostic checks and overseeing the gradual assembly, were frequently moving from the machine to the office in twenty minute intervals. Cooling down as often as they wished. It made Rory feel sorry as he watched the operators at the new machine try to make sense of the buttons and levers without proper guidance, all the while running the old machine, trying to keep up with production as well as retaining what they were being taught.

Rory went to use the truckers' washroom by the shipping office and got a quick splash of water from one of the communal cisterns. He noticed the cooler that was used to house the bottled water was ajar, and, for curiosity's sake, kicked it open to see if it had been stocked yet. The cooler was empty, and when Rory looked up and again caught his co-workers at the new machine, still in a state of disorientation, he decided he'd seen enough.

Rory made his way towards Trent's office which was located in corner of the shop, apart from the main offices, adjoined to the maintenance office and storage closet, and burst through the door without knocking or announcing himself or his intentions. The room temperature was a crisp, air conditioned twenty degrees Celsius, and it almost sent Rory into sudden hypothermic shock. No one was in the office, but it wouldn't have mattered if there were. Rory was on a mission. Cases that had twenty-four bottles of water each were neatly stacked in front of Trent's desk. Rory grabbed one and took it out onto the shop floor. He tore away the plastic wrapping and tossed the bottles into the cooler.

He then strode into the office, right past Trent, who was flirting with a new clerk, and took two bags of ice from the office staff's fridge freezer.

"What do you think you're doing?" Trent said as Rory walked by in the direction of the plant.

"Something you should be doing, Trent," Rory responded.

No one followed Rory out, and he dumped the bags of ice into the cooler before he could be stopped. Rory knew that the bottles wouldn't get cold before his shift was over, but at least there was water. The temperature of it only matter if it scalded, and even then the workers might not have been able to tell the difference. At least compared to the choking mugginess of the shop the bottles already had a chill to them from being in Trent's air-conditioned office.

As he went back to the brake he told those he passed that there was water if they wanted it. Comments like, "That will piss Trent off right quick", "Atta boy", and "Thanks buddy, just what I need" came from his fellow workers and Rory felt a great sense of appreciation for having done it.

An hour later, Rory went back to get a bottle for himself before he took his afternoon break, only there was no cooler. Trent had dragged it away in retaliation.

The action had Rory ready to pop, and this time he moved towards Trent's office door with violence on his mind. When he tried to open the door he found it to be locked and the lights to be out. Rory became even more furious, but rather than have a fit and react impetuously, he shakily went into Wyatt's office and told him that an emergency had come up at home and that he had to leave.

When Wyatt asked for details, Rory gave none, even though he was certain the shop gossip had already gotten to Wyatt.

Rory changed quickly, got into his car and off the property, spinning his tires in the gravel that produced a screech once they gripped the pavement of the city street. He clenched the steering wheel and turned corners as fast as he came at them. In his wake, he left the sound of honks and the skid of locking tires. There was no brushing off the blatant insult and frivolity this time. He could not believe how Trent's ostentation went without criticism. Rory punched the steering wheel. He did it again and again until the skin on his knuckles began to peel like finely sliced sandwich meat.

In his mind he knew he shouldn't be driving in his state, so he pulled off the street into an empty parking lot, got out of the car, and paced. The air was thick with heat, and he began to sweat fiercely. The outrage was subsiding, but the adrenaline still pumped into his system. He wanted to yell out but stopped himself because a few people had gathered in the lot across the street and were watching him with interest. He took a few deep breaths and looked past the bystanders at the store where they stood.

Liquor Mart.

There was no talking himself out of it this time. Rory needed something to take the edge off. He got back in his car and turned the AC on full blast while he waited for the people who had been watching him to leave. Once they had left, Rory got out of his car, jaywalked across the street, and entered the liquor store. He went for a half bottle of Wiser's. He felt weird and out of place, standing in line with the rest of the afternoon consumers. For a fleeting moment he thought he felt a slight tug at the bottom of his shirt, but when he turned around, there was nothing.

On the way back to his car, he felt his phone vibrate in his pocket.

"INCOMING CALL . . . WORK."

The outrage started to flare again, but he swiped to answer the call anyway. "Hello?" said Rory.

"Rory. It's Wyatt. Everything okay?"

"Just fine. What do you want?"

"Whoa, no need for hostility," Wyatt said. "You just left rather quickly, and I'm just checking in. I, uh, heard about your little encounter. That wouldn't have anything to do with you leaving, would it?"

"I told you I have an emergency to attend to."

"Okay. That's fine. I just want to let you know that I will be docking your pay and writing this little incident up for your personal file and we'll review it together tomorrow."

"Those fucking cases of water are five fucking dollars each. And that lazy sack of shit gets to pick and choose when we get water out there! It's hotter than hell in that place."

"No need for that kind of language, Ror."

"You can call me *Rory*. Got it? Now if you'll excuse me, I'm driving, and you're making me break the law." Rory hung up his phone and turned off the power.

It felt good to say that to Wyatt, to hang up on him, but Rory knew it wasn't going to last. He'd have to face the music on this one, escaping censure was not going to be easy, and the thought of how the ingrate Trent would laugh about it like an uppity hyena made the rage flood back into his face and fists. Rory cracked the bottle of alcohol and took a long pull from it. It hit him directly. He capped the bottle, put it back in the paper bag, stuffed it under his seat, and started home with a lightheaded buzz—his mania momentarily impaired and distracted.

He tried to separate himself from the events as best he could before getting into the house. He dragged his aggravation behind him at a distance, but he couldn't stop it from slithering in before he shut the front door. He bypassed his normal acknowledgement of Anna and Chelsea and went straight to his room, and hid the bottle under his pillow, and changed into his I-couldn't-care-less-about-my-appearance sweats and hoodie.

Chelsea met Rory in the kitchen, but he immediately buried his head in the fridge, pretending to look for what he could make to eat so she wouldn't catch a whiff of his breath.

"Hi, Mr. Gunn. You're home early."

Rory didn't answer. He kept clanging around half-empty jars of jam and pickles, trying to get her to leave him alone.

"We went for a walk today and stopped by the store to get some spaghetti sauce. Anna said she wanted it for dinner. I also took out a package of ground beef from the freezer earlier and left it in the sink. I think it should be thawed by now."

"Thank you, Chelsea," he said, unwilling to face her. "If you don't mind, I'd like a little quiet time, so you can go on home. It's not you or anything, but I'm just not in the greatest of moods. You understand, right?"

"Sure. No problem. You're welcome for the sauce. Anna's in the living room with another colouring book, just so you know. See you tomorrow, I guess?"

"See you tomorrow. Have a good night."

Rory listened while Chelsea gathered her things and said goodbye to Anna. It was not until he heard the front door shut behind her that Rory could leave the kitchen. He carefully poked his head around the corner so as not to break Anna's concentration. He didn't feel like trying to have conversation with someone who could make it feel like he was the only one in the room.

He went back into the kitchen and rummaged around in the cupboards, looking for a package of spaghetti, but all he could find were old lasagna noodles and some elbow macaroni. He thought it absentminded that Chelsea had gotten sauce and no spaghetti noodles but settled on the fact that Anna probably wouldn't even notice the difference if he cooked both kinds of pasta and told her it was a new type of spaghetti. It wouldn't hurt anyone, and Rory was not going to the store.

Rory thought it best to prepare dinner so he wouldn't have to worry about it later, and he filled a pot with water and set it on the stove to boil. He took out a large skillet and turned up the heat so as to brown the meat, whose frozen core still needed melting. The meat sizzled and spit as he broke it into smaller chunks with a spatula, and after breaking it enough he placed a splatter screen over top of the skillet and lowered the heat to simmer.

With the water heating to boil and Anna busy colouring in the living room, Rory retrieved his bottle of whisky and slipped into the bathroom to take another swig. He refused to look in the mirror as he took his first sip. And then he took a second, followed by another that was more like two. The alcohol stung and tranquilized as it drained into him and was absorbed. He clanked the glass of the bottle hard against the sink, and when he turned his head to see if he had cracked or chipped off a piece of the ceramic finish, he caught his appearance in the mirror. A shadow of himself looked back, and turning away from it, he took another swallow.

What are you if not her father, came from his conscience—the shadow of the shadow he saw in the mirror, *You're a coward if you give up on her now.*

The sudden kick of booze on an empty stomach hit him like he'd been spinning in circles for a minute and come to an abrupt stop. He tried to stand up straight, but gravity was pulling him towards the floor—it wanted him to sleep his decision off before he went out and played father. The foolishness set in and the regret came quickly. He ran the faucet and took large gulps of water in an attempt to counteract what he had done.

As he drank, his shame came again, asking him, *So what is it? Father or coward?*

Breaking his soliloquy of self-pity, a wail cut through the walls and he stumbled to his feet and towards the origin.

Anna was by the stove, screaming. She had touched the red-hot element that boiled the water for their dinner. White and red blisters bubbled on her middle and index fingers. She stood stiff, all her wretched sensations on high alert, shrieking like nothing Rory had heard before.

The only thing that he could process was that her hand needed to be under cold running water. He grabbed her by the forearm and pulled her to the kitchen sink, forcing her hand under the tap, but her hysteria would not lessen.

"What are you doing, Anna?" he yelled. "Have I not told you that you are not to touch the stove? What is wrong with you?"

Anna toned down to sniffles. Her face beet red, and her expression tortured. What Rory had just done didn't register with him at first, but once he took his hand off her arm and saw the marks he'd left from squeezing, he dropped and began to cry. Anna followed and sobbed as quietly as she could, balling herself up on the kitchen floor.

"Oh baby, sweet, Daddy is so sorry. Are you all right?" He opened a cupboard and took out a large mixing bowl and filled it with cold water. "Here, honey, put your hand in here. It will make the pain not as bad."

Anna gave her injured hand to her father but did not look up at him. She rocked back and forth slowly and, after a few minutes had passed, didn't make a sound.

Oh, fuck, what have I done? Rory thought.

He asked Anna if she wanted anything, but she didn't respond. He told her he was going to the bathroom to get the first aid kit and that she was to keep her hand in the water until he got back. Again there was nothing.

The whisky was still trying to knock him off balance, but he got into the washroom, retrieved the first aid kit, and looked for the burn ointment and some dressing.

He kicked the bottle of his recklessness, and it spun on the tiled floor. He looked down at it, and sadness battled with anger. Most of the whisky was on the floor. He threw a towel on it to soak it up, and then he dumped what was left down the drain. He looked at himself in the mirror again, into his own eyes, in search of some sort of verdict for what he had done.

How can you go out there and face her, you idiot. You negligent, selfish bastard. That little girl trusts you, and that's how you treat her?

"I didn't mean to," he said into the mirror.

Prick. I suppose it was bound to happen again. It all starts some-where, right? A beginning never forgotten. Or did you just feel she needed to be reminded of it?

"I . . . I . . ." Rory said.

Save it. Go to her. You might be a complete fool, but she definitely doesn't need to be alone right now. Even if the only thing available for her is a fool.

* * *

Dr. Abbott called towards the end of August. He had gotten into the groove of directing the Webb facility, and had told Rory that there was indeed a place for Anna at Webb. The doctor was adamant and insistent that they come, for if nothing else, at least a tour and some much needed time off.

It was no surprise that Chelsea had chosen to take the position at Webb. She said it was the hardest decision of her life to make, and had stayed for as long as she could to assist with Anna, even putting off her departure twice because of how hard it was for her to part with Anna, but ultimately had left not long after Dr. Abbott had called.

Chelsea was more persistent than Dr. Abbott was, with the pursuit of getting Rory out West. And the constant nudges were forming a bruise on Rory's conscience.

He wasn't going to drive. The old Nissan would never make it. That left the only option of flying. And Anna had never been on a plane, let alone Rory for that matter, and he teetered with the idea of how that would go over. It excited him, and maybe she would enjoy it too, looking down on the clouds from above and watching the cities get smaller and bigger as the plane took off and landed.

In Chelsea's absence, a temporary caregiver was hired through the nanny-on-call agency he dreaded having to use again. The woman they sent spoke roughly and had a dead personality. She smelled like a mix of borscht and joint lotion, and the strong smell of cigarettes suggested that she smoked pack after pack in a tiny enclosed room with no ventilation. Her wrinkly face and bad teeth were frightening to Rory, and he didn't wonder as to why Anna had a difficult time taking to her. Searching for permanent care had become a night-mare. Chelsea truly was one in a million.

Nervous concern had made his nights sleepless. It was during one of those nights, in tangled restlessness, fraught with guilt and indecision over the e-mails Chelsea had been continually sending, that he got up and sent her one back, telling her that they were going to come out as soon as possible.

He went into Wyatt's office the next day and told him he would need one of the next three weeks off and that there was no way around it.

"These talks we have are starting to become pretty routine, don't you think?" Wyatt said. "I'd really be putting my neck out for you. Again."

The events surrounding Trent and the water cooler debacle had still not gone away. And Wyatt made it clear that changes in the behaviour of his employees was suspicious to him and that he would not have his leniency regarding suspensions for insubordination taken lightly.

"I'm going out of province," said Rory, "and I know I'm springing it on you without adequate time to organize around it, but I can't get out of it, and I'm sorry for that, but it's the way it is."

Wyatt turned in his chair and looked out his window. He folded his hands together and made his pointer fingers into a steeple that he pressed against the groove above his lip and below his nose. "I see."

Rory didn't wait for official permission, and he grabbed the proper paperwork from one of the many administrative cubbyholes in the office and proceeded to fill it out accordingly. Not a word or a glance passed between the two of them while he did it.

"Where are you going? If you don't mind me asking."

For the sake of salvaging some sort of amity in the exchange, Rory decided to tell him, but not the whole truth. He didn't mind lying to Wyatt. "Alberta to see some family that is in a tight spot," Rory said.

Chapter 10

Rory tried putting the implications of the trip out of his mind. He tried explaining it to Anna, but she didn't show interest. In an effort to help her better understand he got out his copy of *Airplane!* and dressed it like they were going on an adventure. He got so into it and carried away, goofily pretending to fly around the room with arms outstretched. His silliness got Anna smiling like she used to and looking at him like he was the only thing in the world. He soaked it up, trying to embed the image in his mind. She began to play along, spreading her arms and motoring around the room with him in mock flight. He wasn't sure if she completely understood what was going on, but the enthusiasm was enough for him.

The hustle of the airport made Anna pensive—the romp in the living room didn't make the transition. She was drawn out from behind the security of her bear by the roll of suitcases on the tiled ground and the clicking of high heels and dress shoes. She watched carefully as the people snaked through the ribboned maze to the check in, and she watched their luggage move off one conveyor to another, dragged at a steady pull to an abyss that gobbled them up at the end of the line.

Anna clung to Rory's hand as if they were fused together. She had never been in such a busy place. The woman at the counter tried to make her laugh, but Anna only peered at the woman like she didn't know how to speak.

Rory was keeping an eye on the situation in case she became volatile, but she was locked in idle fascination rather than fear of what she didn't know. Rory wondered if that was what Dr. Abbott had been talking about when he'd said she needed to "experience more group interaction," as an isolated environment would eventually become the norm, and the older she got, that antisocial comfort would be all that she could handle.

The security check went fine. The lights on the metal detector caught Anna's eye, and the security guard on the other side who was waving people through with his handheld wand smiled at her.

Rory tried to take Mr. Boo from her, but she looked up at him like it might turn on the waterworks if he did, and with a little explanation and a sympathetic bend of the rules, the staff let her keep her comforter while she passed through the towering portal.

Boarding the plane was easy, too. The attendants were all smiles, and it seemed to make Anna feel safe. She became more animated with every minute. Because Rory and Anna were allowed on before anyone else, she watched everyone go to their seats and stow their luggage in an orderly fashion. It was by another stroke of luck that no one sat in the aisle seat of their row, and Rory thought of how that eased the process even more, and how it cut down the probability of a close quarters disturbance.

The discarnate voice of the captain had Anna searching quietly and all around for its origin, and she watched the demonstration of wearing the seat belts and using the oxygen masks intently. Anna was more interested in the body language than the actual safety of the demonstration, and she laughed along with the other passengers when the attendants made lighthearted jokes to relax everyone, even though she didn't understand them. It was like a live action cartoon for her.

"Oh how she must love you," said the woman in the aisle seat opposite of theirs, "She hasn't been more than an inch away from you the whole time. That giggle of hers is infectious. And such a cutie pie too."

"Thank you." Rory said, "Anna darling, what do you have to say to the nice lady?"

Anna hesitated to speak and instead of words she just nodded and smiled brightly at the lady in the aisle seat.

The plane began to taxi into position for takeoff, and Anna struggled to lean over her father in an attempt to look out, but she couldn't see anything and gave up without hassle. It was a beautiful, sunny day, and a strong sense of hope that everything was going to be fine blanketed Rory.

The plane quickly built up to a high velocity. Anna looked to her father for reassurance, and he ran his hand over her head and gave her a wink. Once they were off the ground, she strained in her snug seatbelt to see out the window again.

"Just wait, honey. I'll let you see soon."

When the plane reached cruising altitude and the seatbelt sign was turned off, Rory let her climb into his lap. She was immediately transfixed, and without making a sound, watched the clouds for a solid two hours. No one would have been able to get her to look away. Even if the plane were falling out of the sky.

The attendants came and went, commenting on how well-behaved she was. The praise was like an uppercut to Rory. He had become the one that didn't know how to respond. It was all so unexpected and new to him that all he could do was return a congenial thanks and wonder who the little girl sitting in his lap really was.

Anna didn't want to relinquish her window spot for the descent, so Rory took the middle seat. He strapped her in, and again she struggled to see out the window a little better, but Rory told her it wasn't safe, and she began to fidget and pout.

Twenty-five more minutes, he thought.

Then the cabin pressure began to drop.

Anna clutched at her ears in a useless attempt to stop the

blockage from building in her head, and she began to tear up in discomfort. She writhed and clawed at her seatbelt. Rory fought to keep her hands from accidentally releasing the latch, and then she began to wail like she was being pummeled. The screams were at a shrill, crowd-dispersing pitch, and the passengers in the row opposite theirs now looked upon them with pity.

She kicked at the chair in front of her furiously, and Rory could see the top of the passenger's head loathingly shake back and forth.

Rory rubbed her head and her legs, but she was inconsolable. He remembered being told that gum might help, but he didn't have any, so he tried to get the attention of other passengers in an effort to procure some. He signalled to them in poor sign language over Anna's screams. One of the passengers nodded and reached into his pocket and handed over a stick. Rory unwrapped it and tried to administer it to Anna, but she batted it away and scratched at his arms, looking at him angrily like he was inflicting the pain on purpose, again.

Another tactic Rory remembered being told of was to hold your nose and blow out the pressure, but there was no hope of conveying that either. He would only look like a fool to her, making a funny face when she was clearly not having any fun.

The plane hit the runway with a bouncy skid. The enormous sound of the engines reverse thrust did little to drown Anna's bawling, but Rory had her tight in his arms, hoping she would tucker out from struggling. He stroked her head in an attempt calm her while her sobs were projected through his clothes, into his body. Her amazement at the world of clouds had been forgotten, replaced by pain and tears.

Rory waited while the plane emptied. He graciously acknowledged the words of support from some of the passengers as they deboarded. But he also felt the quiet displeasure of others who thought of children as a scourge.

Anna's loud cries had died into a shallow weeping, and Rory continued to do his best to shelter her from the pain in her head. His heartbeat was steady but strained, and he hoped that if she could feel it, hear it, pass from his body to hers, that it might help to slow down her own.

An attendant came after the plane was empty and let Rory know he could take an extra few minutes if he needed it. He thanked her and said they would be ready shortly.

The attendants smiled as Rory and Anna debarked, but their eyes weren't as bright and welcoming as they'd been when the two boarded.

Chelsea had told him that she would meet them at the airport. At first Rory was going to let it be a surprise for Anna, but she was so closed off after the trauma of landing that he decided to tell her to see if the news would snap her out of it. There was a glint of registration at the mention of Chelsea's name, but Anna remained disturbed and disagreeable.

They got through the arrival gates well enough, but by that time, Anna had shut herself off and did not look up from the floor.

Rory took a seat away from the throng that waited by the turnstile for their baggage. He didn't want the activity to affect Anna, and he did his best to make them invisible. He also didn't want to catch the murmurs of the people around them who had taken the same flight, so he turned on his phone and scrolled through his contacts, pretending to be checking e-mails or missed text messages.

"Who's that bear? Can that be *the* Mr. Boo?" Chelsea said, coming up behind them. Picking up on the trouble, she hunched down to console the shaken child. "What's the matter, Annsie?"

"She took the landing a little rough," said Rory. "Cabin pressure, it was bad."

"Oh, my poor little buddy. You need some fresh air." Chelsea looked to Rory. "You mind if I take her outside?"

"By all means, if you can get her doing something rather than stew," Rory said. "You should have seen her before we left and in the air after takeoff. All alive and interested. Shot to shit right quick."

"Want to come outside with Chelsea?" she asked the clammed-up child.

Anna did not look up, but she nodded solemnly and held out her hand for Chelsea to lead the way.

"We'll be waiting for you," Chelsea said.

"All right," Rory said.

* * *

The ride from the airport towards the mountains, bringing them into glorious focus, was humbling—a sight missed in the descent. Rory sat in the back with Anna who was staring out the window, not one awed gasp or question about the mountains came from her; the majesty of wide-open nature did little to cure the mood set by the airplane landing.

The radio was faint, playing some neo-hippie indie love song. It normally wouldn't have bothered Rory, but after the experience on the plane, he wanted to rip the stereo out of the dash and throw it out the window—imagining his hands around the lead singer's throat, throttling him, screaming to stop being so happy, but Rory kept his cool—breaking things was a ludicrous way to distribute his agitation, and he was a guest now. It wasn't his radio knob to turn.

Chelsea hadn't said much during the drive, and he kept catching her glancing at him in the rear-view mirror. She seemed to be holding something back. Their eyes met again, and she couldn't stay quiet. "I booked you in at a place a little way away, outside Canmore," she said. "Really nice, like you asked for."

Rory rolled the dollar signs around in his head and decided it was better not to think about the expense he didn't consider when he had asked her to book lodgings for them. "Thank you, Chelsea."

The hotel where Chelsea had made the reservation had been built when Canada hosted the 1988 Winter Olympics. It was initially used as a dormitory for athletes, but the end plan had always been to convert it into five-star lodgings with condominium-esque luxuries in most of the rooms.

A deluxe, swanky spice emanated from the place, and Rory fought not to flinch like a classless interloper when they walked into the grand foyer. Everything, except the Chinese designer carpet, was white or a shade of it. Ornately carved Ionic pillars lead up into vaulted ceilings forty feet high that were designed with a layered three-dimensional effect that made the ceiling look like it was breathing if you stared at it long enough.

The polished and veneered oak reception desk popped out against the white walls, as did the black on black suit worn by the clerk behind the oak desk. He was lanky and Rory thought he resembled Mick Jagger. There was something about the clerks half mouth smile that gave him a snobbish texture, like he thought Rory was only in there to ask for directions to somewhere else and was too cheap to buy a map.

Chelsea told the man who gathered no moss Rory's name. The clerk turned up his lip and rolled his eyes as he typed Rory's last name into the computer.

"I've got this," Rory told Chelsea. "Why don't you two go and check out the lobby for a few minutes?"

"A two-bedroom facing Mt. Rundle. Lovely view from there," the clerk said like a waiter reciting the special of the day. "Of course, there was no credit card given at the time of reservation, and I'll need one to go on file before I can check you in. You're lucky it's the time of year it is. There's no way you'd get a reservation like this during the busier months."

Rory handed his card to the clerk with confidence, like a person with disposable income would. "There you go, *Mr. Satisfaction.*"

"Beg your pardon, sir?"

Who is this guy? He's been in this thin air too long. Rory thought. *Too much huffing of the extravagant pheromones, convincing himself he should be in the company of his patrons. I bet a couple bills greasing his hand and a sly wink between them is all it takes for the venom to start the veins swelling and the heart pumping . . . Asshole.*

"Nothing. Don't worry about it," Rory said.

The awkwardness between them was shattered with an explosion of cheers from behind a door that had "bar", stencilled in old English lettering, across the glass.

"What's going on in there?" Rory asked the clerk.

"Baseball, I believe. There is some sort of playoff significance taking place, if I heard correctly."

"It sounds like there are fifty people in there," Rory said.

"There is a symposium going on this weekend, and apparently a lot of baseball fans are attending." The clerk handed back the credit card.

"What kind of a symposium?" Rory asked.

"The resort's union holds seminars and workshops for members from all over the country here periodically throughout the year. This is the last one, I believe, and I guess everyone got out of class a little early today."

"Thanks," Rory said, forgetting he didn't care for the guy.

He drifted towards the bar door as a recovering alcoholic might, with heavy steps that tried to prevent him from going in and taking a swan dive off the cliff of sobriety.

"Excuse me, sir. Your key," the clerk said, reeling Rory in and away from the crack of a bat and the mixture of voices and empty, thick-bottomed pint mugs being brought down on hard wood tables.

"Yes, of course." Rory took the key, grabbed his bags, and motioned to Chelsea and Anna that he was ready to go to the room.

They were by a fountain in the middle of the foyer. In the centre was a magnificent sculpture of a woman—an imitation goddess—swaddled in her own hair, all the naughty bits hidden from the eyes but not the imagination. The two of them were flipping pennies in and making wishes. Anna had since become a little more approachable and, to Rory's relief, seemed to be letting the terrifying experience from the plane ride wear off.

Chelsea gathered Anna and joined Rory in the elevator.

"Whath fwoor, Dwaddie?" said Anna. "I whanth to pweth the butt-on."

"Card says fourteen-twelve, darlin', so I'm guessing press fourteen."

The number was too high for Anna to reach, and Chelsea lifted her up a little so that it was easier for her to press.

"The guy says we can see a mountain," Rory said.

Chelsea didn't answer, she wasn't allowed the opportunity to. The elevator moved so quickly and unnoticeably that by the time Rory finished his sentence, they were already at their floor.

The room was about as big as Rory's living room and kitchen combined. The bedrooms were separate and there was a mini-kitchen complete with stove, sink, and a close to full-size refrigerator. The living room area had a couch and recliner, and they weren't the kind that looked hard and uncomfortable. The flat-screen television was five times larger than anything Rory had ever owned. And the paintings on the walls were abstract and looked expensive. They called to Rory, begging to be interpreted, but he kept his distance, just in case he were to somehow knock them from their places and have to pay for them.

"Wow, this is really something," Rory said, looking out the twelve-by-twelve plate window and onto the side of the mountain.

"It is," said Chelsea. "I really love it up here."

They all stood in silence for a moment, letting their tiny existences pale in the glare from the sun off the serrated snowy peaks of Mt. Rundle.

It was true beauty, true greatness. But something still nagged. Like the kind of itch you get on your ankle when you're wearing skates or high boots, and you can't scratch it unless you take the whole thing off your foot, and even after you've gone through the whole ordeal and are back on the ice or wherever you're going, the itch doesn't stay scratched. The commotion in the bar and the chance to fraternize with union workers had piqued Rory's interest. He wanted to go back down and mingle a little bit. Perhaps down a beer and maybe even walk around and take in the grounds for an hour. He wanted to erase his responsibility and feel, if just for a moment, like he really was on vacation.

"Chelsea?"

"Yes?"

"Would you mind hanging out with Anna for an hour or so while I go catch the end of the game?" Rory asked. "Is there a place to eat around here besides the bar?"

"I think I could do that. I'll take Anna to the roof. There's some cool stuff up there and a restaurant, too."

Rory handed Chelsea a fifty-dollar bill for something to eat and knelt down to kiss his daughter. He told her he wouldn't be long and that Chelsea was going to take her for a bite to eat.

Anna didn't protest, and she looked at her father like she wanted him to leave for a while—the plane ride was still a little bit his fault, and she needed some time to rebuild her trust in him.

Rory got off the elevator and walked into the lounge without purpose in his step. If it was one thing he knew well about bar etiquette, it was that the regulars always sensed the outsider.

It wasn't white on white in the bar. It actually reminded him of "The Woodbine", only a little brighter, and he half expected Linda to come out from the back. But this bar made him feel more at ease. It was far more modest and inviting than the reception area, and he no longer felt like he didn't belong. It was encased by a dome of glass like it was a snow globe. He took a seat at the bar top and asked what the most popular local brew on tap was and ordered a pint. After letting the head settle for a minute, he took a big swig and enjoyed a few at bats before attempting to engage any of the other patrons. He'd been out of touch with the proper way to seek out new acquaintances for a while, and it didn't help that he wasn't the biggest baseball fan—he had to feel the crowd out for the favourite. The team playing defence was getting a lot of praise for their efforts, but Rory didn't know how he was going to disguise his lack of knowledge of the players or the significance of the game at hand, so he chose to remain neutral for a little while longer. He figured his butterflies would fade by the time he was through with his drink.

The final out of the inning was made, and the advertisement clip rolled. Rory decided to seize the opportunity and try to get in the mix.

The man who sat two stools away was hefty, and his moustache was so thick that it looked like it could be used to sweep a filthy floor clean. It hid his upper teeth from view when he laughed, and he wore a bomber jacket with a giant *U, S* and *I,* stitched in blue and yellow, on the back. A half-full pitcher of beer in front of him.

Is that what he uses for a stein? Rory thought. "Been a good game so far?"

The man turned to Rory with a hardy smile and rosy cheeks.

"It's been a hell of a game," the man said. "Blue Jays need this to squeak in."

"Playoffs?" Rory asked, remembering something the clerk had said.

"We'll see if they get out of this one first," the man said with a grunt.

Rory let a few seconds pass. Then he introduced himself with an extended hand.

"Gus Roberts. Pleased to meet you," the man replied. "What brings you up to the tits of heaven, Rory?"

"Just a little family vacation," Rory said. He wanted an acquaintance, not a social worker.

"Ah yes, the much-needed vacay. I can't live without them myself. Tend to think I'd strangle the old lady if I couldn't get away once in a while," Gus said with a laugh. "I don't mean that. I'm only joshing you."

Rory smiled and took another sip of beer. The game came back on, and attention again turned to the television screen. Half the people in the bar didn't seem too interested in the game. They glanced here and there, cheering when the die-hards cheered. Only those at the bar top intently watched the pace of play.

The first batter struck out, and Rory heard Gus murmur something to the person beside him.

"So what brings you up here, Gus?"

"Business, I guess you could say," said Gus—not taking his eyes away from the screen, "There's a convention of sorts for my union. Unity Steel International." He got up and proudly displayed the back of his jacket right in Rory's face.

"Yeah, the clerk at the front desk was telling me."

"I bet he did. That guy's about as pro-union as an ass massager in a manager's office chair. You a union man, Rory?"

"I am not," Rory said.

"Does that mean you're anti-union?" Gus asked—taking his eyes away from the game and running right through Rory with an inexorable bulldozer stare.

The silent inquisition was rattled apart by the reaction of the bar toppers to the second batter taking an eighty-nine mph pitch right in the middle of the spine. Gus and Rory's attention was back on the screen in time to watch the slow-motion replay of the player take the ball in the back and twist his torso in 180 degrees of agony, before staggering out of the batter's box.

Rory wasn't dressed like a stuffed shirt, but being in a hotel with $190 a night rooms, he was beginning to feel like one. Out of place and under the heat lamp and uncomfortable for no reason.

"Not that, either. I'm a steel worker, though. Press brake operator to put a name to it. Our shop is non-unionized. Never had the numbers, I guess. If you don't mind me asking, how is it that a steel workers union has members in a hotel?"

Gus looked Rory over and then returned to the game. It was difficult to tell if Gus was sweating Rory out, waiting for a sign that he was a stoolie or imposter who got a thrill from being one-of-the-guys on the weekend. Maybe Gus thought Rory would go back and laugh with all his corporate cronies about how he'd infiltrated the ranks of the common man and got the skinny on union dealings from some drunken blabbermouths who'd felt compelled to chant their union's name and business for all to hear.

"Doesn't matter what you do. USI takes on lots of workers. Any workers. Paper. Rubber. Hospitality. Energy. Steel. It's industry Rory. And where there's industry, you'll find people like me. Plain and simple," said Gus.

Rory didn't like the idea of being thought of as the one that others couldn't be sure of—he wasn't lying about his job—but Gus made it seem like there was a password, or a handshake, Rory should know that would expedite the ice breaking process between people whose dirty, hard, hurting hands were one and the same.

Then it hit Rory: the name that Dom had written on that piece of paper that Rory discounted had the same initials as Gus's jacket.

The Policy

Rory felt ecstatic—he'd found some common ground. "Come to think of it, I have heard about you guys," Rory said. "One of my co-workers was contemplating a drive a little while ago, but getting the train moving is easier said than done. Know what I mean?"

Gus continued to watch the game like he wasn't buying Rory's story. "You want to know how to get a union in?" Gus finally offered.

Rory didn't want to come off as too eager, so he let Gus formulate what he was going to say and gave him as much time as he needed.

"First off, you need someone who can talk and is well liked by all the little cliques," said Gus—following it with a burp. "Secondly, you need management to fuck up big time to cause some sort of unrest that pisses off the majority of workers. Lastly, you need to get the cards signed—the more, the better. Once those things are all completed, you run them through your head manager's office like a blade that's been sitting in hot coals for hours. You need to cauterize that wound around that blade quickly, before management can pull it out and make you pay. You know that whole 'bite the hand that feeds' saying? Well, it's one thing to get away with it, and another when the hand catches you and starts pulling out your teeth for the offence, you get my drift?"

Rory nodded—soaking in every word Gus had to say.

"The corporate types think the dog food they give us is prime rib and that we're just a bunch of greedy ingrates that have forgotten how to kneel. The truth of it, how I see it anyway, is that a union means more than money, but to them it's all about money, so they're incapable of understanding why folks've been organizing for over a century now. They believe that they're guiltless because they are generous and we are ungrateful, undermining invertebrates that have taken up residence under their skin as constant agitators that impede business." Gus's diatribe on the separate ideals wasn't giving anything away, and it would be enough to instill a little fear into Rory if he were a poseur.

Other members behind them yelled for Gus to pipe down and stop talking shop. Others agreed and said that they were in a bar, not a classroom. A few others jokingly interceded about Gus's dramatic way with words, and others yet affectionately referred to him as the Pie-Eyed Piper—a sentiment that he returned with a hand gesture over his crotch.

A crack of the bat from the surround-sound broke the interplay up, and the bar gasped as they waited to see if the ball was going to make it out of the park. As it slipped through the left fielder's mitt and behind the wall, the crowd detonated into cheers. The excitement swelled as a few high-fives were passed around, and the few who were rooting for the opposing team, or just shit disturbers, cupped their mouths to amplify their boos.

Gus leaned over the bar and tapped the girl tending the drinks. He whispered something to her and thumbed towards Rory. She filled another pint and replaced Rory's empty one.

Gus pulled out his wallet and gave the girl a hundred-dollar bill and motioned to the others at the bar top as well.

"Couple rounds on me," he said to Rory. "You can thank the Toronto Blue Jays."

"Cheers," Rory said, raising his glass. "To the Jays."

"To the fucking Blue Jays." Gus tapped his glass against Rory's and then the bar before downing the entire glass.

Rory looked around for a clock but couldn't find one. An image of a little girl appeared in the stands at the baseball park, and Rory was jolted back to reality. He asked the bartender for the time, and she pointed over to where the Gran Marnier and Southern Comfort resided. It had been almost an hour since he'd left, but Rory figured he deserved a few more minutes. He didn't want to insult Gus by taking off without finishing the drink—not that the old man would've noticed. Inebriation had set in, and Gus started to unbutton his shirt. He left the bar top like he was in vertigo and began to make the rounds to any table a woman was at.

Rory finished his drink and looked at the clock. Another half an hour had passed, and he figured he had been away long enough—he didn't want the girls to worry. He threw a twenty on the bar to pay for his drinks and told the bartender to keep the change. He was compelled to say goodbye to Gus, so he went over to the booth Gus had slumped into.

"Thanks for the drink, Gus. I've got to be getting back to my room," Rory said quickly, trying not to get pulled into any drunken antics. The women at the table rolled their eyes when Rory didn't scoop Gus up and take him away.

"Rory! I want you to haff soming," Gus yelled with a slur. He got up and swayed after Rory, producing a card from his pocket which he handed to Rory. "If you guys at whurever you work want to unionize, ghiy me a chall. I'll poin you in the rye direction."

Rory expected a wink and a sweaty handshake, but Gus turned right back around and sauntered off, like the ladies he was headed for were not balking at him but begging for more.

Rory laughed at the spectacle and went to elevators. He vowed not to forget the power of Gus's earlier words. It wasn't the way they were said; it was how they'd made Rory feel. They made sense in a weird way, like they were an identity ready for anyone to take on if they had nerve enough to follow through. Gus's discourse had made Rory feel in control, and *in control* was a concept Rory had been so far removed from that the words were like an illusion.

Rory was murmuring an incoherent soliloquy to himself when he opened the door to the hotel room. He had a spring in his step, and an innocuous expression stretched across his face.

Chelsea had Anna on the couch, laughing as they watched a show about farm animals.

"Feeling all right?" Chelsea asked.

"I feel great. Met a gentleman down there that was a riot," Rory said. "How's my baby girl?" He sat on the couch snuggled up beside his daughter.

"I'm fwine, Dwaddie," Anna said. "You smwell fwunny."

"Oh, my little angel. Dad just had a couple drinks downstairs. I'm okay." Rory stroked her head.

"I hope your daddy can get up in the morning," Chelsea said. "We have a big day tomorrow."

"I'll be okay. I'll have a few glasses of water and be right as rain in the morning."

"Whair awre we going tuhmorroh?" Anna asked.

"Do you remember that nice doctor you met a while ago?"

Anna nodded blankly, like she knew it was the answer her father wanted to hear but didn't know why it was the answer.

"We are going to his playground," Rory said, dressing up the idea just in case the word *hospital* or *facility* came out of his mouth and spooked her.

Anna looked to Chelsea to bolster his statement. Anna may have her impediments, but there was still a cleverness to her. She had good instincts when something was amiss, and she'd get confrontational if she thought she was being taken for a fool.

Chelsea tickled her a little. "Does that sound like fun, munchkin?"

Anna giggled. The aftershock of the plane ride was a distant memory, and Rory smiled, admiring his daughter and how bright and alive she could be. It was the times like these that made Rory never want to let her go, buzzed or not.

"I'll be here at 9:00, out front," Chelsea said. She wriggled into her tight brown leather jacket that had about a dozen zippers.

"We'll be ready."

Chapter 11

Webb was a twenty-minute drive from the hotel, and when Chelsea arrived to pick up Rory and Anna the highway was still slick from an early morning misty rain that had blanked everything—like some God had emptied a giant can of aerosol from above.

Rory had never been more than a few hundred kilometres outside his home town, and he didn't have any other kind of morning atmosphere to compare the gloriousness of the mountain range to. He left the back window to Chelsea's car open an inch to allow crisp air to pass over his face. He had sought this kind of relief before with a trip to a beach that was a forty-minutes outside the city, but he was only met with the throngs of city folk who migrated there in the summer, seeking the same thing he did, and who instead added to his already semi-sullied notion of what a calm place to unwind was.

Off the highway they turned at a road that had a stone foundation sign welcoming people to Webb—no indication of what Webb exactly was. It only bore the words "CARE, COMPASSION, and CONFIDENCE" beneath the name.

Dr. Abbott had not alluded as to actual acreage on which Webb was built. The physical facility looked like a university. One huge building was conjoined to a smaller one by a skywalk that met them at halfway up the tallest and close to the top of the smallest. Concrete footpaths, lined with mid-sized shrubs, went in all directions, around, away and towards all the entrances and exits of both buildings.

Rory followed one path to a playing field that looked like it could accommodate every sport played on grass, and another that headed for a scaled down amphitheater half-concealed by some large trees that were part of a forest of unknown extent. As Rory watched the tree line a group of children and adults came out of the wooded area from what he thought must have been a hiking trail.

"This is beautiful," Rory gasped.

"It really is, isn't it?" said Chelsea.

As they got closer to the parking lot, Rory could make out the portly figure of Dr. Abbott approaching, waving them in excitedly.

Rory barely had time to get out of the car before the doctor was upon him.

"I'm so happy that you made it," Dr. Abbott said, his usual grin of excessive delight in place.

The absurd notion that maybe the doctor had been taking a few of his own prescriptions flashed in Rory's mind, and he chuckled quietly to himself. "Good to be here, Doc," Rory said. "This place is something else."

"And so good to have you. Now, where is that precious child of yours? Oh, there she is," Dr. Abbott said, making a funny face through the window at her. Anna reacted to the playful buffoon like she was watching monkeys at a zoo.

"Come on. Let's get inside. I can't wait to show you around."

The atrium was spacious, with walls of windows that let the sun in from the moment it peeked out from the east in the morning to the last ray of light before it set behind the mountains. The heat from the sun kept the temperature inside the grand entrance snuggly warm. And depending on the season, and hours of the day, the receptionists needed to wear sunglasses to protect them from the inescapable blaze of light.

A multitude of potted plants adorned the vast entrance that, upon first impression, made Rory think he'd walked into a conservatory. Pots with ferns, palms, peace lilies, anthuriums, and orchids hung from the ceiling and lined the walls in orderly but beautiful fashion.

Anna gazed in wonder. It looked like a painter had taken a sea of variant greens, spotted and lined them with white, and then lightly stroked certain sections with different shades of reds, purples, and blues.

"Is this even real?" Rory asked when he came upon a pot of what looked like something manufactured for show.

"Why yes, Mr.Gunn," Dr. Abbott said with a smile. "Those are schefflera plants. The exterior looks very waxy. I do agree, but I assure you they live as we do. Here at Webb, we believe botany, and its derivatives, to be a key tool that encourages tranquility and pleasantness. We even employ a horticulturist. Dr. Eggart curates the Plant Life Project, as we call it, and that includes maintenance and basic education about not only plant life but life in general. We have a substantial nursery where we grow many species of popular flowers, vegetables—which we use in the kitchen—and house plants. We even sell much of what we grow during the warmer seasons. It has proved to quite a successful and self-sustainable program."

Rory didn't get it, but he had never been one to stop and admire patiently cultivated verdure. All he ever noticed were nuisance weeds in the cracks of his driveway and large boughs that would be torn from trees during storms, blocking traffic or taking down power lines. He'd once bought an aloe vera plant—he remembered his grandmother using one on his scrapes and cuts as a young child—but he didn't care for it enough, and it eventually withered and died. He looked at the array of greens and tried to find what it was Dr. Abbott meant when referring to the plants as a "key tool" for tranquil pleasance.

The receptionist's office was bordered by a carefully wound lat-ticework of creeping vines that grew from a trough of soil beneath it, and as they passed, Rory received from the women behind the long desk, the most genuine smiles and waves he could ever remember having gotten from strangers.

Any remaining cynicism that Rory harboured was quickly filtered out of him like it was as toxic as carbon dioxide or xylene, and was being replaced with a spirit that made him feel like he was a long lost family member being welcomed home after many years of estrangement, without question or unreasonable doubt as to why.

"We encourage responsibility to the fullest, and if you take something as delicate as plant life, which needs tender attention to survive, you can see how rewarding it is when a person understands that. And it helps us more easily explain to our people, in some cases, the nature of their situations.

"I believe that responsibility and relation are much the same as subjective and objective thought. If the subject can relate to the object and understand what makes them similar and different from each other, then you have started on a path of greater responsibility, not only to yourself, but to whatever is around you."

Rory nodded his head in agreement, but he still didn't quite grasp the concept. And as he rolled it around in his head he thought of Richard, and what his take on the statement might be.

Dr. Abbott led the party through some doors, and they snaked through a few hallways. Muffled sounds of interaction came from inside the classrooms as they passed.

"This way leads to our children's wing," Dr. Abbott said, pointing down another hallway that looked like a tunnel to a cartoon world: construction paper, large sheets scribbled all over, and crafts of Styrofoam, pipe cleaners, Popsicle sticks, glitter, and macaroni were hanging on the walls as representations of achievement. Most were abstract, and some were quite thoughtful pieces of art. They weren't separated in any way, the good from the bad—they were all left together, creating a sense of acceptance no matter what the ability.

"Chelsea," said Dr. Abbott, "why don't you take dear little Anna and show her the playroom while Mr. Gunn and I tour the rest of the grounds?"

112

Chelsea nodded, knelt down to Anna's level, and whispered something to her that made the child's eyes light up like she had just been told every day was going to be like Christmas.

Anna skipped on down the hall, devoid of the anxiety that normally came to her in unfamiliar places. She caught the joy and colours that decorated the walls and took off without saying a word to her father.

Dr. Abbott watched as Rory's shoulders slumped. "Her short term memory inhibits her manners, I see."

"It happens more than you know, Doc. It used to hurt, but I think all that is getting calloused over," Rory said.

Dr. Abbott patted Rory on the back. "Some of these children have such damaged wiring inside their little heads."

The thought made Rory recall the memory of the toy racetrack he had as a kid: The cars went around and around on an electric charge that passed to the car through the track. He remembered the one car that had stopped receiving the relay, and when he'd asked his father to fix it, all that could be done was to blame "shoddy wiring."

"Come, Mr. Gunn," said Dr. Abbott. "Let me show you the rest of the facility."

The constant reference to the inhabitants of Webb as "our people" put even more of Rory's apprehension to rest. He heard words like *research* and *tests* used only with positive connotations. The facility didn't smell like bleached degradation from hiding the shamed; it was polished with pride. It was as though one by one Dr. Abbott was pulling all Rory's cons about letting Anna stay, out of his head.

Some residents came to Webb already as adults, from families who no longer knew what to do, or just could not bear the struggle anymore. Others came as adolescents who had too great of a learning curve to overcome and whose parents just wanted to see them smile with others of the same persuasion. The rest of the residents were children, no younger than, due to policy, seven years of age.

"We try to keep the wings separated by age as closely as possible. As of the end of last quarter we are closing in on three hundred and fifty residents, with forty staffers on hand. And that includes a few maintenance people and some cooks," said Dr. Abbott.

"How many of those are children?"

"If memory serves there are seventy-five youngsters. Your Anna will be the youngest of them too, by the way"

"How often do you have visitors?" asked Rory.

"As much as possible. Those who live closer come more often, as you might suspect. We even have some, who don't chiefly reside here, that come to us for therapy a few days a week from Calgary and surrounding areas. Our people mostly come from the West of the country, but I'd say around ninety come from out East. Folks tend to visit on birthdays, many come in on major holidays, but for those whose distances are greater to travel, the visits are less frequent."

Rory thought what kind he would be, often or less frequent, or maybe even never. Then he thought of how that reflected Anna's on-an-off focus, and how she could travel thousands of kilometres away without leaving a room.

"You'll excuse me if I come off a little uncertain here, Doc, but I'm still having a hard time understanding how this deal is no strings attached. I'm old enough to know nothing is free."

"Well, to be clear, it won't be completely costless to you. As we will be waving out normal fee for enrolment, there is still the matter of supplies, clothing, and the like. It will be around what you would have paid Chelsea or any other personal caregiver you have employed in the past.

"To be perfectly honest, Mr. Gunn, I don't like making absolute guarantees. No one can give those kind of numbers without risking foolishness. And I don't believe in it because that is just not how life plays out. But I can make certain assurances in this case.

"Webb has been working to get where it is now for twenty years. It has taken much time and patience, and a great many hurdles that needed be jumped to get what you see now.

"Initially it was some very affluent benefactors that funded the start up, and the facility was only the main building. It has only been in the last ten or so years that additions and expansions have been possible. The people who started Webb also ceaselessly lobbied for Federal and Provincial grants. From the beginning, those involved believed in this place, they still do. And they don't believe they've finished.

"If it will help to dispel some leeriness, I can give you a round price, just in case it ever does become a discussion we need to have one day. But please don't let it cloud your judgement. Webb has a fee of sixteen thousand five a year. It makes us semi-inaccessible, I appreciate that, but now that we are starting to come out of the red, we have a chance to extend a little charity of our own. We don't want to cater to a specific demographic. That is quite contrary to what we do here.

"Mr. Gunn, Anna is the first candidate ever considered for beneficence of this kind from Webb. And there were many discussions concerning the use of such aid. And as I can attest, it didn't take much convincing the board, but it took some. As do all sorts of deliberations such as this. Something you're accustomed to as well, I imagine."

Rory gazed out a window onto the playing field where a group of teenagers were chasing a soccer ball. "I can't just ask her. It's impossible for her to make an informed decision. She won't even be able to put it together. And she can't fathom any of what I'd have to explain. How can I say no to an offer like this when she'll just get worse with me anyway? At least you're equipped for this."

"That, Mr. Gunn, is precisely why Chelsea is also a huge part in this. She has agreed to take primary care of Anna, a guardian of sorts. They won't joined at the hip per se, but they will be sharing quarters. And that's a major component of why this will work so well for all involved. I hope it eases you knowing that you wouldn't be leaving Anna here as some sort of orphan. The two of them have become quite attached, wouldn't you say?"

The incidental motherly influence Chelsea had developed with Anna wasn't lost on Rory, but he never wanted to try to breathe too much life into it, in case he chased Chelsea away with such a weighty and selfish imposition, but what developed between them was beyond his control.

Rory became dizzy. The room began to sway. He had never known generosity like this, which made accepting it a far harder reconciliation for his conscience.

They went outside and upstairs, around corners, and down the path that led into the forest Rory had seen driving up. Behind the trees there was a small lake with a dock that had a motorboat roped to it. There were also several overturned canoes placed in an ordered fashion along the rocky shoreline and Rory thought that never in his childhood did he ever get to experience anything so serene. It looked like a postcard.

Not much was said between the two of them after they got to the lake. And to allow Rory some space and a moment alone to ruminate, Dr. Abbott excused himself and went to speak with a grounds man that was repairing a riding lawnmower by a giant shed.

Rory looked out on to the water. The sun spilled across small waves generated by a light wind, and the glare forced him to squint like it would help him to see further, but in the trials of the past that he was searching through, he'd already seen all he could see. He had heard all that he could hear. All that remained was how much Emily was going to rebuke him if he went home alone.

He hadn't told her about any of the real reason they'd gone on the trip. If fact, he hadn't told her about anything to do with Webb at all. The scrutiny that his sister would no doubt dole out had him imagining her words to be no less corrosive than battery acid. And while, in his head, she railed against him, he thought what it was going to be like, having to live with the possibility of never being able to convince people that leaving Anna at Webb wasn't a cop out. That it was most definitely the best, and only, decision he could make.

Dr. Abbott returned and broke Rory's trance. "Mr. Gunn, if you please, I'd like to show you the last stop on our tour: the children's indoor activity area. The girls should have had enough time there to tire by now." They walked back out of the forest in silence. Rory was grateful that it wasn't in Dr. Abbott's nature to blabber on about nothing during moments of unease.

The activity area was an auditorium-sized room, a good two

floors out of the main building, that had walls of glass just like the atrium of the building did— Rory felt like he should be paying admission for it. The room was built around a massive fortress that had slides, ropes, and swings—everything that could distract a child for hours—and it had access everywhere that made it easy for adults to navigate. The hazardous aspects were nonexistent: everywhere Rory looked, there was something that would cushion a fall or cover a corner that could cut or gouge. Rory counted fourteen adults supervising an innumerable amount of children that were dashing back and forth, in and out.

"This is Castle Comfy, as the children call it," Dr. Abbott said.

Rory tried scanning for the pink corduroy coveralls Anna was dressed in, but the playroom was so colourful and the children moved so quickly that it was impossible to track anything. "I wish there were places like this when I was a kid," Rory said. "This is incredible."

"We like to indulge their playful side as much as possible, and as many of our staffers can attest, it gets quite exhausting. But it is integral for development, and it makes the children more accessible and open to challenge themselves. We believe that many of life's root behaviour can be addressed in a playroom such as this. Cooperation, patience, problem-solving, and even moderation can be taught with this kind of therapy."

Rory couldn't have imagined any greater environment to be associated with emotional healing—the smiles, laughter, and screams of delight, mixed with the green-apple fragrance of the playroom. It was a contagious atmosphere, and Rory wouldn't have been able to remove the smile from his face if he'd tried. He again revisited his own childhood, and were it not for his grown man code of conduct, he would have kicked his shoes off and joined in the ruckus.

He sat down against the wall, partly to relax, partly to revel. He chased the children around with his eyes as they played tag and rolled around tickling each other, not one child alone. Not one child in fear of anything. They wandered like feral animals, and from the bustle, Anna popped out of a slide, a couple meters away from him—the arm of her stuffed bear firmly held in her tight fist.

The joy on Anna's face was so free. It was like she had been chained to the same spot for years in some dark, horrible place, and at last the sunshine was warming her cheeks.

Chelsea came out of the slide next, and Anna made a sharp turn right back into her arms. Like something was trying, unsuccessfully, to break the permanent fusion of their atomic bond.

"I don't think I have much of a choice here, Doc," Rory said. "I'm never going to be able to tell her she has to leave this place."

"Would you at all be averse to letting Anna spend the night? Just to see how she deals with it." Dr. Abbott suggested.

"I don't see why not," said Rory.

"Splendid, well, with that decided, I must say we have reached the conclusion of our tour, Mr. Gunn," said Dr. Abbott. "I'd be happy to answer any questions you might have."

"Not a thing comes to mind."

"I'm glad to hear it," said Dr. Abbott. "Now if you'll excuse me, I have some business that requires my attention."

"Of course. Thanks again. It really means a lot."

"You are very welcome. Oh, and one more thing—will you be able to join me for lunch tomorrow to go over some particulars?"

Rory pretended to flip through an imaginary day planner, "I've got nothing penciled in, should work." He caught Anna smiling at his silly antics from behind her teddy-bear bodyguard.

When they got back to the hotel, Anna was still daydreaming. Once in the elevator she jumped up and slapped at every button that she could reach. Rory and Chelsea giggled, admiring the mischief.

The door opened to the floors of the random buttons Anna had pressed, and she tried to take off at the first few, but Rory grabbed her before she could get away. At the fourteenth floor, Anna looked to her father for confirmation, and when he nodded, she darted out and spun in circles, moving her hips like she had an invisible hula-hoop that she needed to keep from hitting the floor.

"I truly can't believe the transformation," Rory said. "And you didn't even drug her."

"It's a funny way to put it," Chelsea said, "but Webb is like that. The people there are like that. It's a place of building character, for everyone. It truly is something special."

"Do you think this is what I should do?" Rory asked as he opened the hotel room door.

"I think you know what the right thing to do is," Chelsea said, smiling. She turned and called for Anna to join them. "We have to get your jammies, darling."

Anna rushed past them into the room and made a beeline for her suitcase, and together they gathered her sleeping attire, toiletries and a change of clothes for the next day.

Rory walked them back to the elevator in silence. And he recorded every movement his daughter made as she skipped, hopped, and spun towards the elevator.

"Tell your father good night and that you love him," Chelsea said.

"I wuv you, Dwaddie," Anna said, wrapping her arms around him firmly. "Gwood nigh." She kissed him and ran into the elevator and again jumped up and hit all the buttons she could.

"We'll come get you in the morning around 11:00," Chelsea said. "Sound good?"

"Sure, sounds great. See you in the morning."

"Rory?" Chelsea said. She leaned in close and kissed him on the cheek. "You are a fantastic father—not *were* or *had been*. You *are*. It's pointless to blame anyone or anything and worry yourself about what could have been done differently or if these are the right choices you're making now. Anna loves you, regardless of how she expresses it. There are a lot of roadblocks and locked doors inside her little head, but behind those obstacles is her memory of you and how much she loves you. If you choose to let her stay here, don't go home and take it as a failure. Your little girl will always be here, and I will not let her forget you."

"Thanks for that Chelsea. I think it was just what I needed."

Rory went back to the room, sat down on the recliner, and mindlessly surfed the channels on the television. He couldn't focus on words, their meanings, or what to think. Images of news shows, cartoons, movies, serials, and reality television blended with the images of Chelsea, Dr. Abbott, and Anna.

Everything was background noise and distanced. Chelsea's words were like an anchor shackling him to contemplation, while what still functioned of his consciousness floated around the hotel like an apparition getting used to its surroundings. He was avoiding the only two words that held any water—*yes* and *no*. Both seemed so final and he struggled to lift either to push out of his mouth and into the real world. He thought that they both could be construed as selfish, but from another point, they were selfless. Hollow shame battled with forgiving practicality. It terrified Rory.

He ran the water in the bathtub at a scalding temperature, filling the bathroom with steam. He wiped the condensation away from the mirror, and he stared at himself until his image disappeared again. He wiped it away over and over again, trying to catch something he might be missing. Finally, settling on the fact that if there was something missing, it was out of his depth to recognize.

Despite the emptiness of the hotel room, the next morning was bright and hopeful, and Rory felt replenished. Half-asleep and hazy he went to the room Anna would have been in to wake her, and for a moment the uninhabited bed alarmed him. But soon it registered where she was.

There was a lot of time to kill before Chelsea and Anna came to collect him. Rory decided to order a big breakfast from room service and eat a quiet meal alone against the backdrop of the towering mountain range of the Canadian Rockies.

He had the lumberjack special: sausage, bacon, hash browns, toast, and eggs over easy. A jug of orange juice and a pot of coffee were brought up as well. He knew there was no way he was going to drink all of it, but he felt like indulging his inner glutton.

After the hearty meal, Rory started to think and question himself again. Did he deserve to look upon such a backdrop? Was it the right moves or the wrong moves that had gotten him there? And what would he be without Anna around? But what sane person would ever consider prolonging a local disaster until it became a pandemic catastrophe?

Chelsea's words about him being a good father ran laps in his head. He felt like he was sweating and that his body temperature was too high. He went to the thermostat to check if he had accidentally turned the heat up, but it was set at room temperature.

Still in his pyjama bottoms and hotel monogrammed house-coat, he burst out of his room like he was being chased. When he got to the elevator, he pushed the button to the observatory deck. Once there, and the door opened, he fell out onto the floor. He got up clumsily, stumbled towards the open air, and leaned against the railing, inhaling heavily.

It was a chilly morning, but Rory didn't notice. There was no one else was on the deck, but it wouldn't have mattered if there were. Rory was seeking something that concerned only himself, and his appearance and manners were the last things he was worried about. No one else existed except for him and a cleverly hidden answer that he was having the hardest time finding, even though he knew it was in the most obvious place.

He had no idea where to start telling his daughter, who could barely recite the alphabet without cues, that she wouldn't be living with him anymore. It had nothing to do with the fact that he was letting go of his princess—what really scared him was she wouldn't react to the news with dismay or objection or a fight to stay with the person who knew her best, who shared her DNA, who had loved her before anyone else did and before anything was known to be amiss with her.

Rory raised his arms up in the air like a parishioner in a revival tent, imploring for some wise entity to lead him out of the maze of hesitation. He had reached the summit, but he was still having trouble taking that last leap of faith. He wanted so much to be told what to do, but no veiled apparitions came to guide him, and no whispers of influence were carried to him on the breeze that blew through the mountains and down into his lungs. The only direction left to follow was instinct and instinct alone. He had postponed the inevitable for long enough. It was time to say the hardest words he would ever have to speak, and that power made him feel faint and unhinged.

His sense of disembodiment was broken by a tug on his house-coat. A hotel maid stood behind him, eyes wide.

Rory's bearings were as unreliable as a compass sitting atop a magnet. The maid looked astonished, and when Rory finally realized that he was almost over the edge of the balcony, he knew the maid's look of concern was warranted. He didn't want her to get the wrong idea—that he was some nut or suicide case to be reported to the hotel manager—so he quickly calmed himself and told the maid that everything was indeed all right.

"Just getting some air," he explained with an abashed look on his face. "The mountain air is so fresh, got a little lost there for a second. Thank you for snapping me out of it."

The maid seemed satisfied, and she went back inside to her cart of linens and cleaning supplies. She pushed them towards the elevators, away from whatever crazy was really going on outside on the observation deck.

With Rory's reset back into awareness, the chill began to creep into his housecoat. He decided to go back to the room for a hot shower and await his escort back to Webb.

By the time he was finished he had a half an hour to kill before the girls arrived, and he went down to the lobby to wait for them. He ambled into the bar, half hoping to see Gus. But the bar was empty, save for the bartender taking daily inventory, so Rory decided to take a little walk around the grounds. Trails went every which way, and he could hear the rush of a river somewhere close, but out of eyesight. There were no signs of ski lifts or manufactured slopes, and when Rory asked about it, he was told that a shuttle took skiers to a different location to sculpt the mountains.

When the girls drove up, Chelsea reached over, unlatched Anna's seatbelt, and opened her door, and she bolted for her father and jumped into his arms.

"Hi, Dwaddie," she said. "Chewlsea and I had so muttz fwun last night. Can I stay wif her some mwore?"

The Policy

"I think we can arrange something like that, baby."

Chapter 12

Excitement spread across Anna's face like crayon scribbling across a living room wall. Her continued buoyancy was just the reinforcement Rory needed to live with his decision to leave her at Webb.

They ate lunch in the cafeteria with residents and employees alike. The noise was distracting to Rory, but Anna sat patiently, watching the other children. She ate her grilled cheese sandwich without protest or incident.

Not much was discussed besides the eating routines at Webb. Dr. Abbott wanted to be sure Rory knew that nutrition was highly important and that the children weren't fed cheap, freeze-dried, preservative-filled, steroid-enhanced wholesale garbage. There was a kitchen staff that prepared everything. Most were basic staples like cereal, pancakes, toast, hash browns, fruit, and eggs for breakfast, with pork products making special appearances. Lunch consisted of a variety of sandwiches, soups, and salads, but it was dinner that was the most anticipated: pastas, pizzas, chicken, beef, fish, vegetables of all kinds. It was a veritable high-class restaurant, and Rory was extremely impressed.

"The only things we prohibit are stimulants like pop and overly sugary candy," said the doctor. "We have desserts occasionally, but many of our residents react badly to them, so we keep it to a bare minimum—plus it's very unhealthy. Of course, our staff aren't restricted—they can have what they want in their private quarters— but it is discouraged to have on the campus grounds.oh, and non-meat diets can be prepared if you think that is something you'd like for Anna."

After lunch, they took a leisurely stroll outside and ended up once again in the jungled entrance. Dr. Abbott's office was tucked in the back, through the secretary station. It was a very modest room, at least compared to the size one might think the curator of such a magnificent institution would have.

The shelves were lined with books on psychology and medicine, as well as books of fiction and books that weren't; all in no particular order. On the walls hung the doctor's degrees and commendations, along with pictures of the doctor and his family or various colleagues.

The office resembled a room in the midst of transition from the seventies to the eighties. The ugly oranges and sickly greens of the furniture blended horrendously with the flat, characterless browns and black of the carpet and walls. The designed simulated wood-grain walls, like the kind you'd find running down the sides of old Plymouth station wagons, reminded Rory of his parent's living room. He looked around for baseboard heaters. They'd been common when he was young, and it all brought to mind memories as a kid; drinking tonic water and eating croutons while he watched television after school, warming his bare feet on top of the heaters.

The office had only one window, and it could be cracked open by winding a small lever system at the base. The desk was wider than it was long, and it had documents, requisition forms, pens, pencils, paper clips, and sticky notes strewn about it. In front of the desk there were two tough leather chairs that looked like they were made for a showroom display more than they were a place for one to actually sit.

"Pardon the mess. I'm not in here with visitors too often. I have a different office for more formal purposes. Not to say this isn't a formal meeting, I just know I forgot what I need for you in here. This is more of a private sanctuary, for when I have time for such a place. And please forgive this gaudy colour scheme," Dr. Abbott said with a hint of red in his cheeks. "It's a vestige of my predecessor. He had a penchant for retro design, something I don't much care for. And I haven't had much of a chance to get properly established, there is just so much going on. Please have a seat."

"Not a problem, Doc. Doesn't bother me in the slightest."

Rory's hands had become clammy, and he tried wiping them on his pants, but they wouldn't dry. He fidgeted in his seat, as he couldn't find any comfortable grooves to fit into, but it helped, seeing Dr. Abbott in a disorganized setting, to recede Rory's anxiousness. It made him feel like they had more in common than he once thought.

"Let me just find the paperwork. I could have sworn I asked for it to be brought in . . . ah, here it is. If there is anything that you need clarified, just let me know."

Dr. Abbott handed Rory a file folder that had colour-coded stickers coming out of the side indicating the pages requiring a signature. Rory went over everything, searching for a stipulation that might ensnare him or fine print that suggested hidden costs to be incurred in the future, but he found no such trap in the legal jargon; it was all pretty straight forward.

Satisfied, Rory and the doctor emerged from the office and met with Chelsea and Anna who were waiting for them outside and appreciating the plants.

Dr. Abbott patted Rory on the back, followed by a round of relieved smiles and hugs between the four of them. There were no tears; there was no need for them. Rory would not let his wounded pride take away from the revelry.

Rory and Chelsea embraced and took turns improving on each other's fractured explanation to Anna that she wasn't going home with her father and that she was to live with Chelsea and that Webb was to be her new home.

Anna laughed and nodded. She said she knew already and that it was okay. "Dwaddie will bwe fwine wiffout us."

There it was—that semi-truck of Anna's misconception, blazing the highway hauling a full load of weight behind it and slamming right into Rory's chest. The driver never saw him crossing, he imagined one witness saying.

Anna didn't understand what she was saying, but there was no point in correcting her. The important thing was that she was content. The future was uncertain, but it no longer looked frigid and scary—to any of them.

Rory spent a few more days at the hotel and Webb, wandering around and meeting people and generally just relaxing and taking in the atmosphere. He went on some hiking trails and had found the source of the rapids he had heard before.

It occurred to him that he'd neglected his phone completely, leaving it in his hotel room turned off. When he finally realized that he had ignored it the whole time, the idea of detaching himself from the extension that bound him to everyone else, no matter where he was or what he was doing, was as freeing as pardon for a crime he'd later been found wrongly accused of. So he decided to leave it off until he got home.

The time he had spent away from work with Anna and Chelsea had given him as close of a sense of family as he'd ever had. It occurred to him that missing that connection had damaged him more than he'd thought possible. He needed to start looking for normalcy again—it was not lost, just a little banged up and dirty.

When the girls took Rory to the airport, Anna was just as inquisitive as when they'd first left—the landing had had no lasting effect.

The phantom hug that Anna gave him before his departure hung around his neck the entire plane ride home. The feeling of independence didn't hit him until he got into the cab outside the airport.

He was alone.

Chapter 13

Rory wasn't on home soil for more than twenty minutes before he turned his phone on, and it went off like a blasting cap after he did. A deflating way to come home— peppered with an onslaught of voice mails and text messages—but it didn't surprise him.

A few of the messages were from Emily and Richard, but the bulk were from Dom. Some demanding an explanation of his whereabouts and what was going on. Others were apologies for being rude in previous messages, but that were still spoken demandingly because *people want to know that everything is okay.*

Dom had left a couple incoherent and indecipherable messages, more than likely while intoxicated. He had dredged up the old truculence and vigour he once aimed at the managerial coalition of Dambar so regularly. The straps on his muzzle had loosened from quietly working his jaw against the binding. His old self re-born. And with it came heavy, dangerous stress when he repeated, *things are going down*, in almost every message.

It was a hope Rory had, to keep the revised image of

himself that he acquired in Alberta, for longer than a few hours, but the gloom that came with thinking about the shop resurfaced.

Rory called Emily first. Dom and everything that went along with Dambar could wait.

Emily's voice sounded taut when he called her. "You said you'd call when you got there and I get nothing. Then your phone sends me to voicemail. What was I supposed to think? How am I supposed to react?"

"I'm sorry. We were having fun and it slipped my mind." Rory said.

"Well, that's good to hear. How's Anna doing? Did she like the airplane?" Emily asked.

Rory couldn't answer. The confession got stuck in his throat, not having decided on the right way to speak it, and stifled his voice. He didn't want to explain why his daughter wasn't with him over the phone, so he dodged the question and arranged to meet in a coffee shop by Emily's place. Being in public would cut down the chance she would make a scene.

When they met and Rory explained what he'd done, she looked at him like he was explaining mathematical algorithms, and that she, a layperson, was absolutely supposed to understand them. Rory watched her expressions cycle through shock, sadness, inquisition, and mannerly poise.

"What in God's name are you thinking? I mean, I know that what's going on with her isn't something that can be treated with a pill or an injection or surgery, but shit, Ror, fuck. I feel your pain, I do, but..."

Rory explained it all to his sister thoroughly, and he highlighted the fact that anyone who accused him of jettisoning dead weight from here on out was going to get a hammer fist of reasons about how it wasn't anyone else's plight, nor was it anyone else's decision.

"I hope you can appreciate why I didn't tell you. I didn't want anybody else's opinion about it in my head. It was hard enough as it was," said Rory. "But it made a lot of sense, and in the end I couldn't justify taking her away from that place and from Chelsea." He gripped his coffee cup like a holy chalice, speaking into it like he was seeking divinity in the hot, caffeinated liquid. "I need you now, Em, not a bunch of crap about doing something stupid. This freedom is fucking scary."

"Well, I'm not going anywhere," Emily said, "Whatever you need, I'm here for you. I'm sorry. I just wish there was more that I could've done."

"Webb is *the more* you're talking about, trust me," said Rory. "And we can always go visit."

After the chat with his sister, Rory didn't want to contact anyone else until the day before he was scheduled to be back at work. He needed the time to pack Anna's clothes and some of her toys to be shipped out West. What toys that had no place, clothes that had no use, were tossed into a box marked "goodwill". But in each article of clothing, every stuffed animal, being sent or not, Rory found a reminiscence to delight in about events that took place when they were purchased.

He remembered the lady who became disgruntled by Anna's lack of cooperation when they bought the jeans with flowers stitched into the legs, and how Rory found it funny because to him Anna was being cute difficult, not ugly difficult. And how his amusement had encouraged her, and caused Anna to run with it, which caused the lady further, playful, grief. Or the time Anna wouldn't leave the toy store without a penguin she had procured from a chest of stuffed animals, and how that penguin now played second fiddle to Mr. Boo.

Once everything was ready to go, all that was left in her room was a bed, some smudges from dirty fingers and indentations and punctures in the drywall from her knee, foot or little fist, or where a toy had been thrown in aggravation.

Without Anna around the house, conduct of what it was like to be single slowly started coming back to Rory. The idea of being able to fill the sink up with dishes or leave his clothes where he wished and not follow a laundry schedule wasn't exciting to him, but the territory was different, and there was no need to set an example anymore.

After his trip to the post office to ship off Anna's things Rory stopped by the store to grab some groceries.

On his way out of the store he noticed a sign, protruding out from the side of a motel/bar that shared the same lot as the grocery store. It read, "Cold Beer"; suggestive and blandly attractive; it displayed an arrow indicating to customers in want that they had to come to the back, down an alley way, to find the entrance.

What's the harm? Rory thought, *It'll be nice to keep a few cold ones in the fridge.*

He bought a twelve pack of Kokanee and returned home. It hadn't occurred to him at the time but he had inadvertently bought too much food—the amount he normally would have if Anna and Chelsea were around. Among the excess were some muffins and juice boxes and other things he probably wouldn't consume on his own. And there was enough of everything else that he wouldn't need to go for groceries for a while.

Once everything was put away—muffins in the freezer to be forgotten, juice boxes on the floor of the pantry to collect dust—he turned on the radio, cracked a beer and settled into the couch.

That cheated feeling that accompanied dwindling holidays and a rotten anticipation of back-to-work, floated away on a sudsy buzz with each sip Rory took, and a quarter dozen beers later, he decided to call Dom—confident that there wasn't much that his contentious friend would be able to say that would mess with his softened frame of mind.

The phone rang a few times, and just as Rory went to press *end,* he heard Dom on the other end. "About goddamn time."

"Hey there, bud," Rory said like a loosened up corner store wino. "How's it been?"

"Hectic and stressed. I hope you had a fine vacation, because have I got an earful for you."

Rory cracked another beer and nestled back into the couch. His body was limp, like a drunk driver who was entering a hundred-kilometre-per-hour rollover but remained in a state of slow motion while everything around him toppled over itself, out of control.

He listened to Dom go on breathlessly about a few new guys who'd come in by way of a headhunting firm who didn't have to start at the bottom doing grunt work. They came right in and started at jobs some guys had waited years to get a crack at. One of them was working at Rory's machine, but the sense of threat that Dom laced his revelation with didn't concern Rory too much. Dom also spoke of a new corporate policy that effectively ended a two-hour paid grace period the employees had previously been allotted for appointments.

"Guys are pissed about that one big time. Another thing—the guys on the line have been told that the twelve-hour rotations and running that new machine twenty-four-seven is mandatory now. And there's talk of an overnights foreman. Huge stink there. Those line guys account for a big percentage of the force, if you get what I'm saying."

After ten minutes of Dom, Rory needed another beer. He got up and went to the fridge, half listening to Dom, half reciting Led Zeppelin's "In My Time of Dying," which played faintly on the radio. On his way back to the couch, Rory took his wallet out of his back pocket and threw it on the coffee table and returned his attention to the diatribe firing out of his phone speaker. After Dom had made a few more passes around the track, words like *organize* and *union* reminded Rory of Gus, and he pulled out the card he had been given and inspected it like an artifact.

"Hey, Dom, shut up a second. You'll never guess who I met while I was away." Rory made it sound like it was a mutual acquaintance— that Gus was your friend right off the hop, no résumé or get-to-know-you period needed.

Rory told of the encounter in the hotel bar and noted that Gus was from the same union Dom had researched. Through the whole story, the other end of the line was quiet.

"That's fantastic stuff," said Dom. "What do you think now?"

"It's neither here nor there at the moment," said Rory. "But I will tell you, the guy made a convincing case."

"Just wait until you come in tomorrow."

"I guess I'll see you tomorrow then. You know if I'm on days?"

"Yup. I hope you're well rested, because now it's back to the grind. Goodnight." The phone clicked over to the empty tone. Rory with felt like he'd been hit in the flank, made *it* in a game of tag, one he was unaware was being played.

Chapter 14

It didn't take long for the shop's scent of salt, handled pennies, and charred barbecue to end the furlough that Rory's lungs and sinuses had been granted in the open mountain air.

The construction crew had finished ahead of schedule and had cleared out their gear in the week Rory was at Webb. Behind them they left an intricate network of rebar, concealed within concrete, that went ten meters deep in the ground. Fortified enough to prevent the new machine from sinking into the earth from the great force of its pounding mechanics.

The incessant noise that they added to the already insufferable volume of the plant was a gratifying departure—noise that, at its worst, had made it so the workers could barely hear each other if they were side by side. A few of them had taken to communicating on paper pads and using crude hand signals to deliver messages from the crane to the floor, but most of the time it was still a swipe of the hand under the chin or a single extended finger.

Although the reprieve from the jarring discordance was

welcome, the decreased decibel level didn't last long. It was soon replaced by another terrible clamour as the new machine was brought to life after being completely assembled. There was a feed site where the steel began the flattening process. And if someone was unfortunate enough to not have hearing protection when the coil of steel reached its end and the tail slammed into the reinforced guard plates, it would feel like thousands of microscopic miners had entered their ear canal and were dismantling the cochlea with sledgehammers and pick axes. The ringing could last for hours, and the damage was irreparable. There were signs up everywhere indicating that hearing protection was compulsory, and the corporate manifest had policies in place, but there were still some who did not wear the ear muffs or plugs provided. Double standards that started to create animosity between workers from different departments— where one, in a quieter area of the shop, caught shit for not wearing proper P.P.E., and who would watch as those in the loudest area escape reprimand for the same breach of policy.

Rory had overheard some guys call the workers on the cut to length line "elitists" because management didn't want to do anything to upset them—using placation and amenity to keep anything from interfering with production. Rory wanted to say the paranoia was unwarranted but he wasn't sure he could say it without a little doubt in his voice.

The new cut-to-length line, from loading end to finished product sheet stacker, spanned nearly thirty meters in length by five meters wide. Once trolleyed into position, and secured on an expanding wheel that insures control and prevents looseness, the 25,000-kilogram coil's lip is carefully fed into the mouth of an entry shear that crops the malformed ends off. Next begins the straightening of the steel into stiff, inflexible sheet by a series of shafts and hydraulic cylinders inside of a flattening cassette that is powered by a wired mash of high tech gear boxes, linear voltage transducers, electronic encoders and micro-processors that were controlled by dozens upon dozens of buttons, levers, dials, knobs, switches and sensors.

Between the two massive hydraulic towers is twelve meters of table rollers that are affixed to a collapsible bridge that, if disengaged to allow for tension release, would descend into a pit that went as deep as the construction crew had dug. The three-meter-thick towers spanned the width of the machine and reached almost as high as the ceiling. They clamp down with 2.5 million kilograms of pressure on the corners and could stretch a few more centimetres out of the steel with a million kilograms of force (if it was necessary), making the once rounded casting as flat and level as possible—reducing noticeable imperfections caused by deviant waves or buckling, and thus generating product accuracy within millimetres of precise tolerances.

A grid of invisible ultra-violet light curtains and fences with magnetized electronic triggers and safety railing beset the more hazardous areas where one could suffer serious injury from pinch points, or anything else the unforgiving mechanics might be capable of. If any one of the triggers or curtains were to be tripped while the machine was running the whole thing would shut down and have to be manually reset before production could recommence. All that was missing was razor wire, the workers would joke. It was the most elaborate safety equipment in the whole shop, and it got Rory thinking about where the company was placing their priorities and why.

Beyond what Rory thought it could mean it was still a magnificent sight and he couldn't help but stare in its direction—glistening and proud against a backdrop of worn age and dismal shading—while he walked to the brake.

When he turned in the driveway, finally able to pull his attention from the new machine, Rory saw someone he didn't recognize standing beside the brake, examining it. The man was wearing a yellow hard hat, and his coveralls were a darker, fresher blue than the ones worn by the employees of Dambar. An outsider brought in, for sure. Rent-a-worker written all over him. A guy who got made ten dollars less than what Dambar paid the agency that sent him. More proof that overhead was the great unassailable excuse when it came down to shucking the maximum profit out of something.

But there was something different about the guy in the yellow hat. The way he stood poised for inspection, hands behind his back, chest high and forward, boots planted firmly—not one noticeable aberration in the perfected, time-developed stance. It was too rigid to be the posture of the usual fly-by-night rummies, the dwellers of the fringes of society that weren't motivated enough to work forty hours a week. The regulars Rory was used to seeing at Dambar. This guy wasn't going to be that kind of temp. The kind that developed a good rhythm, got to know their way around the machine, and then vanish. This guy in the yellow hat was too focused— unsettlingly staring at the brake, almost as if he was communicating with it.

Dom's forewarning hovered over Rory. It would be careless to approach without a fair bit of mistrust, but he had already decided that he wasn't going to come in and bombard the new guy with negativity about Dambar so he'd lose interest and ambition and stop showing up all together—something his co-workers would do if they felt threatened. But a warning was a warning, and Rory had to play it cautiously. So, instead of saying something gruff like, "And who might you be?", or "Can I help you?", or some other sort of circum-spect question that's ingrained with an attitude already decided on building a barrier, Rory just dragged the soles of his boots across the shop floor to alert the man of his presence.

"You must be Rory," the guy said, startled but readily cordial. "It's a pleasure to meet you, sir." He extended his hand to shake. "I'm Edward, but you can call me Ed, and I'll be your new helper."

Rory was stunned by the formality; Ed was obviously a decade Rory's senior, and that kind of reverence in a steel factory wouldn't get anyone anywhere quick. *Fucker, asshole,* and *dickhead* were about as conventional as it got between workers on the shop floor, and those were the most pleasantly neutral ones.

"Pleased to meet you, Ed, but there's no need for the *sir*. The only rank I hold here is a certain pungency after a long and sweaty day," Rory said, trying to set the tone and see if Ed had a sense of humour. It was going to be a painful partnership if he didn't.

Ed chuckled, but the joke didn't loosen him up too much. He just continued to stand, unflinching, like iron rods ran from his heels to the base of his neck.

"Is this your first day?" Rory asked.

"No, sir. I spent last week working with Matthew."

"That must've went well," Rory said. The sarcasm was completely lost on Ed, who told him that indeed it had gone well. "And please, Ed, Rory or Ror will do just fine."

Ed apologized. It was a habit that would be hard to break for him, and they were not in the right place to be focusing their minds elsewhere, so Rory figured that he'd just drop the issue.

"Let me just get organized and then we'll get started," Rory said.

The first half of the day was easy. There were a couple of small jobs—nothing too complicated—and Ed caught on quickly. He said that it was kind of difficult working with Matt, to which Rory responded it would pass, that Matt was a good guy, and it was just a matter of getting used to each other.

The better chance to find out more about Ed came in the second half of the day after some sweat and a few laughs unlocked Ed's hardened exterior. He told of his family: two teenagers and a demanding wife, that he had spent time in the military (stance explained), and that he bought, flipped and sold houses in a more uncouth area of the city. That was his passion, he said, and it was easy to tell because his excitement rose when he spoke about it. An excitement that dipped back down again when he explained that he was just starting out and his first house still needed work, and that he couldn't afford the building supplies yet to complete the job, and that it was hurting his investment. His big plans were yet to be.

Ed also revealed the agency he had been brought in by—Oakner Work Services—and Rory knew the name. It was a headhunting firm that was hired by companies to find certain kinds of people to fill specific jobs, and the thought made fresh Rory's wonder after Dom's warning.

But the red flags that Rory expected to pick up on were never waved, and he started to think that Dom was up to his old conspiracy theories and paranoid assumptions. If it was one thing that never wavered, it was Dom's penchant for pigeonholing—like he had been present at the casting of the mould. If he thought nothing more of a person than just blood, bone, sinew and muscle whose purpose it was to be torn, broken and replaced. A judgment that never changed, even if Dom was proven wrong. It was a flaw Rory told him would get him into trouble, but to Dom, advice about how to manage his misconceived notions was about as effective as bullets from an air rifle would be at penetrating a Kevlar vest.

It wasn't until after the shift that Dom appeared. He was out by Rory's car, leaning up against it like he'd been waiting outside a prison on discharge day. He wore a determined and undeniable look of triumph. "What did I tell you?" Dom said.

"Ed's all right," said Rory. "Don't know what you were talking about last night."

"That guy's after your job."

"And how the hell would you know something like that?" Rory asked.

"It's a pretty plain grab, if you ask me, and you ain't got shit protecting your job from some sidewinding asshole that will do whatever need be to take it from you." Dom sounded like a crazed mountain hermit—declaring arguable truths from his falsely sacrosanct pulpit at the mouth of his cave—to passersby that just kept on passing by. "You need to give that contact of yours a call. This place is a pressure cooker right now. Oakner is sending people here now? I bet that's where the crane operating temp came from. I'm telling you, man, we gotta strike while the iron's hot here, and we need you, brother. I've told you before that these guys trust you. Your push, your breath on the sail, is all we need to get close enough to the shore and get the anchor in the sand."

It was a compelling sell of a caustic idea, Rory admitted, but had no immediate reaction to it. Other workers had come out from the back entrance, into the parking lot, and had no doubt heard what Dom was preaching. It was obviously not taboo among the guys who were leaving. All they wanted, Rory guessed, was a nod—some sign of approval from him that didn't reek of apprehension.

"I told some guys about your encounter over your holiday," said

Dom, "and I must say it was met with optimism."

"What the hell else has been going on around here?" Rory said as he turned to address his departing coworkers, trying to gain some insight from their facial expressions.

"Trust me, Ror. It's a big fucking barrel of worms, but now that thing is in the ground we've got an advantage. You can't deny that," Dom said.

"Man, I need to see something for myself. This can't just be a screw-management vendetta that we leave them to clean up afterwards. This kind of thing requires our involvement too, you know. We need an actual threat to our jobs here, and we need to research this stuff. Educate ourselves. Not just pull a pin and hope for the best."

"Hey, man, I'm just relaying info."

It was like they were standing at the foot of a great pyre with the management team, corporation incarnate, bound to the giant stake at the centre; Dom passing Rory a match to set it ablaze. Management's pleas of mercy drowned out by the baying and chants of the masses behind them.

"I'm going to need to think about it, man," Rory said. He got into his car and rolled down the window, allowing Dom to stick his head in.

"You seen Bill from the line today?" Dom asked.

"No, I have not."

"Well, you should. He's not who he was. You know that guy won't stop working even if it's killing him. Management knows that, but they won't say a thing about him working the way he is. He can barely walk properly for shit sake. Are they waiting for him to collapse? These fucking disability claims people really burn me too. Protocol they say. Policy they say. Procedure they say. There's nothing we can do about it they say. Bullshit is what I say. The time is now brother, or else. These are our lives. Think about it. I'll see you mañana."

Dom's departing words were urgent, and they stuck like a spitball. Rory drove off to digest all of it. Dom's eloquence was becoming more acute and pointed. Unionizing wasn't going to be easy; it was a sudden shift, but at the same time it was apparent that it was a long time coming.

Rory got home and slumped into the couch, not even noticing that he had automatically grabbed a beer from the fridge. He stared blankly at the wall, burning a hole into oblivion; peeling away the layers of paint and drywall and deconstructing the nails and boards and insulation behind them. As he sipped from his can he tried to piece together what had everyone's feathers ruffled, and what would happen once the easy dreams were to wane and the workers displeasure found elsewhere to set up shop.

His far off thought educed scenarios about the general disapproval; playing out in his head like a courtroom drama. The plaintiffs and bailiffs were various figures from work, and the jury box was made up of a fifty-fifty split of management and worker representation that howled "guilty!" and "innocent!" at the each other, never being heard except by themselves.

For some, the prime concern was parity and the right to gain seniority that would afford them peace of mind when it came to job security. Others flailed about, decrying that greed was so often the catalyst of sedition. The immodest and grungy corporate types wore snakeskin boots and oversized cowboy hats that exemplified their extravagance, and their belt buckles were imprinted with their own wide, guiltless smiles. While the workers were smeared with dirt, wearing ragged clothes, holding rotten food in their hands.

Through all of it came the image of his daughter—and not because he associated her absence with the demand for deliverance or with his reluctant acceptance that he was to be the head for the body of protest. He thought of her because normally he left all the office politics strewn among the steel dust on the shop floor. He didn't like that it had followed him home. There was nothing around to keep his mind off of it.

This must be what it's like for Dom, he thought—going home or to the bar, trying to drown the effects work had on him but only strengthening it by concentrating on the nature of the torment. It no longer escaped Rory what it was that made Dom such a volatile man: It was a repressed fear and an indistinct need to challenge the authority of men who were superior only because some college had given them a piece of paper assuring them they were.

Pedantic castrators of other people's ambition was what Rory thought Dom must think of them, but he tried to divert his resentment because he couldn't define its source and ignore the haunting x factor—the what-ifs that could throw the gentle construct of Rory's universe into a dryer and set the timer on eternity.

The rest of the week continued smoothly and, despite the spread in the plant, Rory successfully fought off Dom's communicable treason. Ed showed promise and was excellent to work with. He was diligent and possessed a savvy that Rory might have admired in himself, had the roles been reversed. Ed deserved more of a chance than was being given. He had a family too.

The last stretch of Friday's shift was coming to a close, and they had gotten ahead on their orders, so Rory decided to kick back behind the machine and kill that last hour chatting with Ed, who was coming out of his shell and freely spoke more in depth about himself.

Ed had enjoyed his time in the military, but for others he knew it was not an easy experience. His understanding of society and *what really matters* was broadened greatly by his time in the service. It was there that priorities were defined for him, becoming a man with a lot to say but no questions to ask. He then moved on to discuss his family and his sons more. Ed took as great a pleasure when talking about them as he did about his renovation business. Rory could tell Ed had the recital of accomplishments at the ready for whenever an interested ear or opportunity to talk about them came up. The kids were geniuses, and during high school they were in all the advanced classes. Ed was proud that they wouldn't have to follow in their father's footsteps and join the military or work as a labourer. "There's no sense forcing a kid—that's how they get away from you" was how he explained his approach to parenting.

Rory could relate to Ed, and he felt comfortable enough to share about Anna. It was hard at first, figuring out the right way to explain it, but Ed was empathetic and told Rory that he was a strong man for making such a tough decision. It was reassuring, and Rory talked with him like they had known each other for twenty years.

"You know, some guys in here told me to be careful around you," said Rory. "Said that you may be after my job." He followed the outrageous idea with a little laughter.

"Hell, no," Ed chuckled, "Not at all . . . I mean, don't get me wrong here, the plan has always been to train with you and eventually get hired on as a brake operator, but as far as I'm after your job? No way, man. Matt on the other hand . . . Wyatt made mention of his days being numbered."

Ed's admission jerked Rory back into awareness like he had drifted off the road into the wake-up notches that lined highway lanes—designed to keep fatigued drivers from perilous wandering.

"Oh, really?" was the only thing Rory could think of saying without having the lighthearted banter turn into an investigation.

Ed's certainty of his future at the plant nudged at Rory as though it was someone's pointy umbrella jabbing into the small of his back on a crowded subway—and he didn't know how to politely ask the passenger to hold it by his side, not under his arm, like a normal human being would.

Rory staved off the impulse to back Ed into a corner and set him straight about what would happen if he disturbed the status quo. But there was nothing for Rory to stand on, and he was definitely not in a position to feel the warmth of security—there was nothing protecting his job and nothing he could do to discourage a guy like Ed from schmoozing and sweet-talking his way into management's favour.

Rory excused himself and went to the bathroom. He wanted to wait. Play it cool until the horn of shift switch sounded and Matt was at the brake so they could talk.

Ed didn't seem to suspect anything out of place when Rory got back. He continued to blather away, incriminating himself more with every syllable. Rory discredited him and tried to erase any connection they'd made on the human level. Ed was now an enemy, a weasel that would keep up the charade until he achieved what he wanted and then show his true form, and it enraged Rory to think that this guy whom he thought once harmless, and deserved a chance, had transformed into a prevalent danger with one sentence.

Rory felt used and duped, and his contempt towards Ed became like an allergic reaction. Rory couldn't wait for him get out of sight.

The bell finally went, and Ed saluted Rory goodbye and said he'd see him on Monday. *Not if there's a God, you won't,* thought Rory. *I'll be damned if I let you screw with my friend's livelihood.*

Matt, walking with a limp, passed Ed in the driveway, and they exchanged a bland acknowledgement.

"What's with you?" Rory asked.

"Nothing," Matt said, shuffling passed, clearly uninterested in having a discussion about anything.

"That's a hell of a thing to say. You get hurt or something?"

"It's nothing, all right?"

"Okay, then. Listen, I had a chat with Ed today. Did you know he was training to work here at the brake with us?"

"He said something along those lines, yeah. What of it? I'm really not in the mood for this."

You never fucking are, Rory thought. "All right, then. It's just our jobs."

"You're starting to sound like your buddy Dom," Matt said.

Rory couldn't tell if it was a shot or a genuine observation.

"I'm in," said Matt, "if that's what you're after."

"In what?"

"The union stuff. Dom told me already. You bring me a card, and I'll sign it. Something's better than nothing, right?"

"I suppose so," said Rory—thrown off by Matt's lack of misgiving. "You have yourself a fine shift, my friend."

Matt didn't respond. Rory knew pledging allegiance was difficult for him, and he'd did it without being prompted or coerced, and he seemed to mean it. The revelation from such a meek man had Rory thinking more brazenly about the undertaking. Matt was definitely a push in the right direction, but unionizing still wasn't foolproof, and Rory knew anything less than guaranteed was very dangerous.

Rory went to the back to change and took his time, mulling over options and trying to determine how each of his co-workers would react if he were posed the question to sign a union card. Rory looked at them in passing glances and in his peripherals as they laughed and joked while changing into their street clothes.

He's a definite. He would sign. No way he would. Without question that guy would. No point even bothering with him.

The generalizations and assessments drowned their raucous behaviour from Rory's ear and mashed their images into an abstract, multi-coloured mass. They took their turns in the "bird bath" wash up station they all shared like a miniature oasis. They filed out and said their *see ya laters* and *have a good nights*, and Rory hadn't even washed the layer of carbon dust off his arms or his face yet, but no one seemed to notice he was dragging his ass.

"Would it really work?" Rory asked himself aloud. His attention snapped back to focus at the opening and shutting of the lunch-room door.

Marshall had walked in, and he had more gunk, dust, grease, and crud all over him than normal. It was in his wrinkles and so heavy on his arms that it looked like it was his natural skin colour.

"Running a little behind, Ror?" Marshall asked.

"Kinda. I guess."

"I'm getting too old for this shit. These machines in here are getting too old. Like a fifteen-year-old, three-legged coyote. I don't know why they had to keep the old line after the new one got up and running."

The analogy didn't make sense to Rory, but he laughed anyway. "What makes you say that?" Rory asked.

"Seems like we do more work to the old Triton than we actually accomplish with it. But hell, if they want to pay me my wage to roll around in the dirt, then I guess I shouldn't complain, right?"

Rory felt opportunity shove him onto the dance floor. Marshall was the best unaffiliated worker to run the idea of forming a union by, but Rory couldn't figure out the right way to keep the conversation neutral. They had moved to the bird bath and were lathering their arms with a cherry-scented industrial soap that removed the layers of filth from their skin like turpentine would take paint from a board.

Rory decided to strike at the conversation. He already knew Marshall was a little more prone to a revealing interaction in a one-on-one setting, and there was a vulnerability between people at the bird bath—like it was a confessional.

"What do you think about this place nowadays?" asked Rory. "You've been here, what, twenty, twenty-five years now?"

"Has it been that long? Kinda depressing when you think about it, eh?" Marshall said.

"You know what I find depressing? How this place has been doing solid and steady business for the past eight months now and we still haven't heard about those incentives being reinstated."

Marshall continued to scrub away at his blackened, foamy arms. "What exactly are you thinking about doing about it?" he finally asked.

"I really don't know," said Rory. "All I know is that there are things going on in here that just don't seem proper. I've heard things that I can't substantiate, but I've also witnessed certain behaviour that leads me to believe these presumptions I've heard are not groundless."

"What kind of things have you heard?" Marshall asked.

"I heard they are going to be making you guys run those machines all day, every day now, and that those twelve-hour shifts are mandatory, and only at the line."

Marshall rinsed his arms. He dried off and went into the change room without saying a word. It made Rory queasy. He couldn't tell if he had just thrown the ticket in the trash before he knew if it was a winner.

"If you're talking about what I think you are, then you better know what you're doing. I'm not eighteen anymore," Marshall said as he walked out the door.

Chapter 15

Over the weekend Rory called Gus and was put in contact with Pete Nichols: president of USI's local branch, and a meeting was arranged for lunch on Monday at a downtown sandwich shop.

It helped that Rory was on the evening shift. If he wasn't digressing from routine, expected to be one place but being in another, the chances that the semi-covert meeting would dig in under anxious skin and compromise his ability to hold it together and see it through, was less.

He knew it was a fool's wager to think that management didn't always have their ear to the ground, listening for faint traces of a schism forming, readying to rupture. That they weren't prepared to squash a threat as soon as they find out. It was why Rory went alone. Deniability. Publicity needed to be held off for as long as possible.

Pete didn't attend the meeting. He sent two of his regional organizers, one fat and tall and one skinny and short. They came with a handful of pledge cards and a memorized precept that they rallied back and forth and to a T.

"First thing you should know right off the bat is, do not

seek signatures on company property," said the fat one.

"That would not only be a violation of union policy, but it would also constitute unfair labour practices in the eyes of the company. In other words, it is against the law of labour standards," said the skinny one.

"This battle, bringing in a union, can be a long and disheartening one," said the fat one. "You've got to be ready for setbacks and be in it for the long haul."

"You will also find out who your true friends are, that's for sure," said the skinny one.

"Just give me the cards and I'll contact you when it's finished," said Rory.

The organizers cracked smiles and told Rory that if he thinks it'll be that easy, then by all means, go for it. What the organizers didn't know was that the formation of dominoes was ready to be set off by the weakest of touches on the first tile, but still they smiled and jabbed at each other with their elbows and snickered to themselves while they ate their pastrami sandwiches—thinking about the world of disappointment Rory was in for without their help.

At work Rory was quiet. Dom was texting him for an update and all Rory typed back was: *Meet at my house after my shift. Bring Cy and Reg and tell them to get all the line guys they know will sign to come too. Richard will be there.*

All together there were fifteen Dambar workers at Rory's house in the early morning hours of Tuesday, and there would be eight more stopping by after their shift ended at 8 a.m.

There was no need for phone calls of solicitation, like the organizers said there would. No need for in-person house calls to plead the case. Rory, Dom, and Richard had worked out the logistics and executed them with the precision and speed of battlefield surgeons.

To avoid the policy and legality warnings, Rory offered his home as the place to sign the union cards. It was off the radar, and not having to look over their shoulders set the more addled and squeamish personalities at ease.

Only after passing the required percentage of fifty-one did they start canvassing the on-the-fencers, the indifferent, and the timid. The ones who feared being blackballed jumped on the bandwagon with little need for convincing. The last group, the hardcore gossip-mongers and office snitches, were avoided altogether. Once anyone had signed a card, they were instructed to stay mum about the movement when informers were around, but if they could, not say a word about it until it was over. The day that the finks could no longer gain clout within the office by selling out their comrades wasn't a long way off, and many took great pleasure in being elusive around them—making them feel like they had once made others feel.

Over and over again, Dom was calculating the percentages like he was a gangster's crooked bookkeeper: number of signatures divided by total number of workers employed times one hundred. Even if the number hadn't changed, he obsessed over the equation like a fiend. It was the most math Rory had ever seen him do, and if it kept Dom's claws retracted and his mouth shut, then the fixation served a purpose.

As the week progressed, and more workers signed cards, Dambar got quieter than anyone could ever remember it being. It was a wonder that management didn't make anything of it.

By the evening of the fourth day, Rory felt like a conga line was shuffling all over his last nerves. They had more than enough supporters, but the possibility of exposure was still high. All it would take would be for one person getting cold feet, one man to back-pedal out of fear, to end it. Nothing reduced support and fanfare for an insurgency more than the execution of the leader of a cause, and Rory would be the one to suffer that fate.

Despite the gut-wrenching paranoia, Rory made it to Friday to hand in the cards to Pete Nichols' fat and skinny organizers; 73.8 percent of the workforce had signed, enough for an automatic certification by the provincial Labour Board under the Unity Steel banner.

"I'll personally get this down to the Labour Board and make it official within the hour," said Pete. "If your bosses didn't know already, they surely will when you go into work tonight."

Management was completely blindsided, T-boned, sucker

punched and violated. There was no time to coordinate opposing propaganda to sway the cautious and malleable. It was all done too quickly—even from the union's standpoint. They hadn't heard of organization and initiation happening that quickly since the days of heavy and physical labour disputes. The fat and skinny organizers were amazed. And they called Pete Nichols to their office so he could see for himself what had been done.

Before getting to the brake to start working, Clive came up to Rory in the driveway with his hot-off-the-presses literature of dissuasion. A vain and inconsequential attempt, but an attempt nonetheless.

"The company is aware there is a union drive going on," said Clive.

Rory wanted to say he'd already driven the bus through the wall, but he held his tongue. He wasn't sure how safe he was from retaliation. The grace of anonymity was far more comfortable—cloaking him from crass prejudice and fiery tempers.

Clive eyed Rory like a suspect, but Rory gave away nothing.

As Clive walked away, Rory noticed Dom sitting in his crane, watching the panic unfold as management frantically tried to perform damage control. His maniacal laughter was hidden by the roar and hum and bang of the machines and equipment, and he looked almighty in his perch.

Disapproval from the office, mostly launched by Trent, came like venom from a spitting cobra, intended to blind, but it lost all momentum and potency almost immediately after release. Their natural order had been upset. They were being forced to endure the scourge. They had to defend their den by default. Because underneath it all, as a symptom of contact high, they longed to fit into a niche of avarice, to one day be an insider, an accepted, even though they were just as disposable and replaceable as the workers.

"You have no idea what you've done" and "You are fools" and "You'll regret this" were the most common things that were heard, but the workers on the floor walked with a silent pride, knowing they'd become a nuisance with a name instead of a number to blame.

The dust settled in late November of 2010. Nothing was going to happen immediately, and Rory spread the word for his union brothers to remain patient while acclimating to the new two-tier system. Those first few weeks were a tentative period for all; many still reeled from the surprise attack. Clive's shutter blinds, which had once been open enough to see into his office, were now tightened like a bomb shelter door.

Wyatt's once unlocked, open, and inviting office door was being locked at night, and new distorting panes of glass had replaced the old wire mesh panels he had before. He too pulled down the shades in his office that looked out onto the shop floor, and one could watch as his shadow paced about in a downtrodden sulk, as though he'd been unjustly betrayed. Wyatt would never be able to turn a blind eye again lest he didn't mind having it snatched out of its socket.

When the time came to elect the various positions within the Dambar union membership, Rory was voted the unit chair. At first he was reluctant to take it. He thought Richard was the best candidate, but Richard said that his emotions would run too high, that he was too old and nearing retirement, and that might prove costly to the movement. Instead, he offered his service in the capacity of unsanctioned emissary and veiled counsel.

There was no way Dom could have taken the position; he was far too likely to resort to guerrilla tactics, like littering people's driveways with roofing nails or throwing bricks through front windows during the dead of winter if something didn't go his way. One could take Dom's insinuations as high-octane, hypothetical threats, but putting him in charge was like chancing tinfoil or metal utensils in a microwave.

Besides, the position gave Rory something new to nurture, and he wasn't feeling half empty anymore. He had people's spirits to keep up and dispositions to stimulate. He was like a gardener, the way he coddled and coaxed solidarity at the shop, and he found it fun trading barbs with management without fear of consequence. He wanted them to know he wouldn't be baited with controversy, and that the aftershocks would not knock him down.

When they spoke, before it all unfolded, Gus had told Rory that management was going to "come down with a squall of intimidation" but that it was "packed with flaccid muscle and large, threatening words that most people didn't understand" and that it would be, at times, difficult to weather.

"I'll think I'm prepared for that," Rory had said.

"Are you a religious man, Ror?" Gus had asked.

"Not by choice."

"Well, you might want to start believing in something, some totem or talisman, because I'll tell ya, once the shoreline erodes and there is nothing left to use as traction, moving in that wet sand becomes quite the chore. Convenience is often not convenient, you get me? It's then that you might need something, anything, for moral support."

Although tensions gradually eased between the unionizers and management, there was still some apprehension among the workers who had not been approached to sign cards. Day after day, they came in faceless and frightened. They had no idea what the changes meant for them. They tried to integrate themselves with the triumphant body of the majority, but were given the cold-shoulder. It didn't help that those who had signed were now sporting the attitudes and style from teamsters and gangsters in movies. What disturbed Rory the most was that they starting to emulate Dom, and that could prove to be a catastrophe all on its own if it weren't dealt with quickly.

In one case, Todd Foree, another crane operator, had started to run down a few of those once called apple polishers and informants. He told them that their games were over, and it was their turn to worry. Rory saw what was happening and interceded. He stood in front of Todd, and reassured the group that they would not be persecuted, and that the union would fight for them just the same as if they had signed the pledge cards.

He then turned to Todd and told him they weren't in the business of fear-mongering and browbeating. They were one now, and as soon as the word *unity* lost meaning, the mountain they had conquered would be no more than a tiny hill anyone could scale.

Rory didn't like feeling that he was stepping on to a battleground every time he punched in for work, but management adapted to the change of culture as such. They wanted sycophants and the acquiescent and the spiritless lining their ranks, not the intrepid or the tenacious. It was because of such values that Rory figured they disassociated from the affectation that there was a human side to their positions. It led him to believe that somewhere behind a translucent window in some classroom, in some university or college, there was a corporate ethos written on a whiteboard that said, "Hire them smart enough to do what you need but stupid enough not to say anything about it."—Business 101.

The branch manager, Grant Campbell, wouldn't see Rory at first. Campbell took the union drive as a slap in the face, and he had barricaded himself away in his office. Rory imagined he was stewing in seclusion, biding his time, planning out how he could decapitate Rory and get away with it.

The two of them didn't even know each other aside from a few passing glances or a slight nod of the head—or an ineffectual, palm down handshake at the distribution of Christmas turkeys, when Campbell would say a lackadaisical "season's greetings" followed by Rory's name, which was read from his uniform.

It was a week into December before Campbell finally gave Rory an audience. Campbell did most of the talking, and it was more like a dictum than a discussion.

Campbell's chair looked like it had been built for a monarch. High-priced cushioned leather that made a rude, interruptive squeak every time he repositioned himself while Rory would speak. The chair also had some loft to it, so it appeared to anyone that sat opposite him, that Campbell had the higher ground, looking down.

The topic discussed had nothing to do with the newly minted union, nor was it pocked with any kind political sparring. It was mainly to inform Rory that, in the coming week, the company was planning a showcase of the multimillion-dollar cut to length line they had installed. All the bugs had been worked out, and the operators were confident they knew the machine well enough to handle demonstrations.

It was a big deal for the company as well as Campbell, and he had decided to shut the plant down for half a day to accommodate the event. And in what he thought was an enormous display of generosity, also decided to not excuse those on shift, but to instead pay them for the time they would be sitting around.

The new cut to length line made money hand over fist. It was faster and more reliable than the older model, and in taking on the more difficult requests asked of it, was luring away business from competitors.

It was no secret that Dambar was poised to become the biggest supplier of plate and sheet metal for Western Canada. Rory had seen for himself how many more trucks were coming in and taking full loads to one destination and not dropping small loads off at several different ones. It was occurring every day and sometimes twice. And when he thought about how much money that generated, the ratio of Campbell's generosity against production time that would be lost with a half day shutdown, was like comparing a basket of apples to an orchid.

Before leaving, Rory tried to broach the subject of a few safety concerns, but Campbell said he didn't have time and that Wyatt or Clive were more than capable of sorting out whatever it was Rory needed to talk about.

Campbell got up and opened the door for Rory with a spurious smile on his face—the kind a washroom attendant at some fancy restaurant would have after being forced to endure the seasoned rancidness that came from the stalls and act like it didn't bother them.

Management continued to brush off Rory in the lead up to the open house, and it was getting irritating, but Christmas was also approaching, and Rory gave them the benefit of the doubt that it was because of preoccupation and not blatant avoidance.

Once Dom was told about the exhibition he wanted to sabotage it by letting rats loose in the plant or rewiring the machine to run in reverse or loosen a hydraulic oil hose so it that would burst mid demonstration, slicking the floors and covering the suits in golden goop. Although it would have been like watching a slapstick gag reel, and the idea wasn't immediately shot down, Rory told him to stop putting ideas in people's heads. There was no need to affect outside business. No orders meant no work, and no work meant no jobs, and that was easy enough for Dom and his band of saboteurs to understand.

When the day came the demonstration went off without a hitch, and the turnout was impressive. Managers, purchasing officers, and sales reps from rival companies as well as current customers had shown up to get a glance at the prototype machine in action.

The majority of the workers were relegated to the farther removed areas of the plant, where the suits wouldn't be poking around. Rory thought of it like a plantation hiding its *help* when guests were present. Only the most disciplined and courteous were on display. No one took that as personally as Rory did. Most were content getting paid to sit on overturned pails and poorly constructed stools made from broken and warped two-by-fours and playing cards or dozing off.

A couple of days after the open house, memos were sent out as to how well the presentation had gone and how valuable the employees were to the company and how knowledgeable the guests thought the operators were. The buttery words came off sounding like a bow gliding over a violin's heartstrings in an attempt to disarm the union members and trick them into feeling guilty about what they had done, and the closer that it got to the 25th of December, the more vulnerable they would be to the suggestion.

Rory reviled the tactic. He had to continually remind the guys that words like *sincere, important,* and *appreciated* were emphasized for a reason and not to get caught up in the glamour of neon signs that sold a different product than the one advertised. It was difficult to convince people not to let their resolve weaken just because of the holiday. And the daily reminder was all he could do to keep the guys from having a change of heart about the union and becoming soft, even though it had just gotten off the ground.

* * *

The weather was getting colder. An arctic vortex that would last a month or more, said The Weather Network, made everyone irreparably crabby.

Amid trying to keep the spirits high in the shop, Rory was trying to stave off the sting of spending his first Christmas without Anna. He used to cherish the shopping and the sneaking around, hiding gifts, but without her around the holiday took on a bleak tone. He started making up ways to stay away from the house as long as possible after work ended. He didn't want to have to pass her old bedroom and look in on nothing. To distract himself he wandered the crowded malls, drove around the perimeter of the city, took in movies he didn't want to see, and went to out of the way bars for a long drink or two, all in a bid to clear his head, but it didn't stay clear for long. He wanted to see the girls. Nothing was going to erase that.

He had been in regular contact with Chelsea since leaving Webb, and he talked to Anna as much as he could too, but between things at work and her schedule, those talks quickly became fewer and farther between. And since the subject of being invited for the holiday never came up, he thought it inappropriate to ask. He didn't want to be one of those bothersome people who invite themselves places.

Just about a full calendar week before the 25th, Rory snapped out of his insecurity and decided to call Chelsea. He couldn't let the idea go. He had to hear a definitive yes or a no about visiting for Christmas.

When Chelsea told him that coming out was a fantastic idea, his heart melted. As soon as he was off the phone, he booked his flight, made a reservation at a hotel, rushed out to the shopping mall, and picked up a stack of colouring books for Anna. It didn't matter if his vacation would be approved or not. Rory was ready to quit if it was the only way to go see his daughter.

Chapter 16

Rory took a car service from the airport to the hotel, and the same one again to Webb. Chelsea called after he landed and apologized for being unable to pick him up. As much as it hurt, he assured her it didn't matter. Rory just bottled it up; not wanting to make a big deal out of it.

In the few short months that Anna had been at Webb, a more specific diagnosis concerning her problems had been considered. Dr. Abbott hadn't told Rory earlier because he didn't want to cause undue stress over an unconfirmed hunch, but now that they were in person there was no point in withholding it. The doctor was convinced Anna's problems weren't just from FAS; he theorized that she'd also been showing evidence of having early-onset Huntington's disease.

"It would explain her stifled personality development, her problems with focus, and even the complications with her common sense," said Dr. Abbott. "Huntington's disease is a disorder in the DNA sequence that is passed on from the parent. As of this moment we have taken a sample of Anna's blood and are still waiting on the results."

"And you would like to take a sample from me to see if I'm

the source?" Rory asked.

"Well, it's not imperative, but if you want. I mean, obviously if it shows up in hers and not yours then . . ."

"Yeah. I get it." Rory knew where trail of the doctor's suggestion lead. "Tell you what, Doc. I'll give you my blood, if it'll help you understand this better, but I don't want to know the results. Okay?"

"Sure. Absolutely. Whatever you'd like," Dr. Abbott said. "I'm sorry to have to tell you such a thing now, at Christmas."

"How come *now*, Doc? How have none of the doctors I've seen before you thought of this? All they ever thought would help was a sedative to knock her out at night. Got to let it run its course, they said. Nothing to be done, they said."

"Well, the only conclusion I can come to is that the FAS diagnosis clouded their judgment. It would be easy to confuse the two, let alone look for both. Most cases of Huntington's are only detected later. Around the thirties is normal. And in children, the symptoms would be less pronounced as it's a creeping deterioration."

The doctor's words took some time to set in, and Rory couldn't do more than stare at the corner. He felt exhausted, like a boxer who no longer had any strength behind his strike. He was punch drunk, concussed by the newly revealed charge of complicity. The emotional bill of shame had collected interest that needed to be paid.

He shook off the trance, reset himself, and asked Dr. Abbott a few quiet questions about how living with the disorder long-term would affect Anna, but every answer he received was indeterminate until they knew for sure. His lack of concentration went unnoticed as the doctor rattled off data and what they would try to do for her.

It was foolish to act like he understood everything that was being said, but he nodded anyway. He would much rather have had Chelsea explain things to him, but he would just run it by her later. It wasn't that he didn't trust the doctor, but Chelsea was closer to him, closer to Anna, and it was more comfortable to get bad news from someone who was like family, not an official.

"This wasn't exactly how you'd thought your visit would start, was it?" Dr. Abbott said.

"Not at all, Doc, not at all. Would it be possible to speak with Chelsea for a moment before I see Anna?"

"Of course. I'll have her paged."

When Chelsea showed up, she gave Rory a big hug. A stillness passed between them as they stayed in the embrace for a few moments. After finally letting go, she suggested that the two of them walk and talk.

"Anna's at the other end of the building doing some interactive exercises. She should be done in fifteen, twenty minutes." Chelsea said.

"So, how's it been going?" Rory asked.

"Oh, Mr. Gunn, it's been marvelous. If what Anna had been at home was a cocooned caterpillar, here she's a butterfly."

Rory thought about how what Chelsea told him was, in a way, in direct conflict with what Dr. Abbott had said. But choosing her analysis of the situation, over that of the doctors, was a no-brainer for Rory. "That is amazing. I love to hear things like that. I don't get to hear enough of those kinds of things anymore. Fantastic."

"I told you about her progress with the alphabet and numerical sequences, right?"

"I believe you did."

"Okay. What else? Oh yeah. Her memory for characters in movies is astonishing. I really think she is a visual learner. I think it's easier for her to grasp things that way instead of fighting to form them in her mind," Chelsea said.

"How about the outbursts? Have they gotten any better?"

"Well, besides the initial period of getting used to the new surroundings, they've actually gotten a lot less intense. And they don't last as long as they used to, either."

"Does she ask about me?" Rory said.

The pain in Chelsea's eyes wasn't well masked. "You're her father," she said. "You always will be . . ."

Rory didn't want her to finish, but it was useless trying to avoid reality anymore.

"It's not that she doesn't love. It's that her expression of it isn't quite what you or I are used to it being. She might not know why she should love, but she definitely feels it. It's all around this place."

"I get it, Chelsea. It's one of those things that's hard to say and hard to hear. I have to accept it. I don't want to, but I have to. I guess I thought that I could leave her here for a bit, everything would get fixed, and I could take her home. Dr. Abbott told me about the blood tests."

"I'm so sorry," Chelsea said.

"Don't be," he said. "If Anna wasn't here with you, it would be a different story. That's my comfort. If you're here with her and she forgets me, then that's all right. I'd have it no other way. Love and setting it free, right?"

"I suppose you've got a point," Chelsea said, wiping a tear out of the corner of her eye. "Well, here we are. Anna's in there. She'll be out any minute now."

"Will she even know me?" Rory asked.

Chelsea shrugged.

The doors to the room opened, and a crowd of smiling and happy faces flooded the hallway. Rory waited, patient and resigned. Once he spotted her, he took one last shot at optimism and prayed that she would recognize him and jump into his arms, but it was Chelsea she noticed, not him.

Anna turned to her father in timid reluctance while Chelsea whispered into her ear about who it was that stood before them. She looked at him like she was trying to decipher a word that had been written in pencil and erased, leaving behind a smudge of something meaningful but illegible.

She dropped her knapsack and rummaged through it until she found her bear, Mr. Boo. She held it out and pointed it towards her father. She connected that bear to him, and if it was the last thing left that kept him as part of her life, he wasn't going to let it bother him. That stuffed animal and he were one and the same.

Anna didn't speak. She just rolled her eyes, smiled, and giggled while he made funny faces and giggled with her. Rory took in every fragile millisecond, appreciating the levity through a slow motion lens.

The rest of the vacation Rory relegated his somberness to his shadow that followed. After she pulled her bear out, it made him think of Mr. Boo like it was an urn with his ashes in it, and that in time, all that Mr. Boo would represent would be a muddled and forgotten childhood, locked away in a toy box, buried.

Rory enjoyed as best he could, what he figured would be his last Christmas of presents and laughter. They ate a fabulous turkey dinner with the other residents and their families, and everyone sang songs. There was even a hired Santa's sleigh ride, and beaver tails and maple syrup taffy pops that they made in the snow.

Dr. Abbott spent the holidays in the city with his family, but he left a message for Rory saying that as soon as the blood tests were in that he'd let Rory know the results—even though Rory said it was something he'd rather not be told.

When it came time for him to leave, the girls drove him into the city, to the airport. He gave Anna the biggest and tightest hug, "I love you, baby."

"So do whi," said Anna.

It was a dry goodbye, and there was little more that Rory wanted Chelsea to know before he left. He hugged her tightly too and uttered a nearly inaudible "Thank you" and "Take care of her."

Rory took his phone out and snapped a picture of the three of them—genuine smiles across the board, like a family photo already in a frame. Not a hint that anything was wrong.

The girls waved to him as he passed through security and into the terminal. Rory waited for half an hour to board and divided his time between examining the photo and taking in the majesty of the mountains in the distance. It was cathartic to watch them; they were immovable, eminent, and they stirred something in Rory, like nature was bolstering him.

He knew he had to go home and face the industrial declaration of war he had initiated. It wasn't just going to sort itself out, and if the movement was left to swerve all over the road or allowed to stagnate in the hands of the less capable, then everything would have been all for naught.

Part III: 2011

Chapter 17

The spring thaw revealed the destruction caused by snow ploughs and the contracting and expanding of concrete during the extreme freeze of Northern winter. The streets were torn up, potholes and broken curbs everywhere. The leftover sand and salt whisked into Rory's eyes when he walked anywhere, and the piled mounds of cleared snow were covered so thickly in it, that they wouldn't melt until May.

It was late March, and the seasonal temperatures were below average. Everyone was salvaging what they could out of the longer days and the retreat of the snow. People were determined to get outside and air their houses.

The only thing that remained frozen were some abilities that the company had. Firings being the most important one. The provincial labour board was watching their moves closely, ready to swoop in and extricate any who chose to challenge its authority.

Rory, Dom and Richard were safe from amercement, but that didn't mean they weren't also being monitored for the slightest of mistakes that could be used against them later. All the temp workers were let go once the new year started. The union argued that management should hire them if they were essential, but management was not interested in adding to the workers' numbers.

Ed let Rory know what he thought about it by running his thumb across his throat. "You're a real piece of shit, you know that, Rory?"

"Not my problem," Rory said.

"You'll get yours someday."

"I'll be waiting."

Corporate types from Toronto and Vancouver were flying in for plant inspections and boardroom meetings more than the workers had ever noticed before. At first, having so many suits around was intimidating, but soon the anxiety dwindled. One mogul even went so far as to shake all the workers' hands and chat with them about their jobs for a few minutes. It took many by surprise, and reactions were mixed.

"Playing the PR game is what it looks like to me. I bet you this is why they were so quick to renovate the back rooms. They didn't want these big wigs seeing the decay we had to eat and change in." Dom said.

"I don't know," said Rory. "Seemed pretty above board to me. And who cares why we got a new lunch room, all that matters is that we did. What do you think, Rich?"

Richard constructed his answer tentatively, closing one eye and stroking his chin. "They definitely aren't like the suits we've got here, that's for sure. To be perfectly honest, I don't know what the score is. It would be stupid on their part to try to put the scare on us now. And I don't think those renos were for the top brass as much as they were compassion leverage for Campbell."

"Does it occur to either of you that maybe that's what they want you to think? They're all just keeping up appearances. Every one of them. Especially those broad smiled bastards that run this place." Dom asked.

"Yes. It does occur to me, Mr. Dom," Richard said flatly. "I'm not saying let them set up camp. I'm saying I don't have an opinion on it yet, and that they aren't stupid."

"Okay, guys," said Rory. "Same team."

"Something funny is going on around here," Dom said.

"Sure it isn't you?" Richard said.

"Ha, ha. I'll see you two later," Dom said. He strode away towards his crane.

Once Dom was out of earshot, Richard leaned in to Rory and spoke softly. "What I really think is that the big boys from corporate aren't sniffing around because of us. I think they smell something rotten in the office."

"What makes you think that?" Rory asked.

"You notice anything different about Clive or Wyatt? Like Dom says, they sure are a lot more chipper when these suits are around."

"What are you getting at exactly?"

"I think this little party we crashed here at good ole Dambar has been off the corporate radar for so long that no one has ever bothered to ask any questions about its operations. They just go by the margin of profit. No problems with employees reported, all dealt with in-house. Nothing wrong on paper means nothing wrong period. You get me?"

"Yeah, I see what you mean. The enemy of my enemy is my friend, right?"

"Whoa. Easy up, young feller. They're all still a bunch of double-dealers. Don't forget that. And don't take no fucking blankets they offer you, neither," Richard said with a coarse smile.

* * *

Every day, the temperature increased by a degree or two, but the mornings were still chilly enough that the car needed a few minutes to warm up and defrost. Rory was on his way into the change room when Anders came out, on way of his own around the building to his office.

"Morning, Rory. How are you today?" Anders said.

"Anders." Rory had taken to hating early-morning pleasantries. He was beginning to adopt the idea that obligatory reciprocation took the sincerity out of actually caring how someone was doing. "I'm all right."

"Hey, listen. I've got a few things I'd like to touch base with you on. Mind coming to my office once you're ready?"

"You mean after I punch in?" Rory said, wanting to punch out Anders instead.

"That'll be fine." Anders said, relaxed.

Rory didn't rush getting changed. He sipped his coffee leisurely, then chatted with Richard. He was not going to enter the plant a second before he had to. If Anders wanted to talk, it would be on company time.

Anders was sitting at his computer when Rory came into the foreman's shack. There were two copies of the morning paper—one on the desk in front of Anders and one on the chair where employees sat when they came in to look for tag numbers, shipping information, or stock statuses or for a bullshitting sit-down that would give them a few extra minutes of break time.

Rory naturally picked up the paper before settling in, but before he could turn to the last section and ogle the daily salacious, bikini-clad model, Anders interrupted.

"Turn to page five. There's an interesting article there I think you should read."

The negotiations between management and the union had started a few weeks earlier, and it had become a running theme for Anders to prod egregiously, hinting that Rory had gotten in over his head.

Anders had alluded to knowing what was happening behind the closed doors, but Rory knew that it wasn't possible. Confidentiality was paramount, and management would never stand, or risk, a leak. If they wanted something out on the floor, they would whisper it to loudmouth salesmen or treacherous floor moles who wouldn't be able to prove what it was they were leaking was anything more than gossip, not to their own managerial staff. But Rory chose not to call Ander's bluff—casual harassment could come in handy later if it wasn't discouraged before it became useful.

Rory turned to the page Anders had designated. The article was aptly titled "Union: A wedge between liberty and capital."

"A bit overboard, don't you think?" Rory asked.

Anders offered no response. He had to use published arguments to convey his stance on a subject. The man's political views were about as clear as communiqué breaking up over a faulty CB radio. He would espouse whatever doctrine he was told would benefit him, whether he understood it or not.

Rory hated playing into the pseudo-psychological management-course bullshit tactics Anders followed as law. That false positive reinforcement didn't work on Rory like it did on others. He thought that it was a form of mind control, treating people like they were pieces of toast, buttering up the ones hungry for approval so they worked harder because they felt appreciated. And on the flip side, let workers in-fight and get mad at each other, and in doing nothing about it, let them go blow off steam by concentrating their frustration into their work. It was reward for the sensitive ones and more gruelling malignity for the aggressive ones. Rory hated how they executed it textbook-perfect every time—the same way to the same people—over and over and over again.

Rory read the whole article Anders had presented him, but instead of preparing his munitions for immediate counterattack, he simply told Anders the article was interesting. Rory wanted Anders to articulate what it was he was supposed to understand about the article to see if Anders even knew himself.

"Don't you think this union business is a bit silly? I mean, what good is it? Are the headaches necessary? We're all here to do a job, right?" Anders spoke like a coy vanguard from a superior army that had come to an enemy's camp speaking of truce, offering a reasonable chance at survival but at the same time provoking the war nerve. The guy had no idea how much of a political eunuch he was considered, and Rory couldn't hold back.

"Anders, I don't think you quite get it." Rory said.

"Don't get what?" Anders said.

"I'm sure you had me come in here and read this because you had some sort of point to make, correct? I hope it wasn't to rub my nose in it like a dog that just pissed on the Kashmir rug."

Anders went quiet and turned away, but Rory wasn't finished. He wanted Anders to understand there wasn't a difference between continuing to think he was right and ignoring why he was wrong about it being *just a job we're all here to do* anymore.

"Have you ever sat down and read through your corporate policies? I have—four bloody long hours of them. To the point where I forget what I'm even reading about. But that's the design of them, right? C'mon man, stop messing around. You keep hiding behind these contrived evils of a union and continually claim that your pristine conscience is a victim of our misappropriated angst. Meanwhile, most of the managers in here ignore some of those policies."

"Which do you mean exactly?" Anders choked out.

"You want examples, eh? One off the top of my head, no bypassing of safety devices. You know full well that my laser system is off more than it's on because it's a pain in the ass to align and goes on the fritz easily. And I said, as well as Matt did, that a laser system from Europe wasn't going to be compatible with a machine built in North America. No one listened to us on that one. And now look, only ever turned on for show when the people with authority pay us a visit.

"Want another one? I got more now that I'm thinking about them. How about the one that requires proper training to run equipment when pretty much everyone hops on those forklifts without any. You're even on the bloody thing, doing work designated for union members, not management. But if the job gets done, right? And what about the one that requires a worker be secured to something when working at heights above three meters? There's no harness system for the guys that are climbing up in the bar and tubing racks. "Those policies mean something, you goddamn well know why too. They serve a purpose. A purpose that gets spread quite thin, wouldn't you agree? Especially now that I've enlightened you on the matter. And the guys notice these things. The small laxities and bends in the rules, which they start bending themselves. How can you set precedent that way? This place has danger by the square foot, Anders. Complacency promotes sloppy negligence, and before you know it, no one observes any kind of standard anymore. And that's when people get hurt and reviews of procedure and prevention are rolled out and discussed and examined until it's forgotten all over again."

"Do you really want management to come down with an iron fist?" Anders asked.

"Don't play the scare card with me, Anders. I could call someone down here today and have them go through the conveniently overlooked violations of this place's corporate ledger. You'd be in the shit, not me. And that has nothing to do with the union. Making this place safer and more rule oriented isn't punishment, it's policy."

Anders had nothing. Rory got up and dropped the newspaper in the recycling bin and went to turn the handle of the door and leave. He stopped a second and decided to stomp on Anders one last time so he would think twice before trying the stunt again.

"It's sickening how the media can stone-cold oppose the idea of a fighting chance for the working man against big money. Especially when all they have to do is string some words together and meet a deadline. And let's not forget, it's also who you know in that racket, too. So why not write the stories that the people who buy the paper, or own the paper, want to read, right?"

Rory knew it was long-winded, but the dumbstruck look on Anders' face was worth it: curt, terse and debasing—just the right way to get him to tuck tail and yield.

"Are we done here? Good. Now, if you'll excuse me."

Rory left the office and was met by Dom, who was ambling southward to his crane.

"Everything cool, Ror?" Dom asked.

"Yup. Just bought us a little time is all."

Chapter 18

Another summer had come and it was hotter than its predecessor. The plant felt like being in an oven. Working indoors in sweltering heat that just built and built made it difficult to think straight and work hard, and it made even nonbelievers pray for rain. People didn't care if the two thirds of their day spent outside the steel kiln was ruined by the rain, they just wanted to work in some kind of comfort. Some may have even secretly wished for the cold of the winter, but no one would ever admit to it.

Rory kept to himself that morning. At lunch, he decided to sit in the sun on the side of the building where the smokers usually congregated. There were makeshift benches made from two-by-fours and a large four-foot circular wooden table that used to have thousands of kilos of wire coiled around the centre. It was laden with insignias, crude drawings, and carved swear words. Beside it, propped against the building, sat two old seats someone had ripped out of a van. Over the years the maroon colour they'd once had faded into that more akin to an old wine stain, and the cushions were splitting at the seams, exposing old, dusty foam that was as yellow as smokers' teeth.

When Rory got outside, there was only one guy there smoking. He was the oldest employee in the plant, and for the longest time, Rory only ever knew him by the epithet Cods—a name he'd been graced with from his days growing up on the East Coast. He was bitter and cantankerous most of the time, but if you had a really funny joke or just said something a certain way, he revealed a hell of a laugh.

Starting a conversation with Cods was difficult because Rory could never tell what kind of mood he was in. Football was always a safe bet, but Cods' team was the Bombers, and the last few seasons had been shit. Rory thought it counterproductive to get Cods started in on a topic like that unless he wanted to hear a half hour of pointless bitching about how they ought to do this or they should've done that. Cods also liked to gamble, the VLTs mostly, although he had stopped keeping track of his winnings and losses ratio a long time ago and just looked forward to the days that the push of the button swayed in his favour and he could walk away feeling like a winner.

Cods sat in silence, pulling on his machine rolled, twisted end cigarette with a dry and wrinkled mouth. He seemed to enjoy the vice, even though every puff he took seemed to suck something out of him instead of the other way around.

Rory remembered the classy rebel image that came with smoking. Not a day went by that he didn't have a residual craving, and he attributed it to the tough-guy roles of movie stars like Mickey Rourke and Humphrey Bogart. But watching the old man puff away and cough thickly while the midday sun beat down on them reminded Rory of the debilitating effects of looking cool.

Cods said he couldn't move in the stifling heat, and that admission conjured up an image of loose and sticky damp flesh clinging together in a wad underneath the oil-stained cotton Dambar garments. Rory stayed silent in hopes that the conversation wouldn't go any further than that.

"How are the negotiations going?" Cods asked.

"Slowly, but okay. Money hasn't been discussed, if that's what you're getting at."

"I don't think we'll be getting any more money," Cods said in a deliberate tone, like he wanted to follow it with *get it through your head.* "And if we don't, there is a loss of three grand a year in those incentives they won't give back. For some guys, that's a lot of money. They depend on those incentives. If they're lost forever, there will be a lot of unhappy people in here." The old man took another pull from the cigarette. "The economy is in the toilet. If you're a market watcher, you'd know that. It's why I'm still here. Can't retire in this."

"I get that, Cods," said Rory—immediately regretting getting the old man started.

"I don't think you really do," Cods shot back.

Rory thought it pointless to argue with him over matters that had yet to be ironed out, but he didn't know how to get out of it. He thought of ways to satisfy Cods—without giving away too much—so that the old man could go back into the plant and spout something that he could claim came from Rory's mouth.

"Cods, I've heard a rumour that . . . now keep in mind, I don't know how substantiated this is." Rory leaned in and lowered his voice. "I've heard a rumour, don't know where it came from, that the office workers get a clothing allowance."

Cods' eyes widened, and he came in closer to Rory, smelling for a lie or a trap. After a moment, Cods seemed satisfied and offered a reveal of his own. "They used to have their cars taken care of in there, too—maintenance, gas . . . the salesmen anyhow."

"Jesus. Really? That has to be at least another two or three hundred a month," Rory said, mixing awe and disgust.

Cods got up and flicked his butt with disdain towards everything but nothing in particular, like a pissed off cowboy who figured he needed to go get his gun and shoot something.

"Sounds like we have been getting the shaft, Cods."

"Yeah. And we had to grease it, too," Cods said, and he slipped back into the thick, acrid air of carbon dust and bullshit.

Rory didn't even want to go back into the plant. The thought of the company picking up the tab for officer workers' vehicles when it was so difficult to get proper compensation for bodily injuries for floor workers, was absurd. He thought about three active cases being mishandled that were causing avoidable personal suffering for employees while he watched a well-manicured, perfectly dressed salesman drive away in an Audi A6 on his way to take an hour-plus lunch break.

How can these fuckers strut around like that, flaunting themselves, when the only fingers they lift around here are for dialing phone numbers? Rory thought.

Rory could no longer think of people in terms other than soldiers, nobles, defectors, tyrants, and spies. It was war to him, all the time, but it was a quiet war. How could he think of it any differently while phrases like "entrenched competitors", "relentless advertising campaign", "propaganda", "taking heavy fire from the press," and "embattled human resources" peppered the language and proceedings of enterprise and business.

It had taken time, but bit by bit, the behaviours that Richard had opened Rory's eyes to were coming back. They started to speak more on heavy topics trying to find the best way to remain positive during the quiet, monotonous go-nowhere battles with management.

He started to understand more fully that deceit was without end, as long as there were people to throw money in the engine of industry like one would coal in a furnace.

He battled also with himself and didn't know if what he was doing was just his own unchecked hubris and acting out a rebellious fantasy. *Am I an invader or a conqueror? Liberator or scourge?* he thought. *Or are they all, in the end, one and the same?*

Even if he could get away with torturing some sensibility into management, Rory knew he would either become just as they were or open the door for more like them to follow. There was little left to do but practice painfully fruitless civil disobedience.

Rory needed to get out of the sun and cool the rush of hot blood in his system, so he got up and strolled around the building. His vision started to become spotted. His skull felt like it was in a vice and that each of his legs and arms were being pulled in different directions. Rory imagined these were perfect conditions for cancer and insanity to set in and take him out of the game, letting the insolent idolaters get off scot-free by having natural causes solve the problem for them.

Cods wasn't the only worker smearing cynicism and speculative misdirection all over the walls at Dambar—others had approached Rory and expressed their dissatisfaction with how slow and hushed the negotiations were. And for Rory, the waiting on tables feeling was growing tiresome with every conversation he had.

It was all the more agonizing because management wasn't offering any kind of diplomacy, and through their evasion, were helping to further foster internal struggle for not only the union's integrity, but for Rory's as well. He didn't know if he had any friends left besides Dom and Richard, and everyone else's apathy was making him draw unreasonable conclusions.

Anxiety was beginning to consume him as he moved seeking shade. He didn't want to be seen panicking, and he quickened his step to get out of sight from the office. After getting around to a secluded corner, he turned his head to see if anyone was in tow, and in taking his attention from where his feet landed, stepped into a deep rut on the corrugated gravel road that was worn by the heavy truck and trailer traffic that passed through daily. His ankle twisted just enough to throw him into a scramble and he fought to keep his balance but couldn't, and he collapsed against the aluminum paneling of the building.

He pulled his cell phone out of his pocket shakily and searched through the memory storage for the last picture he had taken of Anna—the picture at the airport. He needed to see her smile. She was the only thing that could bring him back, the only thing that straightened him out, the only thing that could wipe away his weakness and remind him he was still human and that he didn't need to stoop to any unconscionable levels to battle the demons that were following him around.

After shaking the paranoia away, he checked the time on his phone. He still had a few minutes to go to the back change room and throw some water on his face, choke down a sandwich and regroup. He wanted to loosen up and lower the pressure in his head. He wanted a reset. He wanted to go out with Dom for a night and get so shitfaced that he couldn't think straight. The sooner, the better.

* * *

Rory suggested drinking at "The Woodbine". It was close enough to home that he could walk if he needed to. He might be committed to revisiting the days of his impetuous youth, but driving around afterwards was something he'd rather not do again.

Linda the bartender greeted him with a smile, "Hello there, stranger. It's good to see you."

"Hey there, Lin. Good to see you too. This is my friend Dom." Rory said.

"Pleased to meet you my dear," Dom said.

"You too. What can I get you?" Linda asked.

"Couple Keiths and a couple shots of Bushmills, sweetheart, and keep em' comin'." Dom turned to Rory, nudging him, as Linda bent down into the cooler to get the beer. "What a sight, eh Ror? How come you never told me you knew such lovely people?"

"Thought didn't cross my mind."

"Well, ain't that a shame. No bother. We're here now and that's what counts, eh?"

"I suppose so," Rory said.

The alcohol was coming fast, one after the other, and it was hitting him hard. Being drunk at 7:00 in the evening with the sun still out was an unusual feeling for Rory. He had barely eaten anything all day: toast for breakfast, tuna sandwich for lunch, and for dinner: half a bowl of pretzels, a few paltry chicken wings and the booze.

With every drink he had, Dom got louder. He was going on about personal injustices, moving from trying to pinpoint who exactly was the cause of what in his sordid life. There was a little studded praise for Rory, who, along with himself, "Brought some sort of balance to those crooked corporate cocksuckers' door," Dom raved.

Dom's rants had become progressively worse since the union had been certified, and the alcohol encouraged the idea that everyone should hoist him upon their shoulders. He was more openly provocative because seniority made him untouchable, barring a reason for immediate termination. It was a new side of Dom that wasn't the best characteristic to be consorting with the id of a hardened alcoholic, because he was now cashing in on all the years he thought that he'd been treated as worthless. He had finally won the lottery of recognition after playing the same numbers for so long.

Rory both relished and despised Dom's candour, but he'd never allude to either, because explaining why he felt either way wasn't worth inciting an inquisition.

"You guys need another?" Linda asked them.

"I'm good for now, Lin. Thanks," Rory said.

Linda gave him a look like she was saying "Slow down" or "I've never seen you like this before," but it could have been "Who the hell is this yahoo you brought in here?" Rory couldn't tell. He was too far gone, and he didn't want to stir anything up.

"I'll have another, darlin'!" Dom bellowed.

Dom was practically hanging from the bar, but he might as well have been standing on top of it. His feet were planted on the brass pipe that ran along the bottom, close to the floor. It elevated him seven or eight inches higher, and he stabilized himself with his right hand, which held another brass pipe that ran along the edge of the bar top like a vice. He was capriciously changing the subject between shop talk and what he thought was classy, innuendo-laden banter with Linda at a high enough volume that annoyed the rest of the patrons but that at the same time kept them uninterested in confronting the excitable and obnoxious ape man.

He sat back down when Linda ignored him, and he turned to Rory, his breath reeking. "I learned a long time ago that you can't expect things from people. You can fight your whole life to accomplish something, and the one person you would never think of betraying you completely lets you down. People have their own agendas. You can't read minds, can you?" Dom finished with salty laughter, as he followed Linda movements behind the bar.

"Like Julius Caesar, you mean." Rory said.

"What's that? No thanks, I hate Clamato juice," Dom said. "I'm going to throw some loonies in the jukebox. I'll be back in a minute. Any requests?"

"Nah. You know what I like."

Rory was enjoying the numbness, but his intended deliverance from shop talk never came. He didn't want to hear any of it but he also didn't want to interrupt—things just didn't seem worth pursuing when he was saturated in booze.

"You and Richard have taught me a lot, Ror," Dom said after returning from the jukebox—AC/DC's "Live Wire" started up in the overhead speakers. "I can see what you and Richard meant now. It's not government. It's regime. They have a job to do! A duty to perform! A service to provide! And so do we."

"There was a moment, somewhere, that leaders knew they could turn on their own. Wring the population dry by using gullibility and persuasion against them. The notion of unity, everywhere, under every banner of any ideal, was sold and altered for accommodation. It is easier to trick the masses by giving them choice, right? I mean, if truth didn't conflict with profit there would be more of it, right? The days of believing in an idea so strongly that it beat its way into the history books with brutal, passionate relentlessness have died. Escalation usually means mutual assured destruction these days, my friend," Rory said, giving in to Dom's sermon in hopes to end it.

"Where once words roused and stimulated, and adrenaline was the only meal served, there stood soldiers—men who, though tired from marching, inadequate nourishment and of indefinite compensation—still moved their legs, one in front of the other, to see to the ends of their leaders—following a resolve without concrete knowledge of victory," Dom said triumphantly—pulling himself closer to the ceiling again.

It wasn't like Dom to wax philosophical or to have so deep an insight, but he had an impeccable ability to hide the amount of alcohol he had consumed, with brute occasions of eloquence. Rory figured it just an attempt to impress Linda.

"Where did you read that?" asked one of the patrons that sat a few tables away.

"What's it to you, old timer?"

"On that note then, I think I better be getting home," Rory said.

"Ah, man, come on. I'm just getting started. You can't leave me here to drink alone."

"I'll call you a cab," Linda said from behind the bar.

"I'm fine walking," Rory said, "I need the air and sunshine anyway. I'll come back for my car in the morning. Dom, you're fine."

"Well, I guess I'll see you tomorrow, my friend," Dom said, giving up quickly on convincing Rory to stick around—because there was a woman around who hadn't yet told him to get lost. Dom liked the competition at a minimum, and Rory knew he wouldn't put up a fight to see some of it walk out of the bar. Dom was as solid as any friend Rory had ever known, but if it was friend or female, Dom always went with the latter. Fealty be damned.

"At least finish your drink," Dom said.

"Yeah." said Rory—guzzling back a good two thirds of a pint, cursing Dom's peer pressure insistence on finishing the drink. "See y'all later."

A few blocks from the bar, there was a small convenience store run by a Filipino family. He shuffled through the door and asked where the bottled water was. A nice older lady came around from the till and got one for him, saying something he did not understand between her accent and his drunkenness. At the till, he pulled out his wallet. He had used his cash at the bar, so he handed the lady his debit card.

"No, no. Min-mum ten dolla for deh-bit."

To meet the required amount Rory asked for a pack of cigarettes and a lighter. A request made by drunken reflex. He was slightly aware of what he was doing, but he didn't care.

Once outside the store, he cracked the bottle and took a long, indulgent swig, feeling instantly better as the cool liquid rushed down his esophagus and filled his stomach. He put the water down on the sidewalk and unraveled the cigarettes almost unconsciously and sniffed at the smooth, tailor-made smokes like he'd been deprived of them against his will. They smelled like the first one he had stolen from his friend's brother's desk when he was thirteen—a glorious and forbidden key to early adulthood.

As soon as he lit it up, he coughed and felt ill. For a second he wanted to throw the pack away and reach for the water to wash the taste from his mouth and lips, but he didn't. He instead fought his body's reaction and kept on smoking. He felt like punishing himself. He took a few more drags and could feel the stale hardening of his throat.

Something in the recesses of his mind a voice cried out, *What do you think you're doing?* but he continued on his way, securing the pack of smokes in his pocket, forgetting he'd left the water bottle on the ground.

Chapter 19

Between the headache, the dry taste in his mouth, and the sandpaper swallow in his throat, Rory felt like he had marched through a desert. He cursed himself over and over again for not easing himself back into it without proper preparation— hard drinking sessions took time to temper the body to, and Rory had gone at it like the last eight years had been no different.

The first thing he did was throw away the pack of cigarettes. After that, he brushed his teeth and swished around a few cups of Listerine, but no matter how much he tried, he couldn't wash away the layer of smoke that was inside his mouth. He thought it all the better that he couldn't rinse out the taste. To let it serve as a reminder of his violation so he wouldn't think about taking up the habit full-time again. He vaguely remembered not being able to hold the cigarettes he had bought quite right and how he'd had to relearn how to make smoking look natural.

What was worse was that he had to walk back to the bar and get his car before going to work. His only relief came from the crisp morning breeze. The suffering from self-punishment registered in his nerves, and it had his whole body at attention.

Once at work he meekly traversed the shop, avoiding as many human obstacles as he could, on his way to the brake. The pounding and crashing hadn't gone into full swing yet, and he was dreading how the general cacophony of the shop and his brain throbbing against the plates of his skull would mingle with each other.

The day left no room for error. It was hard enough keeping alert in the mounting heat, and coupling that with a hangover was asking to lose a finger to the jaws of the brake, or fracture a foot by dropping something on it. Explaining those injuries, and getting sympathy for them, from Trent especially, would be difficult, so Rory moved like a snail.

He went to dab a damp cloth against his head in the rising heat, and he smelled the tobacco on his fingers. He remembered once enjoying the smell, but it had since lost its appeal and instead reminded him of the morning after a party—beer bottles with floating butts in them, dry and sticky spills on the floor and tabletops that could be seen only if the light hit them just right. It made him want to vomit.

Drinking nearly three litres of water helped him piss and sweat out most of the toxins by 1:00 in the afternoon, but he still wasn't in a mood to be affable. He ducked every encounter he could, trying to avoid lengthy talks about nothing.

The clock ticked down slowly, and he couldn't believe he had almost made it through the day without any major glitches. But as he was finishing up paperwork in the shaded cove behind his machine, he felt the presence of someone behind him.

By the way the papers brushed against the leg and how the person cleared their throat, Rory could tell who it was. He looked over his shoulder to be sure and then continued with his paperwork. "May I help you, Wyatt?" Rory asked.

"Maybe we can help each other," Wyatt said as he pulled up the less used, more uncomfortable chair. He swiped at it with his bare hand, whisking the dust off, and—in what Rory saw as a vain attempt to prove that he didn't mind getting dirty—Wyatt wiped the residue off on his pants.

"How's that, Wyatt?" Rory asked again as he watched the tiny clock in the corner of his computer screen.

"We have some new corporate policies that we're going to put in place. Basic stuff, but I thought I'd let you have a look before it became official."

Rory detested the way Wyatt said things like he was being helpful. It wasn't doing Rory a service by letting him *have a look* at the policies; he *had* to show Rory. There was no option, but Wyatt worded it in a way to make it look like there was.

It wasn't a new concept to think everybody could be turned out some way, that Rory would one day play ball. And the glib, cocksure way management applied the corporate formula for wearing a person down, just further cemented Rory's resolution to be so incorruptible that the managers' frustration broke them instead of the person they thought could be easily plied to see things their way.

As far as Rory was concerned, management types were just sharply dressed insects who preferred the cover of dark, dank corners, letting the bigger and dumber insects fight over food or get caught and dispatched. They didn't welcome it when Rory decided to change the light bulb they hid from to a higher wattage, because there were fewer places to hide, and even less room to maneuver.

"Well, Wyatt," said Rory. "You brought them to me at a pretty inconvenient time, don't you think? Why don't you just give them to us at the scheduled negotiations next week, like I'm pretty sure you're supposed to."

Wyatt moved around in the chair. "These aren't part of the negotiations. Corporate policy is independent to the bargaining process. You know that. These are to be implemented across the board, throughout the whole company. You can take them home with you if you like."

"Not really how I plan on spending the evening, Wyatt. When exactly are you thinking about issuing them?" Rory asked.

"In the morning," Wyatt said.

Rory wanted to hit him with a heavy pipe. He wanted to see Wyatt's frailty while he pleaded with pillowy hands that he had learned his lesson and didn't want to be struck again, but the synapses in his brain were just not prepared, so he decided he would save it for a day when he was more alert. For the time being, he'd have to let the swine trundle back to his office unscathed.

"Great timing, Wyatt," said Rory. "I guess I'll have to look it over tonight. seeing as I have no other choice." He grabbed the stapled documents out of Wyatt's hand.

"I'm glad you could see it my way," Wyatt said, beaming as he got up and scurried away.

Rory looked at the documents and judged them at a good thirty pages of backwards, confusing lullabies in tiny print that were going to require more brain cells than he had access to. Just when he'd thought his headache was gone and he was in the clear, it came right back and took up residence in his temples.

Chapter 20

The next morning felt good. Rory couldn't remem-ber at what time exactly that he had fallen asleep, but waking up an hour and a half before his alarm, ready and fresh to start the day, didn't leave him with the feeling of being duped out of those ninety minutes of precious sleep.

A sign his lapse into unconsciousness was unexpected and abrupt was that before he did, he didn't have the chance to clear the documents from his bed; scattered pages were crumpled and folded in the sheets and duvet, underneath him, inside the pillow case, and out of order, all over the floor.

He'd tried to read through as much of the redundant text Wyatt had given him as he could, but nothing stuck together in proper sentences. It was all a jumble of words like *propri-etary, compliance, preservation, CEO, COO,* and *CFO*—acro-nyms that meant nothing to Rory in the first place. Phrases like *risk management* and *whistleblower hotline* and *occu-pational illness* and *monitoring changing work environment* meshed together, as though a typewriter had written several lines one on top of the other on top of the other.

He got up and put the coffee on and took a few pieces of

bread out of the freezer to thaw. When he heard the mailbox shut, he went to the front door to retrieve the morning paper. It was drizzling lightly outside, and the illuminated grey that hung overhead signalled that it was going to be an overcast and rainy day.

Rory poured himself a cup of coffee and spread the paper out across the dining room table. The headlines were about as hopeful as the weather outside: murder rates, interest rates, no money down, corruption, cheating athletes, cheating-death remedies, celebrity tidbits. The local paper had started to look like a gossip rag. It distressed Rory that the only articles that could have prevented people from going back to bed and spooning with a shotgun were blurbs that were added only to fill up space. It was no secret what people wanted to read about. After all, who really wanted to read about the canine citizens mingling at a dog park, or an eleven-year-old boy and his seven-year-old sister trying to raise awareness for some distinguished cause, if they could read about scandal and war?

Rory didn't know if that was the intended presentation or if it just seemed like that because he looked for it. Pushing the paper aside he decided to do something productive rather than wallow. He rifled through the coat closet at the front door, found a pair of sneakers a few years old, and decided to take a run—throw the ear buds in, put the iPod on shuffle, and run. Run until all he could think of was the burn in his legs. Run until there was nothing but sweat and pain. Run until everything in his head became a mash like a 400-page paperback after it had been put through the heavy cycle of a washing machine.

He wanted all the shit and nonsense that he was forced to read and listen to everyday to be mulch. He had been telling himself for months on end that he wasn't going to let anything break him, but the binding was starting to become unglued.

He wasn't crazy—he knew that. He wasn't page-one mass rampage material. It wasn't in him. He had to run. He had to channel all his negativity to the source of his reproach. He had to start saying the things people didn't want to hear, because it was unfair if he had to be the only one to feel the pressure from the monotony.

Rory didn't march so much as stride into the shop that morning. He had his purpose. He knew what fires needed stoking, and he figured he would start at the bottom of the corporate ladder with the foremen.

He knocked on the foreman's shack door lightly, like nothing was bothering him. He didn't want to give them any time to prepare. He wanted to go in there, say his piece, and exit.

Anders and a salesman were in the office, and they relayed information back and forth concerning orders that didn't get finished, various problems with workers, what machinery was down, and how they could get around it and stay on schedule.

It was all blah to Rory, and the trivialities had started to sound like someone with a mouth full of food was trying to say something in a foreign language that they had a poor grasp on. He could see what made Anders, and all the rest, perfect material for managers. They laughed when they were supposed to laugh. Showed concern they needed to. Even if it was all sodden with forged rapport.

Anders and his salesman buddy went quiet when Rory walked in. Almost like they had just finished running Rory down. He went for their throats.

"I read these policies last night, Anders. More contradictory shit. No electronic devices on the shop floor, unless issued. I've seen you, and the other managers, on your own bloody cell phones plenty of times out there, so have others. I doubt that will stop across the board, but yet here we are, signing a document that states that it will. And good luck getting guys to sign something that gives the company the right to do background checks. Did you think that through all that shit I wouldn't find that one? You people are un-fucking-believable. And I'm sure there's more I missed because I fell asleep. But don't think that means I won't review."

Rory dropped the stack of papers and left. He made his way towards Wyatt's office, ready to kamikaze.

Wyatt turned in his chair and looked out the window with the phone pressed to his ear. Rory guessed Anders was on the other line, giving him a heads-up. The element of surprise was gone.

191

Rory shut the door carefully when he entered, letting the ease and grace of how he did it flow through him like a meditative movement some Eastern guru had taught him. "Wyatt, would you please hang up the phone?" Rory asked.

Wyatt continued his conversation for a few more seconds, likely so Rory wouldn't take on the notion he was dictating the pace. "What can I help you with, Rory?" Wyatt said, like he didn't know what the topic of discussion was going to be.

"*Help* isn't how I would say it. That word puts too much of an open negotiation context on what I have to say. I just ask that you listen."

Wyatt didn't speak and waited with reserve. Rory suspected the trap was for him to blow a gasket and forfeit the floor with impolite and aggressive behaviour.

"I think you and your fellow managers need to take into account the calculations of defeat more often. There is a need for a little more perspective here. You must forget that even though you may be our superiors you are the bottom rung of the ladder you climb, not the top of the one we do. I read what you gave me. Utterly ridiculous that you think the guys will read, understand and sign it in any less time than half their shift. And if they catch what I caught, which is the exact opposite of how you want it to go, and they ask me what the union can do about it, I have to look them in the eye and tell them, 'Sorry, you've got to sign it, there's nothing I can do.' It's just politics. Then you absolve yourself by saying, 'It's nothing personal', and I'm the bad guy. That's the way it goes, right? I'm not far off. Tough shit for me. Should've thought about that before I did it, I guess. Wasn't paying attention and lost a bet I couldn't cover.

"Well, I must say, this attitude of yours is troubling to me, Rory. Are you well? You know there is nothing I can do either."

"I asked nicely if you'd stay quiet, so please, if you wouldn't mind."

Wyatt sat motionless.

Rory wasn't thinking about what he was saying, he had no idea where to go next, but he decided to roll with it because his lungs felt fuller, his shoulders lighter, chest looser. A few workers walked by Wyatt's window and they peered in, raising their eyebrows and shooting winks at Rory, trying to get some kind of hint as to what was being said.

Wyatt still didn't reply.

"This may be hard for you to understand, but I didn't take on this union business for personal gain, prestige, or accolade. I did it because I live the hardship that accompanies gruelling work and the physical and mental price that comes with it. I did what I did to help those who need it, not suck the marrow out of their bones for my own end.

"And don't think I haven't seen your defect. Your shudder and shuffle through meetings and discipline hearings when you're around Clive or Campbell. Inadequacy follows you around, doesn't it? Follows all of your kind around. Stalling to make things difficult on purpose. You all do it. You're taught to do. Pathetic."

Rory had Wyatt pinched like a nerve, and he hoped that the bastard finally felt like a small part of a larger organism that would, as a prevailing circumstance of self-preservation, sever his dead weight in an instant if he proved septic.

"Who do you think you are?" Wyatt asked.

"I don't know. Maybe a neo socialist," Rory said.

"Being what exactly?"

"I don't know. Someone bent on exposing the brutal fucking raw truth, the fraudulent political mechanism, I suppose. I know grifters can rule the world. They already do, there is no changing that. But power shifts. Always has. And you're a piece of shit for thinking it won't shift on you. You can't hide forever behind policy you don't regard yourself. It'll come for you. Eliminate and reduce risk, right? It's all in the literature, isn't it? It's what you want me to sign and acknowledge, correct?" Rory drew back oxygen, filling his lungs and readying for more ranting if he needed it.

Wyatt got up and ground his whitening knuckles into his desk like he was going to burrow a hole through it. "You're full of nonsense, you know that? I oughta suspend you."

"For what? You got any proof of what I just said? Funny thing when two people are alone and out of earshot, door closed behind them. Anything can be said. Courts of law don't deem conjecture admissible." Rory lowered his voice and leaned in closer. "I'm going to burn you down, Wyatt. Right to the fucking ground. And not just because I can but because you deserve it."

The handle to the door shook and turned open, and one of the shipping office girls came in. "Oh, I'm sorry. Am I interrupting?"

"Not at all," Rory said. "We were just finishing up, weren't we, Wyatt?"

Wyatt glared through Rory. Agitation bloated his face in an intense redness and it was easy to tell he wanted to leap over the desk and rampage. And the presence of the other employee muted Wyatt, and whatever it was that he wanted to say to Rory would have to wait until they were alone again.

Rory walked out of the office and onto the shop floor with his head high and shoulders back in a strut of obnoxious triumph, as though he had deposed a king. There was a slight tug in his gut—he had crossed a line—but he swallowed hard and fought the urge to run back into the office and apologize. The damage was done.

The workers spoke among themselves and shot glances and nods Rory's way. They were likely wondering what had made Wyatt so red and follow Rory like a security camera through his office window.

The tumult was becoming easier to navigate, and all misdirection that management used had lost its subtlety. The rush of the attack excited Rory, and leaving Wyatt speechless felt like a huge boon for the union's confidence. Rory had crawled up into their lair, unde-tected while they slept, and had desecrated their pride. He thought again how the threats he'd slung at Wyatt may have been too much, but for Rory it was justifiably provoked. There was no longer any time to slam the brakes and slow down. It was time to keep the pedal flat until he ran out of gas.

Chapter 21

Contract negotiations between the union and the company were held in a conference room at a downtown hotel. And despite being among the lower grade of high end hotels, there was always inconsequential jabbering about would pay for it or if the cost would get split between the parties. But the company always ended up footing the bill—making a fuss about it was a part of the show.

Besides the union reps, there was one other actual worker who accompanied Rory to the negotiations. His name was Samuel, but most called him "Shammy". Samuel had gotten elected by the membership to the position of grievance chair. The older workers wanted fair representation, and, like Rory, Sammy ran unopposed. He had the proxy of the senior guys for one purpose—to make sure the pension system did not change and that they weren't hung out to dry by the more youthful subversives.

Samuel belonged to the crew that had worked Dambar's machines during the glory days. The time before the fat pensions of old were nixed in favour of something more corporate friendly and not as juicy. Days that saw the stock benefits system make those that were there for it momentarily rich. And even though the dump of shares and payout was a one-time shot, plateauing and never falling to the levels of pre-payoff again, some of those guys still had their heads in the clouds, hoping to relive those days once more.

Samuel was tall and gangly. He had a pencil thin line of hair across his upper lip, and a red indentation at the bridge of his nose where his glasses sat that gave the impression they weighed a half ton.

Samuel was prone to allergies, so he carried around a hanky and used it frequently. Rory couldn't believe that by midday there was any amount of folding that Samuel could do to reveal a clean spot, but he went right on blowing his nose—hygienic or not.

Rory tried to get away from him on lunch breaks—the thought of the snotty rag in his pocket brought about a nauseated heave—but every time it looked like the coast was clear, there was Samuel, ready to suggest a new sandwich place to try.

This particular morning had the union reps and the management brass hashing out a few logistical points of the contract. It was as boring as waiting for fresh cream to curdle but after the language was agreed upon by both parties the negotiations on wage increases could begin.

Dambar's home base was in Toronto and their head of human resources was Joyce Caruthers. She flew in for meetings all over the country, and it was contract time pretty well all across the board—every week she was in a different province for three or four days at a time. It was obvious she'd been living out of hotels—from the creases in her dark grey pantsuit to her poorly applied makeup and quickly styled hair, the mileage of late flights and early meetings were easily noticeable and she wasn't fooling anyone by playing it off like she enjoyed it.

Joyce and Campbell sat in the middle, flanked on either side by Clive and Wyatt, while Rory and Samuel flanked Pete Nichols and Bob Gantry: a union district representative who, like Joyce, was only ever present for negotiation meetings.

Rory let them do most of the talking. It was what they did for a living. Samuel, on the other hand, would pipe up about meaningless things or repeat something that was just said, trying to pass it off as his own original thought. And no one stopped him because it was, after all, a place where calm cool attitudes were to be observed, but each time Samuel did it, Rory could almost hear the sound of every-one else's eyes rolling in unison.

Rory tuned out and fiddled with his pen. He wanted to make his boredom apparent for all to see but also just subtle enough that he would still be taken seriously as an appointed delegate. To do this, he pulled his hotel stationery pad of paper down into his lap at an angle away from any curious eyes and doodled his boredom away under the pretence of taking notes.

Wyatt sat across from him and slouched in his chair, like a teenager in class whose mind was on after-school video games or the Internet instead of his studies. He did not look like a man that should be attending anything formal, ever.

Is he mocking me? Rory thought. *Fuck, this guy loves to play the games.*

Rory recalled a time he was in Wyatt's office and, like a pseudo junior psych student, he told Rory he was taking a class on reading body language. He claimed he was able to decipher the subconscious intention that came with a twitch of the eye, fidgeting of the fingers or tone of voice.

Blow it out your ass, you cuckoo. Explain the hidden meaning of my ripping your arm off and beating you with it, you silly fucker! Rory tried to understand why he was so aggressive towards Wyatt, but he couldn't put an absolute point on its causation.

The drone of jargon went on until 10 a.m. when Joyce announced that it was time to discuss wages. "The company has come up with an offer we think is representative of the current economy and company profit margins." She handed all the union reps a sheet of paper.

"Well, Joyce, the union has also drawn up a proposal that we'd like to share with you," said Bob, who handed management papers of his own. "If you don't mind, I think we'd like to take a short recess to look this over, as we're sure you would as well. Convene back here in say, half hour?"

"Sounds fine. Half an hour it is," said Joyce.

As part of Joyce's "business class" accommodations, she was privy to a smaller conference room. Bob had asked if it was all right if the union were to hold their private discussions there—another slight fuss that always ended up with a "yes" from the executives and a gracious "thank you" from the union.

Rory never felt comfortable in the small conference room but it was necessary to separate to review and form a game plan. It was too much of a hassle to go back to the union offices, come back, find a parking spot, and get in the room again—only to find out the corporates had changed something else that the union needed to discuss in private before agreeing to it.

Rory went over the corporate offer. It was 1.5% annual wage increase for three years with no mention about reinstatement of incentives or end of year holiday bonus. The union's request was 5% annual for five years and no bonuses or incentives.

"Well, this is not good." Samuel said. "We have to get that year-end bonus and the quarterly incentives back. I've been mandated specifically to get those extras back."

"No it is not," Pete said, "But this is how it works. We start high and they start low." He didn't mention the extras.

Rory knew why Bob and Pete didn't want to pursue the bonuses. It was because the union couldn't collect dues off of them—dues drove their interests and it made Rory feel like if a gain wasn't beneficial to the union on a whole, it wasn't going to garner any attention.

"We're going to counter with four point five percent," Bob said.

"Do you really think they're going to want to sign a five year CBA?" Rory asked.

"No, it'll probably be a three year. That's standard," Pete answered.

"We need those bonuses in there," Samuel insisted.

"Look Sam, corporate is never going to agree to write those kinds of commitments into a binding contract. We go for it in wage increases. Don't you think that'll be better in the long run?" Pete said.

"I don't know. Put something in there about bringing back the incentives. Rory, back me up on this," said Samuel.

"I think so too. Lots of guys want those back. We at least have to try. I mean, who's paying who here, right?" Rory said.

Bob and Pete were visibly unimpressed by the way Rory made it sound like a demand rather than a polite ask, and after a few minutes of making the proper adjustment to the proposal the group got up and made their way back to the larger conference room.

"Joyce, the union has had a chance to look over your proposal and we have made a counter to it." Bob said.

"As we have yours. Why don't you give us a minute to go over it and we'll merge the two? No sense in going back and forth all day." Joyce suggested.

"I think that's a good idea, what do you guys think?" Bob said—addressing Rory, Samuel and Pete.

"I'm okay with that," said Pete.

"I guess there isn't really a choice here," said Rory, "You all right with that Samuel?"

Samuel nodded,"Sure, whatever to make the process go more smoothly." A greasily sly smile came across Samuel's face when he said it and his eyes scrunched up so Rory couldn't see them.

"Excellent. just give me a couple minutes to print it off." Joyce left the room with Campbell and when they came back she handed a single sheet to Bob and kept one for her own records. Rory thought it suspect. He didn't like the way it made him feel—like they were the only ones that needed to know what was on the paper.

"Would you give us a quick fifteen minutes in private to discuss and we'll meet once more before lunch?" Pete requested.

"By all means," Joyce said.

Back in the little conference room Rory watched as Pete and Bob looked at the paper first and made quick glances and slight nods to each other. Nods and glances that weren't helping ease Rory's mounting suspicions and mild paranoia.

"May I have a look at that please?" Rory asked.

Bob obliged and slid the paper across the table to where Rory sat.

The paper read: 3% for the initial year, 2.5% the year after that, followed by 2% in the final year for wage increases over a three-year agreement plus a letter of intention to reinstate the quarterly incentives and end of year bonus, but a stipulation was added—twelve hour shifts and a seven-day work cycle on the new cut to length line be written into the contract.

"Nope. This is wrong," Rory blurted, "They can't go back and ask for this. Schedules were agreed upon months ago. Only work being done on weekends is overtime and no twelves. This isn't going to work. I can't believe this shit. And this gradual decrease in the percentage year after year...they save a percent and a half on each workers wage over the lifespan of the agreement. Not even near a hundred grand in the first year to increase us and they want to cut it back for each year after? Assholes."

Samuel took the paper from Rory and examined it while the other three began to argue.

"Rory, You've got to understand something here, what they are offering is quite the deal. I mean, you are getting a letter of intention. Sure it doesn't guarantee them but I've never seen anything like that before since I've been doing this. And yes they can go back, why not? Nothing is binding yet. This might be the chip we need to cash in to get the wages up *and* get your bonus," Pete said with soothing conviction.

"I'm with Pete, Rory, this is quite the offer. Provincial cost of living increases were only one point two five percent last year," Bob interjected.

"No shit you agree with Pete."

"Hey now, no need for hostility," Pete said in an attempt to settle things down.

Bob was staring right through Rory but corked his temper and turned away slowly, "What do you think, Samuel?"

"Can we still counter this with, say, four percent? I mean, I see where Rory is coming from but I also do agree, this is a good deal. Try to squeeze some more in wages out of them if they want these shifts."

"Are you fucking kidding me, Samuel? Those guys on the line

made up thirty-eight percent of our pledges. Without them we wouldn't even be here. This was one thing they all said they did not want, don't act like you don't know that." Rory said, his voice raising with every sentence.

"Okay, okay, okay. No need for this," Pete said. "We'll take them a counter. Keep the three percent and the bit about the incentives, remove the shift changes, and we'll see what they say. But I'll tell ya, we haven't scheduled anymore negotiation dates as of right now, and we don't need people being unavailable because of holidays to postpone this until summer is through. The membership will not like that. Just keep that in mind," Pete said.

Back in the large conference room Pete handed Joyce the union's revision of the offer and Campbell leaned over to have a look.

"Preposterous," Campbell said, "The only reason I added a letter of intent and offered that kind of percentage increase is if those shifts are agreed upon. If you want, I'll go back down to one point five percent period. Not a thing more. And that will be our final offer."

Rory knew what final offer meant. It was Campbell's way of saying send it to arbitration because he didn't care—1.5% annually for three years was more than the economic norm across the country, no arbitrator would award much more than that, if any at all.

"The old snag and haggle, eh Campbell?" Rory said—forcing his way into the conversation. "There's no bloody way we're going to agree to those shifts."

The room went quiet and everyone was looking at Rory like he had just interrupted a funeral procession. Bob was flushed and Pete shook his head in disbelief.

Samuel stood up, "Well, Rory doesn't speak for the union. I say we take the deal."

"No one say anything else," Pete said—stopping all further escalation. "Grant, Joyce, if it would be okay I'd like to suggest we take lunch." Bob marched out of the room to calm himself so he wouldn't wrap his hands around Rory's neck.

"That's a fine idea," Joyce said, "Meet back here at one o'clock?"

"Perfect," Pete said—hurrying out of the conference room

after Bob.

As Rory was making his way to the door, Campbell hurried his step and asked for a private word. He beckoned to put a little distance between them and the others. "Listen, Rory. I just want you to know you don't have to defend those shifts so much. Those guys won't mind with what they're getting in return. I don't see why we can't make this happen."

"Not happening *Grant*, but thanks for the intel."

Campbell put his hand on Rory's shoulder, digging his fingers delicately into flesh, and pulled him in closer, "How's it been for you lately? Does anybody ask you that? I know how trying this process can be. And there's nothing worse when home life takes a hit because of it. Is everything at home all right? With your daughter, I mean," Campbell said—flashing a freshly disinfected smile.

This guy has never said word one about Anna. Rory had no idea how to respond.

"Look, I've heard it can be troubling and stressful having an inept child," Campbell said. "I just wanted you to know that I have some connections out in Alberta, maybe I could pull a few strings."

Connections? Rory thought. *What the fuck is this guy getting at?*

The chummy expression on Campbell's face didn't fade, and Rory noticed they had moved far enough away from everyone that nothing Campbell was saying could be heard by anyone else.

Rory could feel his hands get moist and heavy. The urge to pummel Campbell into a vegetative state rose with his blood pressure.

"It sure would be a pity if somehow some funding were to find itself . . . unavailable, or worse yet, if a junior staffer were to lose their job." Campbell said, still selling it with that duplicitous smile. "Happens all the time, cutbacks and layoffs. I mean, if our negotiations were to happen to stall or fall through, the codes and locks might be changed too, and that in itself can be a devastating state of affairs to a family financially, especially one with such special . . . needs."

Wyatt—that fuck!

Rory removed his attention and looked about the large hallway.

He noticed Wyatt over by the pastry table watching them, playing out what was being said, practically fondling himself over Rory getting the ultimate fall-in-line-or-I'll-end-you speech.

The corner of Wyatt's mouth crooked upwards ever so slightly, and Rory wanted to go over to the buffet table, kick out Wyatt's knee, knock the top off the gigantic silver coffee dispenser, and then pour the scalding liquid all over him.

The negotiations and flex of ascendency had switched into high gear. It was no longer a disavowal of each side's agenda. Life outside of work was being brought into the ring. Rory knew he had started it, but the determination with which Campbell spoke to Rory added legitimacy to his threats. Threats that Rory couldn't tell where exactly they were being directed. If it was Anna and Chelsea that Campbell meant to target, or if they were directed towards Rory and the other workers at Dambar.

Rory said nothing in return to Campbell and dashed from his grip and went right for the elevators without making eye contact or informing anyone of where he was going. Rory felt like his shirt collar was too tight at his neck, and he tugged at it with four fingers so he could breathe.

The light signalling the elevator car had reached the floor that had called it, went out, but the door did not open. The pale indifference that he started the day with turned into a rash of consternation across his face. He pressed the button vigorously and kicked at the steel doors that distorted his form. Rory couldn't tell if Campbell was just having a bit of retaliatory, malicious fun or just perverting the truth to gain a higher foothold.

The doors finally parted, and Rory rushed into the empty elevator. Samuel came quickly and stuck his hand in to retract the doors. "Thought you could escape, eh?" Samuel said jokingly.

Rory shoved him backwards and held the button to close the door. As they shut, Samuel looked back stunned, and Rory raised both his hands and extended his middle fingers skywards.

Rory wanted to scream, but he caught himself when he figured that it might travel up the elevator shaft and into Campbell's thoroughly pleased ear.

The mirrors on either side and behind him shot his reflection a thousand ways in every direction, and he felt overwhelmed and watched by eyes he could not count or see at the same time. One tear could bring it all down and render him weak, but the image of his poor, sweet Anna penetrated his tough exterior, and her visage lovingly tried to loosen constraining fingers that were restricting blood flow back into his heart. She was speaking to him, but he couldn't make out the words. He tried to read her lips, but it looked like a goldfish drawing breath.

His heart rate and blood pressure rose, and all the autonomous functions of his body pumped full blast, making him heave and hyperventilate, leaving him with no ability to repress any of it.

When the door opened on the ground floor, he was huddled in the corner, sweating, and his eyes were red from rubbing them. Anything that seeped out was ground into his skin by his fist. He refused to let the tears stream any farther than the heavy bags under his eyes.

A lady gasped and asked if he was all right and if she should call for anyone, but he darted out, through the hotel's main doors and into the street. The cool wind that whisked through the tall buildings downtown met him there and eased the tightening dread.

Rory vanished into the lunch crowd that was filling the streets. He wanted to be anonymous within the throng. Feel no eyes on him. And for a few minutes he watched hypnotically how others shuffled through the streets, how the cars stopped at lights and passed through timed intersections—*a ballet of tire rubber, brakes, and engine exhaust,* he thought. But it did nothing to help him reset. The flurry made the panic all the more fierce.

To get away from the chaos, he went a few blocks south and sat on a bus bench to try to avoid getting sick in public. He tried becoming someone else, listening in on a conversation a group of strangers were having underneath the canopy of a small restaurant that had a quaint outdoor patio.

He was reluctant to go back—he needed time to compose himself. He'd never thought of a contingency plan concerning Anna because he'd figured he wouldn't have needed one this soon. How could anyone use a poor, defenceless child as a bargaining chip? Those were the kind of tactics that Mexican drug cartels and the Mafia employed.

If Campbell was trying to disorient Rory, it was working. The daftness of thinking Anna was untouchable paralyzed him, as he sat listening to the people under the canopy. He thought it also foolish to take the faint, implicit threat as some sort of facetious provocation that carried no weight.

Pete Nichols had told him stories of how management, in times of strike, would prey upon the families of workers to weaken solidarity, but what Campbell was doing was beyond feigning empathy.

Rory felt persecuted but not pursued. He knew that he would have to go back to work and see those people he'd run out on and look them in the eye and pretend nothing had happened. That what was said had no effect on him.

He thought of getting a new job, even selling the house and moving out to Alberta to be closer to the girls, but if that Campbell truly did have the cards to play, then he might just play them out of spite for disturbing the status quo, even if Rory folded and relocated.

Getting up from the bus bench and walking back to Main Street was hard, and he got lost in the downtown human traffic. The urge to bolt came—run it off again. But ever since he'd gone for that first run, the dull ache that flashed throughout his legs for the last few years had gotten worse and more permanent. He couldn't bear the thought of running anymore.

He decided that going back into the hotel wasn't an option, not in his state, so he got in his car and got out of downtown as fast as he could.

Once home, he had the urge to stand in the shower and let the water run over him. While the water ran, heating up, he caught something in the mirror. His beard was hiding something. He tried pulling at it, looking beneath in an attempt to reveal what he thought was growing out of his face, like one might do if they think there's a zit or a bug bite or an ingrown hair. But no matter how much he combed through. he couldn't make anything out. Taking out a pair of scissors from the drawer, he started to cut the beard away, trying again to centre in on what it was he thought he saw. And before he knew it, the sink was filled with clumps and strands of wiry, birds nest hair. Upon looking back at the shorn image in the mirror, he stood satisfied that there was, in fact, nothing out of the ordinary hiding beneath his beard after all.

"Well, best that I finish the job." Rory said to himself, as he pulled out his razor and shaving foam.

After getting out of the shower, Rory made a few phone calls and asked Dom and Richard to come over. While waiting Rory put in a call to Dr.Abbott.

"Mr.Gunn, how nice to hear from you." Dr. Abbott said.

"Hey doc, how's it going?"

"Peachy, and how are you? And to what do I owe the call?"

"Well doc, to tell you the truth, it's not a pleasant question I have for you and I don't know quite how to ask you." Rory said.

"Is it about the blood tests? I was going to inform you but remembered you telling me that you'd rather not be told of the results."

"It's not that, doc. It's about where the funding that is helping us out is coming from. That board of directors that you mentioned. Would they have any kind of veto power of funding? Something that might cause problems later on for us?"

The phone was quiet and Rory could almost hear Dr. Abbott's brain pulsing— thinking of an answer for the unexpected question. "In theory yes, but Mr. Gunn, please, that isn't going to happen."

"What makes you so sure of that?" Rory said.

"Rory, this is quite disconcerting . . . I . . . what is it exactly that you're getting at here? You have nothing to worry about. I have it under control."

Rory gathered himself and took a shot of reality. He couldn't tell Dr. Abbott about the threat from Campbell—there wasn't even a name given—how could he accuse, much less prove, that what had been implied at negotiations had in fact, transpired.

"You know what, doc. Forget it. Just a touch of the worries. I'm probably overreacting. How is Anna anyhow?"

"She is well, Mr. Gunn." Dr. Abbott said. "Did you want to know the result of our testing?"

"You know what, doc, I thought I might, but no, I don't. It's been nice chatting. Sorry to have startled you with what I asked. Please just forget it."

"Already forgotten, Mr. Gunn. You take care of yourself."

"Thanks, doc. I will. Goodbye."

Rory hung up and sat in silence while he waited for the guys to show up. The first to arrive was Dom—Rory could tell by the heavy pounding on the front door that sounded like it was the police.

"Wow. Bay-bee-face. What's going on, man?" Dom asked.

"If you don't mind I'd like to wait for Richard," Rory said.

Dom nodded in compliance and the two waited for fifteen minutes for their friend to show up. Upon Richard's arrival Rory sat them down and explained the events of the day to them.

"You've got to be shittin' me," Dom roared. "Those fucks aren't going to get away with this."

"Easy. I've got an idea. I think I know how we can use this to our advantage. Campbell made the threats outside of the bargaining room. I don't think we'd be breaching confidentiality by saying anything about it, so here's the plan . . ." Rory said.

Rory spoke for twenty minutes and Dom listened more intently than he ever had in his whole life. This is what he was made for. Richard sat quietly, taking in all that Rory had to say but offering nothing by way of input.

After the story was finished Dom got up excitedly, hollering and battering his fists on the table in anticipation. Rory looked over to his old friend that sat quietly.

"You haven't said a word for a while. I'd give my left nut to know what you think about this," Rory said to Richard.

"Dirty play on their part. Not many reasons coming to me for why they don't deserve to get an earful," said Richard.

"Hot damn. The wise man approves." Dom said powerfully. "That's all I need."

Richard smiled and Rory could tell there was something the old man wanted to say but was holding back.

For a half an hour the three of them hammered out the exact details to a fine edge and then Dom got a phone call from his wife, demanding that he return home.

"Mama beckons, my friends." Dom said loudly. "Tomorrow is a new fucking day!"

As they were leaving Richard slowed his step and pulled out his cigarettes carefully, giving Dom enough time to drive off.

"This is quite the mess." Richard said, offering Rory a smoke.

"It is." Rory said—taking the tobacco.

"Ya know there's something I've never told you." Richard said, opening his jacket to shield his lighter's flame from the slight wind.

"What's that?" Rory asked.

"When I was a boy, before my mom moved me and my brothers into the city, I had to go to one of those residential schools. You know about those?" Richard said.

"I read a little about them, yeah. Horrible places."

"Depends on who and where you were. Some didn't have bad things to say."

Rory didn't know how to respond. He thought it best to remain silent and listen. Richard had them out in deep waters, far from land.

"The ones that said nothing bad were the ones that made the people running the schools feel successful. Made them feel that they reached their goal of what they wanted to do with those places. They cut our hair, changed our names and dressed us like they were dressed. They tried to erase our way of life. Convert it. Kill it.

"But you know what? It didn't happen. I know who I am. And it sure as hell ain't who they want me to be. Sure, there were lots of scars from lots of bad things. But they didn't succeed. No matter how much they tried to insist it was the right thing to do, they couldn't do it. And you know what? Time made them apologize for it. Time won't let them forget what they done. What they tried to do."

Richard let the gravity restore with a long solemn puff from his smoke. Rory could think of nothing except a young Richard getting a smack on the side of the head, or a belt across his back, or worse.

"Look. I don't want to tell you what to feel about what those motherfuckers said to you today, but I do want to tell you that time does serve its justice."

"And what if I'm the one time is looking for?" Rory asked.

Richard smiled and walked out to his car that was parked on the street, cigarette dangling from his mouth like a glued on prop, and he unlocked the driver side door. He looked up and yelled back to Rory, "It's looking for all of us, boy. One way or the other . . . okay?"

"Okay. Thanks," said Rory. "I'll see you tomorrow."

"Get a good sleep tonight. You look like you need it my friend."

Chapter 22

The next day Rory and Dom arrived together, and they walked into the back room with disquieting posture. They deposited their lunches in the fridge, got changed, and traded a few light barbs with their co-workers, acting like nothing was amiss. They went out on to the floor like it was six years earlier and the political tug-of-war that had since become a mainstay at Dambar didn't even exist.

A few questions about the negotiations came from some of the workers, and Rory just informed them all that things looked good and that a contract was going to be ready for ratification very soon. Truth was that Rory hadn't called Pete or Samuel to inquire how the afternoon went in his absence, but the white lie he told his co-workers didn't bother him. It would all be seen soon enough.

Laughing and playfully pushing each other, Rory and Dom came around the corner to the main driveway. Wyatt was waiting there, like a mother who had expected her children home hours earlier.

Rory figured that Campbell and his cronies expected an immediate reaction to what he'd insinuated about Anna, but as much as Rory wanted to let Dom off his leash, it wasn't time to bait the beast. The day needed to roll on.

"How's it going, fellas?" Wyatt said like he was ready to draw a gun at a standoff.

"Fine, Wyatt," said Rory. "Just fine. How are you this morning?"

Wyatt didn't respond. He eyed the two of them, cocking his head. "Fine as well."

"We better clock in—don't want to be tardy," Dom said without a hint of scorn in his voice.

They left Wyatt where he stood, puzzled by the congenial morning greeting, falling perfectly for the plan.

The people around them picked up on their upbeat attitudes and diligence. Some thought it was because of what was going on in the negotiations—that Rory knew something but couldn't unveil it yet. As a result, the rest of the workers put forth more of an effort, and production was smooth and efficient—almost like there was no need for management. Like the shop could run itself.

The normally slow areas were getting a spit shine, and the driveway was promptly tended to and was kept from congesting. The foremen stayed in their shack for most of day, as they weren't getting angry calls from sales agents and order clerks to chase down a problem.

Wyatt rushed around like he was on an important errand, but the same single piece of paper was always in his hand, and he took the same route all day. By lunch, he gave up and stayed in his office, and that was what Rory was waiting for.

At five minutes before the 2:00 break, Dom stopped his crane above the brake. Rory looked up at him, knocked on his hard hat, and made the drinking motion in front of his mouth. Dom nodded and drove his crane towards the other end of the building, where he parked it.

Rory made his way to the water cistern by Wyatt's office. Sweat was beading under his nose—a liquid moustache now in place where there used to be one of hair. He took two big swigs before filling his cup up for a third time, and then he shuffled four steps to his left so he had a clear look at what his target was doing.

Wyatt was on the phone and oblivious to anyone outside his window, but when Rory raised the cup to his mouth, the movement caught Wyatt's attention, and he turned to see what was going on.

Rory finished his cup of water and crumpled it in his hand. The few remaining water droplets leaked into his palm. He just stared back at Wyatt, who mouthed Rory's name into the phone receiver. And then, from out of his pocket, Rory produced a piece of paper. As he unfolded it he brought it to the window and held it up for Wyatt to read.

The paper said nothing more than, 'I'm going to fuck up the cut to length line' and once sure that it had been read in full, Rory shot Wyatt a cool wink accompanied by a middle finger that was, along with the paper, retracted in an instant.

Wyatt stood up, slammed the phone down, and moved quickly through the shipping office before disappearing through the threshold that connected to the main one, where Campbell and Clive would be.

Dom came around the corner with a violent bounce in his step. "Are we ready to do this?"

"He went into the office," said Rory. "Can't tell you if he'll follow."

Rory turned his attention back to the wire mesh window that gave them a glimpse at the doors Wyatt had disappeared behind. Rory hoped that his note was enough to draw Campbell out, but it wasn't imperative that he did. They just needed Wyatt and Clive, at least, and for them to be so wrapped up in the day's activities that they didn't notice what time it was when they came out onto the shop floor in confrontation mode; hunting for discipline.

The plan was for it to get started as the break bell sounded. The workers unoccupied and all the machines off, producing a light purr instead of a drowning roar, turning the plant into an echo chamber.

Rory watched the clock. It was getting too close—if nobody came out within forty-five seconds, the plan wouldn't work. There needed to be an audience. There needed to be witnesses. And if enough time passed before they did come out, most of the workers would be halfway to the lunch room or outside when it did.

Rory strained himself at the slow movement of the second hand on the huge clock and hoped that Wyatt or Clive hadn't made note of the time and decided against pursuit.

Thirty seconds.

Twenty-five.

Twenty.

Their time window was dwindling, and Rory squirmed, but the door leading to the main office burst open, and Wyatt led the charge with Clive in tow.

This couldn't go any sweeter, Rory thought as he exhaled. "Brace yourself, Dom. Here it comes."

The managers came at them with heavy strides, and by the time they reached Dom and Rory, the break bell was going off all around them, and they realized what they had been lured into.

Wyatt was startled by the signal, and his brows rose as they heard the machines power down. He turned back to Clive for a decision.

The bell died, and most of the workers stood in the empty driveway, watching.

Rory heard Clive say quietly, "Perhaps we should wait on this." But there was to be no adjourning.

"Let 'em have it, Dom," Rory said under his breath.

If some had been paying no mind to what was going on, they did after Dom started bellowing. He told a broken story that had an indiscernible beginning to those farther removed, but as everyone got closer and congregated around the managers and their union advocates, the story became clearer.

Dom lambasted the managers for poor interpersonal skills and their lack of tact. He howled about Campbell's quiet threat to lock the workers out and how cowardly the ploy was to put it on Rory in close quarters, especially with all the issues he has to deal with concerning his daughter. Most still didn't know about the severity of Anna's hardship, and the looks of sympathetic anger washed over the crowd as they computed the implications Dom spoke of.

Rory knew better than to give Dom the whole story, so he'd

withheld the flippant bit about Campbell's "friends." Information like that may have incited Dom to an actual attack, drawing blood instead of asking questions that demanded answers. He needed Dom to stick to the issues that affected everyone. Rory needed the outrage to be powerful again. Put management into a corner, diverting their attention and resources.

The managers took a few steps back in sudden trepidation. Rory could see they wanted to run, but everything in their managerial courses had taught them to stay—they could not look chicken-hearted in front of their workforce. It was the absolute worst time, professionally, to risk compromising their authority, nullifying what little trust some workers still had in them and give the union a big boisterous win at the same time.

Rory didn't say a word. He let Dom talk, grinding down the manager's pleas to calm down. And as instructed, Dom used his body language to speak to the managers by turning his back on them, and his words to address his union brothers—the ones who mattered most. The ones who deserved to know what was going on. The ones who really needed to be looked in the eye.

Rory brushed passed Dom and went right up the middle, between Clive and Wyatt, aiming to part the mangers by division. He didn't bother acknowledging them but knew that they were watching him move through them with thoughts of vengeance and horror. He looked up for a second and caught a dim, corkscrewed look on Wyatt's face, and Rory cracked a tiny smile just for him.

Wyatt said something that got lost in the furor, and he broke away and followed Rory outside.

"What is that all that about?" Wyatt said.

"Same thing that all that shit from yesterday and all that shit from the last little while is about. And do not, for one second, play the coy role. I've had enough of it," Rory said.

Wyatt just stood there, looking like he was trying to think of a way to talk himself out of the situation, but was pulled out of it by the click of a woman's high heels on pavement. He turned to the sound that became louder and closer with every step.

"Excuse me," said the woman. "Would you be able to tell me where I might find Mr. Rory Gunn? My name is Ellen Marie from the *Daily Press*."

Her hair was long and natural red. She wore a light brown skirt with matching jacket that was split down the middle by a ruffled white blouse. Her shoes matched her hair, and the sunglasses were straight out of the Jacqueline Onassis collection.

Wyatt turned to complete mush, and the struggle to find something to say grew harder for him. He was in no condition to competently do anything that required brain activity.

"That would be me," Rory said. "Pleased to meet you, Ms. Marie."

"Likewise. So, you wanted to speak?" Ms. Marie asked.

"Ummm . . . Excuse me," Wyatt spit out, "but what is this all about? I'm the plant superintendent here."

"Mr. Gunn had called me and said that there was a story about the organization of unions that I would find interesting," she said, like it wasn't any of Wyatt's business but she would oblige him.

"Yeah, Wyatt. I called Ms. Marie down here to give her a firsthand account of what has been going here. Morale difficulties and such. I hope that's okay, seeing as I'm on break and all. Any objections?"

Wyatt said nothing. He was too incapacitated by lust, heat, and surprise.

"Okay. First off, I'd like to be clear, Ms. Marie, that I didn't just call you down here to pitch the working man's program. I've read some of your articles and I think you're missing the point. Not the whole point, but some of it."

She produced a tape recorder from her purse that was the size of a knapsack, "Do you mind?"

"Of course not," Rory said.

Wyatt just continued to stand cemented to the ground, looking like he wanted to run but couldn't remember how.

"Go on, Mr.Gunn."

"I'm not by any means an expert on the matter, but I think I have a good handle on the deep-seated social incursion on capitalism, or its parent policy, imperialism or conservatism or whatever, it goes by many names, if you ask me. Now, for the sake of starting this off properly so we're not just blindly firing at one another, would I be mistaken to pinpoint the trinity of the successful business model as keeping down operating costs, staying competitive, and increasing profitability?"

"I think most would tend to agree with you but it's not that easy. You need continuous development and growth as well," Ms. Marie said.

"Right. Exactly. And you've said, in not quite the same words, that all those aspects together make it near impossible to balance labour issues and a lucrative business. But I think there are other facets that don't get examined as much, or what kind of effects they have, Ms. Marie. Minimize risk. Escape scrutiny. Satiate and pacify. Principles that both my union and my employer use to gain favour and success."

"So you're saying that the business sector, along with the unions, follow the same guidelines? That they are fundamentally one and the same? I'm sorry, Mr. Gunn, but this sounds like an editorial, not a news article. I report the facts, not conjecture," Ms. Marie said.

"Really? You report the facts?" Rory said. "Not once have I ever read any of your articles that depict unions to be anything but disruptive and a direct impediment on business. To me that's conjecture. You are scratching the surface, not even going deep enough to realize it yourself. The crux of stalemate is the real impediment. And what people fail to see is that unions or not, industry will keep going. Nothing exists without some sort of industry. But never have I heard, or read, one good solid reason why those of lesser means shouldn't be afforded a little more support if the majority of them so choses to pay for it. That's democracy right there. And democracy never promises to satisfy everyone. The same goes for commercialism, and all its derivatives.

"When this began I thought it was going to really help people, take away their fear of reprisal for speaking up, give some confidence back. But as soon as I got more involved I noticed that the union was never going to come right out and tell me the grand ideals were futile. That I was working towards something accomplished decades ago. That now, for the most part, it's about coaxing members to vote for a political candidate that has the bests interests of the union in mind. Even though, behind closed doors, those same campaigners run down the candidate they are tasked with bringing into power. Affiliation is merchandisable, but as soon as a flaw in the goods is discovered each side tries to prove their exemption from liability for that flaw. And that in the end, the blame needs to end up somewhere, that someone pays for it eventually.

"Delay needs to be explained for there to be calm. Inefficiency needs to be rectified in order to improve. People work hard on both sides to keep the machine going. Civilization has indeed been built by the backs of those born broken, but it wouldn't have gotten done if there wasn't someone cracking the whip. And it's the difference between reward systems that determine the results of that hard work, I think. Incentives don't make us equal or encourage team work, they fan resentment. Resentment that fuels motive. Motive that spawns muscle-flexers and fast talkers. Motive that enables tire pumping, ego deflating, emasculating and dehumanizing comments, and subtle threats."

Rory turned and glared at Wyatt whom was perspiring uncontrollably in a feverish stupor.

"It's that behaviour that has turned me apathetic. I can't even try to care about someone else any more. It's been wrung out of me. And for that lost part of myself, I grieve, even though that term and action, to grieve, is empty to me now. And I wonder if that happens to the others. Do they know and ignore, or do they conceal and suffer? As far as society goes I'm pretty sure neither side wants collapse. Does that make a tiered system necessary and equality infeasible? I hope not but I'm not getting much by way of convincing reasons for the otherwise.

"It's a killer to spend time thinking about these things. My head hurts from it. And when I find myself spending too much time thinking about them, I wish for a few moments of peace. Not complete peace, just moments. I wake in hope that things will get better. That people will stop being so fucking petty. But this, in here," Rory said, gouging his finger into his temple, "The tissue and electronics housed in my soft and vulnerable head, in your head, in theirs. Merely clay in the hands of madmen, control freaks, money hungry roaches, prophetic vagabonds and false lords the world over. The attritionists, as I have taken to calling them. From the trained angelic pitch of their voices to the practiced firm handshakes and their fine-tuned smiles of guile, they kill the possibility of peace, of things getting better. Vandalizing otherwise good people's nature and turning them against one another. But we need them. And secretly, we want to be them. As much as I don't want to say it, we do. They are the ones that put food on our plates and pay for our cars and houses and vacations and materialistic hunger. They provide the means for us to restrain ourselves. The unions know this, they aren't stupid, and they have succumbed and adapted because they know there is no real fight anymore, just compromise. Identity politics has made us like trigger-happy, hormonal juveniles at an amusement park where the admission is free, but it's made up for in how much they charge to get on the rides.

"Relay that to your readers. Get them fighting and talking. Get them interested. Tell them it doesn't have to be one or the other, that there is such thing as prosperous harmony but we're too short sighted to identify it from the rest of the blur. See what kind of response that gets."

Rory let what he'd said set in, giving himself a chance to regroup. He caught a little movement by the entrance to the plant but couldn't make out who the eavesdropper was.

"So what I gather," said Ms. Marie, "is that you see the proceedings here as what? A cyclical facade of some sort? I'm still having a hard time understanding your position. It sounds like you want to take the peasant to the prom but wouldn't mind taking the princess home. As romantic as that sounds, Mr.Gunn, that's just not the way things work in the end. There is always going to be one person's foot on another person's head, no matter what side you're on, as you've been saying."

"Hey, I know," said Rory. "I could be completely alone on this. And

I'd totally welcome to be put in my place. Fortunately, as it just so happens, standing here with us is my superintendent, Mr. Wyatt Burnaby. I'm sure he could clear up some of my misguided cloudiness with a concise managerial perspective."

Rory and Ms. Marie turned and acknowledged Wyatt, who seemed to have forgotten how to speak. His mouth hung wide open, and just as he was about to formulate a reply, Rory's phone began to beep, wiping out whatever gibberish he'd been planning to pass off as a valid argument.

"Oh, no," said Rory. "You'll have to excuse me, but I have a meeting I totally forgot about. I've got to go. Wyatt, I'll fill out the appropriate paperwork and leave it on your desk. Sorry to rush off. We'll be in touch, Ms. Marie."

Wyatt was unable to break professional character with Ms. Marie present, and Rory used the convenience to escape the snarky comments that Wyatt would usually deploy after having something sprung on him—especially given the circumstances.

Rory was two steps from vanishing into the plant when he heard Wyatt spit out, "What meeting would that be? I don't recall anything on the schedule."

Rory turned with an amicable smile. "Not that it's any of your business, but it's a personal appointment. Maybe I'm going to the dentist. No, I'm meeting my insurance broker. Or maybe it's my lawyer. You really don't need to know."

The smile on Rory's face devolved into a scowl once he turned his back and hustled to the office. The crowd that Dom commanded had dispersed and were back working away, their break was over, and the machines were again shouting and alive. Having already prepared the paperwork, Rory quickly slipped into the shipping office and placed the sheet in Wyatt's in-box. He peeked through the blinds and saw that Wyatt had stayed outside talking with the reporter., mopping up the mess Rory had spilled at his feet.

It was a clean getaway, but Rory kept looking back, expecting Wyatt, or anyone, to have taken up pursuit, but none followed.

The empty change room was still, and Rory changed quickly. The fruit the last twenty minutes would bear would no doubt be of indelible taste, but how long it would last, he couldn't be sure.

When Rory got outside, Dom and Cy were waiting by his car. Arms crossed and stares transfixed, they approached Rory. Cy looked like he was ready to lunge at Rory and trounce him. Dom didn't share the same fire in his eyes; instead, it was sullen betrayal that he was refusing to believe.

"Dom, Cy . . . how's it going?"

"Where you off to there, Rory? Got an envelope to deposit or something?" Cy said.

"Would you shut the fuck up and let me handle this?" Dom said, placing his arm as a barrier across Cy's chest.

"What's going on, Dom?" Rory asked.

Dom's unusual moment of calm mediation scared Rory more than the man's latent rage. It was like the quiet and tense second before a hunter's snare pulled tight—maybe Rory was about to become a helpless, dangling meal ready to be skinned and boiled down for oil.

"Cy here told me he overheard a conversation you were having with Wyatt and that slag from the paper that's always writing about how bad unions are. Is that true, Ror? You didn't mention her as part of the plan." Dom said with big eyes that begged for reassurance.

"Yeah, Dom, it's true. I was speaking with her. But what exactly did Cy hear me say? Because whatever that woman decides to print may be different from what I said and what Cy thinks he heard me say. You know how the game Telephone works, right? Out of context . . ."

"Then you'll have no problem telling your good friend what you did tell her, because right now I'm thinking that what you said wasn't very constructive," Dom replied. He pinned back his shoulders, and his fists started to ball. "I really need some clarity here, Ror. Tell me this guy doesn't know what he's talking about."

"Take it easy, Dom. There's no need to blow this up."

"Really? No reason, huh?" Dom said, becoming increasingly agitated. "All you need to tell me is that Cy didn't hear you tell that bitch that unions are meaningless and outdated and that what we're doing here is nothing but playing a fucking children's game. That those office types are needed? That we are just like them. I know you don't really think that. Tell me this dipshit is wrong!"

Rory gathered himself and tried to decide which quick plan of defence and exit would be best; it was either back into the building for refuge or bolt through them in hopes of getting into the car before they could do much damage.

It wasn't in his best interests to run. Dom would immediately take that as guilt, and it wasn't beyond him to get in his truck and tear after Rory, shouting obscenities and waving a blunt object around until he got the answers he wanted. Dom's tunnel vision negated the law, and nothing short of road spikes and a SWAT team would slow him down.

Rory was stuck in a sauna, and he didn't know how to turn the heat down. Dom wasn't going to like what Rory had to say, but telling the truth was a chance that he had to take in order to get out of the parking lot.

"I basically told her we are after the same things and to think there is a difference is naive," Rory said.

Dom's face fell into disbelief.

The three of them stood there in silence for a few moments before the force of a swung fist caught Rory in the abdomen, followed by another blow square-on into his right eye, sending him stumbling backwards.

After registering what happened, Rory looked up and saw Dom restraining Cy. Their voices were distorted and mixed and didn't sound like English. As the two aggressors backpedaled, he could make out Dom saying three words: "That's my friend."

Rory seized the opportunity to get out of the parking lot. He got to the car quickly but fumbled with his keys. He was losing clear vision in his eye as the area filled with fluid. By the time he had gotten the keys in the ignition and put the car in reverse, his assailant and defender had stopped squabbling and were watching him drive away.

Rory took one blurry glance in the rear-view mirror to see if they had scrambled to follow, but all he saw was Don's look of rage battling with baffled disappointment.

Chapter 23

"I feel like I'm losing it, Em." Exhaustion laced Rory's voice. "Between the guy who is struggling to raise his drug-troubled teenager or the guy who needs to buy, but can't afford, every new piece of technology when it's released or the guy who lies toxically in order to get what he wants, I can't find the differences in their problems when they're talking to me. I'm somewhere else when they speak to me. They are somewhere else when they speak to me, all the time. Fixated on things they can't control, or can but don't want or know how to. How can I expect any of them to be able to persevere at work when they're being defeated elsewhere?"

The swelling and bruising on Rory's face made him not want to look at his sister in the eye, and he stared out the window, watching drivers mouth curse words as they slowly made their way through traffic caused by street construction.

"What happened to your face?" Emily asked.

"Little misunderstanding," Rory said.

"Looks to me like it was a big misunderstanding."

Rory smiled a little at that, but his focus remained on the

traffic. "You know when you're driving down the highway and you see those old and colourless dormant barns, maybe they're stables, perhaps hidden amongst a few old trees, grass and bush overgrown all around?"

"Ya."

"Sometimes I think about the history of a place like that. How something of magnificence that once stood for shelter and proof of determination that great things can be built, could be left to deteriorate. I picture it when there was nothing around, vast gaps between homesteads and the closest city. I think of the generations that had no highway, and the only road used was trampled and worn into the earth, sometimes undetectable and overgrown, when only a natural sense of direction could lead you out of no man's land.

"I think of that highway being industry and capital, laying down a route to industry and capital. Luring away the family that so depended on that barn and treated it like a temple. A temple to be claimed by antiquity as a relic of hard work. I don't see a problem with leaving, following the fertile soil. You've got to survive, right? Do whatever it takes.

"And then I think about the people. The ones who cared. The ones who had to leave. The ones who had to follow that highway. And then I like to think that maybe there was this ranch hand. An ageless stalwart with one arm; a hermit type who was hired, out of the kindness of the owners hearts, to help where he could, always willing to contribute where he could to repay the kindness. And I like to think he never left. That he could never leave. That he wanted no part in what went on where the highway led.

"When my daydream starts to bother me is when I think about the final image remembered of the barn before those people head on down the highway. That it was standing and sturdy. The paint not showing a sign of peel or wear. No signs of storm damage or the erosion of time. It's remembered as a photograph. To associate it with anything else would be a disservice to the memory. Not just the physical importance of the barn but how it was part of the family that once used it, that it had personality and it was loved.

"Then after, say, ninety or a hundred years, descendants of the family return. They need that barn. The highway took them somewhere unsustainable, and they need something proven to be reliable. But when they get back they can't believe the state of near collapse and tatters it's in. And they turn to the one-armed ranch hand, who's been watching that barn fall apart every hour of every day for every year since they left, and they ask what happened. They look at him like not only did he let that majestic barn down, but that he'd let them down as well. And then he tells them he could've put a fresh coat of paint on, but he had trouble opening a can. That he could've nailed new boards in, replacing the rotten ones, but that he wasn't able to hold them in place. But instead of saying anything like that, the old ranch hand just stays silent, waiting for them to figure it out for themselves.

"All the depreciation is catching up and setting in, Em. Attitudes are becoming more and more negligent to the maintenance. Eventually, there will be no time to stop every girder, every weight-bearing post from weakening and falling in on itself."

Emily had no response. Rory had never spoken with her so beaten and with such destitution before. His words put her on the verge of tears.

"Listen," he said. "I just thought it better that you knew where I was coming from instead of getting the wrong idea from somewhere else."

"You need to get away from this stuff," said Emily. "I don't like to hear you talk like this. It upsets me, and I know that you've lost what it was that was keeping you together all these years, but you can't just wallow. You need to think positive here. Anna wasn't the only one who needed you."

"I understand that," he said. "But I may have put all that in jeopardy over this board game bullshit."

"It might look bleak now, but you've got to be strong. Those people who are getting you all riled up will appreciate what you've done for them eventually. The best kind of satisfaction is never immediate. And if those bastards really would go after a little girl who needs help, then I guess you are right, and they are obstinate, cold-blooded assholes, but you can't go forsaking everything. You are my brother, and I love you, and you are a good man. You don't deserve this, but that's life."

"But what if I've put Anna directly in the line of fire? That is the most irresponsible thing I could have done. And I'll tell you, something hasn't felt right lately—like I'm being surveilled."

"You sound paranoid. You've got to let it go. It's out of your control," Emily said soothingly. "Anna can always come home."

"Can she?"

Rory and his sister were both challenged on how to proceed.

"Listen," said Rory—breaking the stiff dead air. "There's another reason I wanted a little face time. Now, I know you've got a lot going on, and you helped me so much through the years, what with Anna, her mother, and even with the passing of Mom and Dad."

"Are you kidding?" Emily said. "You were the one who helped me through that. I would never have been able to—"

"There's just one more thing I need to ask of you." Rory produced a large envelope and handed it to his sister. "I've been updating a few legal aspects of my affairs. It's been ages since I've even thought about them. Anyway, I was wondering if you would be Anna's legal guardian if anything were to happen. I've also changed the beneficiary of my pension and all that stuff over to you, and I'm giving you legal power of attorney. There's also a second copy of a video I made for Anna to watch on her birthdays, or whenever. Just in case the original gets messed up or lost, then at least I know someone has a replacement."

"Of course," she said. "Is there anything else wrong? Are you sick or something?"

"No. It's nothing like that. I've just heard a few horror stories about people that didn't have their business in order when they needed it to be."

"Better safe than sorry, right?" Emily said.

"Exactly. You know, Em, I hate to sound cliché here, but you're the best sister a guy could ever need."

"You sure you're not sick?"

"Hey, what's wrong with that? You never know when those tiny arteries on the old ticker might blow a tire or a pail of cement falls on your head. Chance, bad life choices, flawed genetics, someone fixin' the wagon. You never know what's gonna get you, but you'll get got by something, and if it's something that comes about by your own doing, well, sister, you gotta forgive yourself and move on.

"See those people out there in the traffic? If we were to go out and stand on the sidewalk, free of doubt and anxiety and worry, we would be no more than a few feet away from the distended bedlam caused by ten minutes of inconvenience. How is it that serenity and disturbance coexist so closely yet distance things so greatly?"

"That's a weird thing to say, Ror. Are you currently taking any medication I don't know about?"

"Nothing at all, sister."

"Whatever. I've got to go. I'm working the overnight this weekend, and I'd like to get a nap in before I start my rotation. I'll talk to you later."

Rory grabbed Emily's elbow as she passed "I love you, Em. Lots."

"I love you too, ya weirdo."

Chapter 24

The next day, face stinging and more inflamed because he neglected to ice it, Rory called in sick. He wanted to go for a stroll and clear his head. He needed to get away from buildings, concrete, electricity, and language. After getting on the computer and searching for a sanctuary, he found the perfect one. A botanical garden at a city park.

The garden reminded him of Webb, and he thought of his Anna enshrouded by the same kind of tranquility and ease he felt when he walked in. There weren't many others around, save for a few elderly people and staff that tended to the garden. He moved to a quiet alcove of lush growth that was in relative solitude, and a wave of sublimity washed over him, and for an instant nothing bothered him, not even the injury on his face.

How fantastic it must be to be in such beauty, day in, day out, he thought.

Rory figured that this was the place where people who didn't want to sully their appreciation for life came to dedicate their energy into nurturing it instead of obsessing over what was wrong with it. The care that went into every little droplet of water, every fragile stem, every particle of soil amazed Rory, and even though the feeling of renewal was fleeting, it sparked his confidence in humanity. Rory finally understood what Dr. Abbott had meant.

On his way home he drove past Dambar. If what the garden represented was the magnificence that judicious toil and patience produced, then the shop was the dark, hidden shed where the old, rusted tools were kept. He wondered how it would look in twenty-five years, when he would be approaching retirement and all the objects of his frustration were long gone or on their way out. And in his thought of the future, Richard's words about time came to him—how it would take care of the aging generations of flesh and machine the same way.

He caught a red light at the intersection by the shop, and the stench of industry wafted into his car through his open window. It made him want to speed back to the garden and bury himself under the moss. And once the light turned green, Rory put his foot down and sped off.

The generic ringtone and vibration from his cellphone startled Rory as it went off in his breast pocket. He pulled it out and glanced at the screen to see who it was. He hadn't heard from Dom since the altercation, and that was a conflict that needed resolution. They had never before acted the way they had towards each other and the longer it was quiet between them, the worse the backwash would be.

The phone registered an unknown caller, but the *781* prefix were the standard numbers before all lines coming out of the union's downtown offices. Rory pressed the speaker button and laid the phone on the passenger seat.

"Hello?" he said.

"Rory. Pete Nichols. How are you, man? Rushed out on us the other day. Hope everything is all right."

"Everything is fine, Pete. What can I do for you?"

"Well, Rory, for starters, I was wondering if you would be able to come down to the office for a chat. A few issues need to be sorted out, and we need your signature on the CBA. Didn't Samuel get in touch with you?" Pete said with an uneasy laugh.

"No, I haven't seen him. Opposite shifts."

"Yeah, I see. You threw us for a loop when you didn't return after lunch, but we managed without you. Finishing touches are always the easiest, am I right?"

"I guess. If you want, I could swing by right now. I took a mental health day today."

"Aha . . . classic. That would be great. The sooner we can get the membership to vote on this, the sooner we can get you guys paid. See you soon."

The line went dead. Rory turned the radio on to drown out the commotion of the traffic around him. It was a new song by Tom Petty and the Heartbreakers he had never heard before, but nonetheless he hummed along like it was one of his favourites.

* * *

By the time Rory got downtown, it was 3:08 p.m. He hoped he would be able to get out of the area before the streets and sidewalks were jammed with people heading home for the day. His puffy eye gnarled his depth perception and range of focus, and he didn't want to contend with the bob-and-weave, in-and-out, sudden braking and gunning it to make a light, of rush hour.

Unity Steel's main centre of operations in the city was located in a building called Union Towers. It was at the corner of a busy intersection. Most people in transit during the week, from all ends of the city, would cut across and through it by either foot or vehicle. Union Towers housed myriad union head offices. They were independent from one another, yet still worked towards the same goals. It had Rory scratching his head a few times, trying to reason why they didn't all just pool resources, but the more time he spent around union types, the more he saw how counter-effective that was for business.

Revolution has become a business, Rory thought. *Or is that what it always was?*

Rory had been to Unity Steel's provincial head office several times, and every time there was never a secretary behind the desk. There were signs that one had been there; a coffee cup with a little lipstick, a half-eaten croissant on a napkin, but never a secretary.

Rory could hear laughing in the back office, and with no secretary present to announce his arrival or tell him if the time was convenient to walk in, he figured there was no need for the formality. The conversation going on in the back office was indistinct, but as he got closer, the words started to come through clearly.

"I'll tell you. That fuck doesn't know what he's getting into," said a gruff voice.

"Hey, is it our problem he can't fall in like everybody else? No," said a voice Rory made out to Pete's.

"Fucking disgrace."

Rory knocked lightly on the open door, and the conversation stopped dead.

"Hello?" said Rory. "Hope I'm not interrupting."

"Rory, come on in. Have a seat," Pete said.

The other man, whom Rory did not recognize, sat with a stern, blank look on his face. The man was barrel-chested and dressed in a thick white button-up— but only two-thirds of the way; exposing a plume of white, curly hair. He wore nearly as many rings as he had fingers, and Rory could not conceive of the need for that many rings.

"Whoa. That's quite the shiner you've got there. Talking when you should've been listening?" Pete said— a hint of derision in his voice, but not enough to deem it contentious. He placed a leather file folder in front of Rory and opened it up. "This is the final draft of the CBA. You should be glad we didn't have to go to arbitration and tack on another few months of waiting before we could ratify."

"Good news," Rory said. "Do I need to go through this first? What happened with the wages?"

"Well, Rory, without you there we made the executive decision to pursue the company's offer on the wage increases, bonus' and shift changes. Samuel thinks it's the best deal, and so do we."

"Are you fucking serious? How do you think you'll get this ratified if you're alienating so much of the membership? It's going to look like I threw them under the bus. You know that, right?"

"You let us worry about convincing your fellow workers that this is what's best for them. That's what you pay us for, right?"

"Doesn't look like I have much of a choice here anyway, again," said Rory. "Complete trust in you, eh?"

"That would be a good idea," Pete said as he hovered over Rory.

After signing the last of the agreements, Rory asked if that was all they needed and if he could be excused. The man in the white shirt made him feel unsafe— giving him nerve turbulence.

"There is one more thing before you go," Pete said. "Actually, it's a couple things, but they kind of become one thing." He closed the door to the room. "We got a call from a rather irate co-worker of yours concerning a little discussion you had with a certain slattern that fancies herself a news correspondent," Pete said.

"And what would that be exactly?" Rory said, fighting not to bolt for the door.

"The man isn't finished yet," said the brute in the white shirt.

"Easy now," said Pete. "You'll have to ignore my acquaintance, Rory. He just gets a little testy on topics such as these."

"What topics are those?"

"Well, Rory, it's like this. We didn't just get a call from one of your co-workers. Grant Campbell also called and corroborated that you did meet with the journalist. It seems as though you staged some sort of news conference and decided it would be a good idea to run down not only your employer but your union as well. Do I have that right?"

Rory sat in silence.

"You've got to help me here, Rory, my man. You've got to tell me this is a bunch of bull and that I don't need to take steps here," Pete said.

"What does that mean?" Rory asked.

"Do you know what it means to be a member in bad standing?"

"No, I don't."

"To be labelled a member in bad standing within the union means that for a time, if any member does anything to compromise the business of the union, then that member may be subject to castigation. And in most CBAs, you need to be a member in good standing as a condition of employment. Essentially, it would be a violation of the agreement for a company to keep that member on their employment roster. Do you see where I'm going with this?"

"Yeah, I get it. You're threatening me just like those bastards back at Dambar try to do."

"Whoa, hey now. *Threat* is a hell of a word, Rory. I'm just educating you on some of the inner workings of a union. It all has yet to be proven, and you're innocent until it is—you know the law, right?" Pete glared right through Rory.

"Am I free to go?" said Rory.

"Of course you are. Just wanted to touch base is all."

Rory got up, as did the man in the white shirt, whom he could not get a read on. It was far too strange for Pete not to have introduced the man unless the point was to make Rory as uncomfortable as possible.

"You know, before you go, Rory . . . it would make me feel better hearing you say that all this crap about bad-mouthing the union is nonsense. If not for my peace of mind, then for your reputation around here."

Before Rory could answer, the man in the white shirt left. The heat coming off his body must've been what made the room so hot, because Rory could feel it radiate as he passed.

Rory waited for the door to close behind the man in the white shirt before he said anything to Pete. Not that it mattered. Whatever Rory was going to say would be undoubtedly told to the other man, anyway.

"I can't," said Rory.

Pete sighed. "Well, that is really too bad, Rory. We'll be in touch."

Rory left the room. He thought he might vomit in the hallway. It was harder keeping it together than he'd imagined it would be, and the lack of introduction to the man in white made the situation much more terrifying.

The Policy

Unions weren't like they used to be. The intimidation racket solved nothing. It had died with the twentieth-century gangsters and the teamsters, even the union breakers. Billy clubs held in hands with scarred knuckles and the rolled-up sleeves that accentuated the bulge of muscle in the bicep no longer proved any points. The steel toes in work boots were for protection, not to be used as a weapons. But some could never see past that image. The man in the white shirt stuck Rory as that kind of person. The sort of person Dom was.

Rory took the stairs instead of the elevator. Being in a confined space wasn't appealing to him. Something had changed up in Pete's office, and he didn't want doors closing behind him when there was no way out except a window that was four stories off the ground.

People were beginning to leave, and the stairwell started to get crowded as all the offices emptied. Rory looked at his watch and realized that he wasn't going to be able to dodge the downtown traffic, but he didn't want to stay anywhere near the union office building, so he settled on taking his chances in rush hour.

Losing sight of where he was going—his bad eye handicap assisting—he nearly tripped down the last flight of stairs but managed to grab the wrought-iron railing in time, and instead of falling, he swung into the triple-thick glass barrier the railing encased, and banged his knee hard against it.

A few people stopped to see if he needed any help, but he said he was fine and that he had always been a klutz. Truth was, his knee ached intensely. He connected it to walking on the reinforced concrete with inadequate insoles, as well as all the twisting and pivoting that came with trying to get steel to go where he wanted it to. Sure, he had magnets and cranes and many other apparatuses to aid him, but the physics didn't always work out that way—especially with the big jobs. And if he planted his feet and tried to manipulate an extremely heavy, hanging piece of steel carefully, all that weight transferred through the long bones of his arms into his deltoids and trapezius', through his back, into his lumbar vertebrae, and down into the tendons, ligaments, and muscles that kept his legs, knees, and feet together and functioning. It was that kind of repetitive movement and strain that had, over the years, worn him, and others like him, down. Leaving their bodies unable to keep up with the self-repairs.

He limped painfully to the front entrance of the building. People pushed past him, and he felt as though he was a pinball that was being lightly bounced, kept just out of play by the spring in the launch chamber.

The sidewalks were packed with people, and Rory couldn't see much above them because of the way he was favouring his knee. He got turned around so many times that he was beginning to get a little dizzy.

From somewhere he could not place, Rory thought he heard his name called out. He spun around to determine its origin, but it did not come again, and he didn't see anyone making their way toward him through the mass of pedestrians that tripled before it had doubled.

While Rory continued to search the crowd, a man came by and accidentally bumped him with a briefcase right on the tender spot of his knee. Rory staggered back, wincing. Behind him a woman was standing, waiting for traffic to pass through the busy intersection so she could cross to the other side. Rory fell into her like a drunk. She reeled in exaggerated horror from being forcefully startled and squeezed her way through the throng to get away from her assailant. Rory tried to follow to apologize, but he collided with another person. This time there was force behind it; through a shoulder and into Rory's back. And when he turned again to see where it came from, he put too much weight on his injured leg and his feet tangled, forcing him to misstep. His injured leg gave out, and he grabbed at the air as he slipped off the edge of the curb in an unbalanced mess.

He remotely heard the gasps, but he definitely registered the car horn as he spilled into the oncoming traffic. There was no time to brace himself for the blow.

Everything went foggy, and Rory immediately felt like he was getting colder. Shadows and muffled voices were fading in and out, and the daylight dimmed like someone was controlling it with a switch.

The Policy

There was no processing what had happened. Everything fell apart and drifted away. There was only one thing that Rory could focus on, that he could sense. It was Anna, and she was clenching Mr.Boo tightly against her chest, smiling at him from the dusky light.

There was no pain. Only joy.

Epilogue

Ellen Marie pulled up and parked in a visitor's stall outside of Dambar Steel. She watched as Wyatt Burnaby herded workers who had taken a leisurely, extra- long break back into the plant. A couple of the workers got onto idle forklifts and started them up.

Weeds grew in the one spot that could sustain them at the front of the building. Their life expectancy couldn't be long, as the patch doubled as a graveyard for broken and odd-shaped pallets and a well-arranged area for new ones that product would be shipped out on. Remnant gravel from the sand trucks that ran during the winter covered most of the area and made the surface uneven where the sand had piled. The pneumatic tires of the forklifts flung dust into the air while dandelions, milkweeds, and thistles were mulched, crushed, and torn from their stems and root systems beneath the weight and friction.

Ellen covered her mouth so she wouldn't inhale the dust.

Burnaby didn't notice her at first, but after a few catcalls from some of the employees he was escorting inside, he realized their attentions were directed at her.

c. i. downs

She didn't pretend not to hear them or look away in disgust. And she didn't slow her stride to allow the zookeeper time to make sure the animals were in their cages before she got any closer. She walked through the noise and sandy cloud undeterred.

Burnaby left the straggling workers to meet her before she got within earshot of them. The last time they had met, he was made out to be a fool. He obviously wasn't going to let happen again. *At least, not with an audience,* she thought.

"Hello, Miss Marie," he said. "Didn't think we'd be seeing you again so soon." His tone suggested she wasn't welcome.

"Yes, well, I've been following up on a story and just wanted to come by to see if I could get a few statements regarding your former employee, Rory Gunn."

Burnaby sombrely bowed his head. "Tragic wasn't it? He was a very valued employee, and his ethic is sorely missed around here."

"I was actually here to see if I could talk to a Dominic Morse or Richard McKay," she said imperiously.

"Well, Richard isn't on shift, but Dom is right over there in that forklift," Burnaby said, signalling Morse over with a wave of his hand.

Morse shut off the forklift, unfastened his seatbelt, and exited the machine. He walked over with a bounce in his step like he was a movie star ready to put the moves on his leading lady and fire up the on-screen chemistry, but Ellen wasn't impressed.

"May I help you?" Morse said, reaching out to shake her hand delicately as he pulled down his sunglasses to flash a wink and a suggestive smile.

"I actually came by because I'm doing a follow-up on your friend Rory—"

"Shhhhh, I know you," Morse said. "I don't have anything to say, so you can stop right there."

"I just . . ."

"No. Not going to have it. Rory is gone, and that's the end of it. I won't be party to whatever you're doing here. You already got a mouthful out of him, and that is not the way I operate anymore. Okay? Good? Now if you'll excuse me, miss, I have to get back

240

to work."

"Wait!" she called out before he could turn his back. "I'm not here for anything like before . . . anything political . . . I want to run a story on the man. Were you aware of his daughter? That she had been placed in the special care of a facility in Alberta?"

Morse stared at the ground and pushed his sunglasses back onto his face, hiding his eyes. "I knew, yeah. What of it?"

"Did you also know about the life insurance policy Rory had taken out shortly before the accident?"

Morse seemed to be searching for words. "No."

"Well," said Ellen, "turns out that the policy he took out is more than enough to support her for as long as she needs it. There was some controversy over the payout. The insurance company tried to prove it was a suicide, but there were too many witnesses who substantiated that it was indeed an accident. By the time the paramedics arrived, he had lost too much blood. And once at the hospital they found that he had signed a DNR order in the case he sustained injuries that would prevent him from living normally.

"When I met him, he seemed very troubled, very erratic and not necessarily the most rational, to say the least. But now that I know a little more about the man, I want to tell his story, because I don't think it went the way he would have wanted it to."

c.i. downs

c.i. downs grew up in Winnipeg, Manitoba, Canada. After high school he went right into the labour force and took few jobs before spending the majority of his twenties working his way up to being a site-trained machinist. He has an immense love for music, and while he listens to an eclectic variety of it, he considers himself a rock 'n' roller at heart.